Taliban Hunter

Taliban Hunter

Douglas Nix

Copyright © 2012 by Douglas Nix.

Library of Congress Control Number:		2012909332
ISBN:	Hardcover	978-1-4771-1787-3
	Softcover	978-1-4771-1786-6
	Ebook	978-1-4771-1788-0

All rights reserved. No part of this book may be reproduced or transmitted in any form or by any means, electronic or mechanical, including photocopying, recording, or by any information storage and retrieval system, without permission in writing from the copyright owner.

This is a work of fiction. Names, characters, places and incidents either are the product of the author's imagination or are used fictitiously, and any resemblance to any actual persons, living or dead, events, or locales is entirely coincidental.

This book was printed in the United States of America.

To order additional copies of this book, contact:
Xlibris Corporation
1-888-795-4274
www.Xlibris.com
Orders@Xlibris.com

I would like to dedicate this book to a great doctor and friend,

Dr. Heath W. Hampton, MD,
and Travis Breedlove, an inspiring friend.

The Taliban Hunter:
The Beginning

Other books by Douglas Nix:

Al-Qaeda Hunter

CHAPTER I

I was happy school was out yesterday. I sat on the side of my bed thinking about a good run and decided to go; it would be daylight by the time I got outside, but I took my time getting a cup of coffee, sitting and thinking about the coming day. I got through, then went for a good run; after an hour and fifteen minutes, I was back at the house getting a shower. Mom told me as I came through that breakfast is in thirty minutes; I stopped and gave her a hug. "You are the greatest," I said as we hugged, and I went to clean up. I shaved and showered; I am only fifteen, I thought, and I had to shave. I wanted a beard, but Mom wouldn't have anything to do with that.

After eating and talking with Dad and Brendon, Mom asked, "Anyone want these last two pancakes?"

"I'll take them," and reached for the plate, and that was more than I needed.

"Any plans for today?" Dad asked.

"No," I said. "What you got in mind?"

He said, "Let's ride up to the mountains and see Cho."

"OK," I said; then he asked Brendon if he wanted to go.

"I got plans," he said.

Mom was listening. "I got shopping to do."

Dad said, "We might spend the night."

"Have fun," she said.

I got some extra clothes and my overnight bag, and we were on our way to Cleveland, Georgia. The mountains were green, and being the first of summer, it meant fresh garden food. The ride was nice, and Uncle Cho was working on a porch in front of the cabin; he would build one on the side later. Dad and I started helping; Dad took the saw, and I carried lumber and did some nailing. We stopped at one and ate; Uncle Cho had meat in the smoker. After eating, we started back; by six we had most of the porch finished, and we stopped for the evening. After eating, we went to the porch and sit and talked; before night, Uncle Cho went to his meditating rock and sat facing the mountain. Way down in the valley, you could see a train working its way around the valley, its lonesome whistle blowing.

It was great to be here. We went to bed early, and at daybreak, I got up thinking I was the first, but on the porch sat Dad and Uncle Cho, talking. Uncle Cho said, "Finally decided to get up."

"I thought I was the first." They laughed. We ate breakfast, and I started on the dishes. Dad and Uncle Cho started on the porch; by three, we were finished, and it looked so good, I felt proud to have helped.

Dad said we would get ready to go home, and I did. Uncle Cho ran over to a tree and ran up it a little way, then flipped backward and landed on his feet. I had never seen that done before. He told Dad to do it. "Not now. It's been a long time."

Uncle Cho said, "Your dad taught me how to do that." Wow, I thought, I would like to do it. Uncle Cho asked if I would like to spend some time up there this summer and help him add a room on.

"Sure," I said.

Dad asked him, "When do you want Chris, Cho?"

"Now," he said, "or when he can come. I'll start the room next week."

"Want to stay now?" Dad asked.

"I'll need some clothes."

Uncle Cho said, "I can take you home one evening and get some if you like."

"Sure, fine with me."

And Dad left. "I'll see you in a couple of days," Uncle Cho said. It was still early, and Uncle Cho asked, "Want to go fishing?"

"Sure."

And we got two fishing poles and his gear, and down the mountain we went. We would stop and get spring lizards in damp places; we had got around twenty, when Uncle Cho said we had plenty. When we got to the creek, we followed it, until Uncle Cho said, "Let's try this spot." We were not on the creek yet. Uncle Cho said, "Stay here," and moved to the creek slowly, then cast upstream, letting the lizard flow back down; then as it got to a deep hole, a brook trout hit it. Uncle Cho let the trout run a little way, then set the hook, bringing the fish in. Wow, one cast, one fish. He motioned for me to come now; I moved slowly to him, then cast upstream like he did. No luck on my first cast. He had moved down a little ways and caught another one; I tried two more cast, then moved below him, moving slowly and quietly. I cast upstream again and got a rainbow trout. Uncle Cho had caught his third fish, and we moved on down the stream until we had our limit; we cleaned them on a rock and put them in a large ziplock bag. We were almost to the bottom now, so we went on down; there was a big place where people swam in, and a family was swimming.

"I'm going in," I told him. "Want to join me?"

"No, go ahead." I took off my shirt and went in the water; it was cold but felt great. After a few minutes we started up the road home; it was farther this way, but the going was better. It was a little over a mile

We got to our driveway; it was six thirty now, and Uncle Cho put the trout in the smoker. He went over to a tree and started kicking it and hitting it, practicing his martial arts. I just watched. After an hour, he stopped and went to a rock, looking down the mountain; he sat and started meditating. I just swung. This was great; I love the mountains. It was beginning to get dark. After eating, we talked about how we were going to build the room.

The next morning, I was up before sunrise, and Uncle Cho was already fixing breakfast, and he put a roast on the smoker for sandwiches later. After eating, I did the dishes, and Uncle Cho started getting things ready for work. He had a bunch of logs cut and drying out; we brought several to the cabin, and he would measure and mark the logs where to cut and prepare the ends to overlap. All the logs had been debarked; he cut notches with the chain saw, then with a wedge took out the pieces to fit on the next log. We placed the bottom two logs on some footings he had ready, then started with the floor. He had bought some floor joist for the floor. We put them in, then started putting plywood down. It was almost one when we stopped to eat. By the end of the day we had the floor completed; it was almost six when we stopped for the day. I was tired. "We did good," he said. "I didn't think we would get this far. You did good," he said, smiling at me. We had a salad and sandwiches for dinner. Uncle Cho had made a jig to lay the log in, and it was marked to put each log into notch. The next day, we had brought the walls up six logs high; it would take twelve logs high for the walls. On Wednesday we had the walls up, and we stopped early; it was only four o' clock. I took a good walk around the mountain and down the road to the mailbox. I started running back up; I enjoy running.

On Thursday we put the ceiling logs up, then started the top on Friday. We had the room frame. Dad was coming in the morning to help put the roof on. Uncle Cho asked if I wanted some ice cream. "Sure," I told him.

I know he made the best peach ice cream ever; we sat on the porch eating and talking. After resting awhile, Uncle Cho started practicing his martial arts. After a good workout, he started toward his favorite rock, looking down the mountain to meditate.

It was almost dark when he came to the porch to sit and talk. "Do you ever miss Vietnam," I asked.

"Oh yes," he said. "I miss Mother and my family."

"Why did you pick America to come?" I knew he, my dad, and Ton had came to escape the Vietcong.

"Since I knew a lot of Americans, I heard them talking about all the freedom they had and all the beautiful places, the opportunity to make money and have something. It was my choice and I wasn't wrong. I love it here."

"Me too," I said. "I love these mountains." Dad had told me how the Vietcong came to their village looking for Uncle Cho and Ton; they knew Uncle Cho was helping the Americans fight the VC, and they had put a bounty out for them. When Uncle Cho learned of this, he was afraid to go back home; he knew they would harm his family, so they had to leave or their family was in danger. Dad was just a young boy, and their mother asked them to take my dad with them, so they came to America. Here Dad went to school and met Mom, and they got married.

I woke smelling coffee and got up. "Your dad will be here anytime," he said. I was glad he would bring me more clothes and I wouldn't have to wash them each day. Sure enough Dad got there just as the oatmeal was ready. We ate and sat a few minutes; then I did the dishes.

We stripped the ceiling logs with lumber Uncle Cho bought, and by noon we were ready for the metal top. That day went fast. We had most of the top finished. We stopped at dark. Next morning we started early; by midday we were finished. The room was dried in. After eating and talking, UC asked Dad, "Want to go fishing?"

"You bet," Dad said, so we got our poles and started down the mountain. We got spring lizards in wet places, and when we got to the creek, UC told Dad to go first. Dad moved up to the creek and threw his bait upstream. It floated back down; then he cast again. As it floated back down, a trout hit. Dad let it run a little, then hooked it. Then we started fishing. I went below them and had caught one as they went by me, and after an hour, we had our limit. We were near the bottom. As we got there, a family was swimming. I joined in the water; it was cold but felt great.

Two trucks pulled up, with five men drinking beer. I got out, and we started to leave, when one man said something smart to us. We didn't pay them any attention, until one threw a bottle, breaking it on the rocks. One hollered to us, "Hay, Chink, what you doing here?"

We were walking away. I was first, then Uncle Cho and Dad; then one threw a bottle near us. It broke, and Dad turned and ran at the man, Uncle Cho behind him. Dad hit one man, then ran at the bottle thrower. Uncle Cho was fighting one man. He went to the ground. Dad had a man knocking him around; then four men were on the ground, and one man was saying, "Mister, I wasn't doing anything." They didn't hurt him.

One man was cursing, "You broke my dam leg." Dad went to him, and he shut up.

"Don't break no more bottles." Two of the men said they wouldn't; the one standing started helping the others get loaded into their truck, and they left. I stood there amazed; I never saw Dad mad like that and fight.

Uncle Cho said, "You almost lost your temper, little brother," and laughed. Wow, I didn't know Dad could fight like that. Uncle Cho said, "Who do you think I used to train with?" We were going up the road to our driveway. It was a good walk. After sitting and talking, Dad said he would be back next week and left. We sat and talked awhile, then ate. Dad and Uncle Cho had cleaned the trout at the waterfall, and when we got back, Uncle Cho put them in the smoker. Then I started asking questions, things Dad wouldn't talk about. "How did you learn self-defense?"

"There was some trees in the mountains twenty miles from home. The wood would burn long and hotter with less smoke. Me and a friend, Ion, would go there and gather wood. We would take a boat most of the way, then walk the rest. We gathered the wood and come back. On one trip I was partway up the mountain and I saw a young man like myself, gathering wood. We waved at each other. As we got the wood, I went over and spoke to him. He was a young priest getting wood for the monastery. It was the first time he had been out for over a year since he went there. His name was McCoo. 'I am Cho,' I said. I ask the young priest to bless me.

"'You are my first person to pray for,' he said. Then he said a nice prayer for me. We talked for over an hour. As time went by, I would go there and we would practice together. I was eleven. For five years we were friends. When the north invaded us, I started training the Americans hand-to-hand combat and I was a scout for them. We would go after the pilots that were shot down. Four years later, the Vietcong learn McCoo had trained me and they killed him and put a bounty on my head. I didn't care, until they learned where I came from and went looking for me. Once they went to the house, I couldn't go back. I was afraid for the family and me. Cho and your dad had to leave and come to America." His eyes were misty, and I didn't ask anything else. After eating, I sat on the porch in the swing for a while, then went to bed.

The next day, we set the windows and door. "Want to go to town with me tomorrow?" he asked. "I have some vegetables to take."

"Yeah," I said. "I need a haircut." The next morning, we got some tomatoes, lettuce, squash, and early peas and went to town. UC let me off at the barbershop; he left a basket of tomatoes with Bill, the owner.

As I sat waiting for my turn, an elderly man started talking about some Orientals beating up the mason boys. "They broke Melvin's leg, and Tommy had a broken rib plus black eye. It must have been a big gang to hurt those mason boys like that."

I spoke up. "It wasn't like that at all," I said. "Me, Dad, and Uncle Cho came down and I was swimming when five of them came up and they were drinking and busting bottles on the waterfall rocks and one threw a bottle at us. Dad and Uncle Cho fought them for doing it. We weren't no gang."

Bill started laughing. "I figure it was Cho. Those mason boys live in the next county and came over here and raise hell. They beat up Old Benny Ricks last year, put him in the hospital. They had a whippin' coming and they laughed."

"I'd love to have seen it," one man said. My turn came for my haircut, and when I was through, he wouldn't take any money. He said the vegetables were enough.

Uncle Cho came, and he talked to Bill, and we left. On the way home, I told UC what they said and that I told them what happened. He looked at me and said, "It doesn't help to tell everything. That event, I rather not tell."

"Yes, sir," I said. We stopped at a house. UC told me he would only be a few minutes. I got out of the truck. Three children were playing—two boys around ten and a girl around eleven. One of the boys came over and asked if I want to play pitch with them. "I don't think we will be here that long," I said. "I'm Chris."

One boy said, "I'm Jeff." The other boy was Albert. The girl just stayed back; she is Barbara. I motioned to her and said hello. Uncle Cho got all the vegetables off the truck and took them in. I helped.

Inside, a lady said, "So you're Chris."

"Yes, ma'am."

"I'm Dorothy and you have a wonderful uncle," she said.

"Yes, ma'am."

A young baby girl was crying. Dorothy went over and picked her up. "This is Sandra. She is new with us." Dorothy went over to UC and said, "You are so kind to us. Thank you, Cho."

"You're welcome and we will see you later." We left, and Uncle Cho explained that Dorothy took in children that had trouble at their home and took care of them.

"None of the children are hers?" I asked.

"No," he said.

"Does she have a husband?" I asked.

"No, she doesn't."

At the cabin, we started cleaning out the spring. We took a shovel and went up the hill a ways. We dug out the spring and fixed a pipe that came down the hill, and a trench was dug to let water flow through the garden. We dug the trench a little, and at the garden we dug several rows for the water to come to. "That's a good idea," I said. "Did you have something like this in Vietnam?"

"No," UC said. "We had to carry water in buckets when it was dry."

"Wow, that was a lot of work."

"Yeah," he said. "Some days that was all we did, me and your father." That evening, we planted another row of squash and okra.

After we finished, Uncle Cho went to his tree and started hitting it and kicking. This went on for over an hour; then he went to his favorite rock and started meditating.

We had ribs smoking, and UC got them out and fixed a salad; he had smoked a potato for us, and we ate. After doing the dishes, I went to the porch and swung. It was time for the train to come through the valley. I went over to UC's rock and sat; then the train came through. The valley, it was like a beautiful picture with a train blowing a lonesome tune.

The next day, I had a good run, then ate, and we got rocks out of an area UC was going to put fruit trees on. We had the tractor pulling a wagon. Each time we loaded the wagon, we would take it and make a wall. We got through loads, when UC asked, "Want to go fishing?"

"I'm ready," I said. We got our pole and started down the mountain at one place. We got plenty of spring lizards at the first big fishing hole. I waited while UC moved to the creek and cast up the stream. He missed a fish and cast again; this time he got one. Then I went to the next hole and cast; on my third cast, I got a brook trout. UC moved below me once. After catching another fish, I moved on down the creek. If you're quiet and move up to the water's edge, the fish won't get spooked. They can see you so easily, and so we always moved slow and quietly. We had our limit before we got to the bottom. Down there, Dorothy was with the children, and they played in the water.

On the way, I saw a pretty flower, a mountain laurel. I picked it and went to the young girl; she was watching Jeff, Barbara, and Albert play. I held the flower out to her. "A pretty flower for a pretty girl." She took the flower. I reached for her and picked her up and started talking. She liked the flower. After walking around a little, I put her on my shoulders and ran around with her. I went over to the boys, and they threw water on me, so I started throwing water on them. "Help me, Sandy." The boys were getting me wet. Sandy started throwing water back. The boys were having a good time. Then Sandy started smiling. I had got in the water now, and we were getting good and wet. Barbara came over and got in the pool with us, and we were all laughing.

UC had been cleaning fish; now he was with Dorothy. She looked at Uncle Cho and had tears in her eyes. "That is the first time she has laughed since she came to us."

The boys were showing me how they could swim. "That's good," I told them. We played a little longer, and it was time to go. Dorothy wanted to drive us home, but UC said we needed the exercise, and I left, with the boys telling me to come back next time with them.

When we got back, UC started smoking the fish; then he went to his tree and started working out. I asked him if he would train me in self-defense. "If you are sure you will follow through with it and it's OK with your dad."

"Great," I said. Dad was coming tomorrow to help with the porch we were starting; it would go around the new room we added on. Uncle Cho got on the floor and started doing push-ups. After he did fifty, he looked at me. I smiled, then got on the floor; I did twenty. Then he got back on the floor and did ten with one arm. Wow, I never tried that, and I tried. No, I couldn't do one. "When you are fit you can do fifty with one or either arm."

"Can you?" I asked.

"Yes," he said, but he didn't do any more.

The next morning, I woke with the sound of Dad's truck. I got up, and Dad was already talking to Uncle Cho. He was almost ready with breakfast. I gave Dad a hug. "This boy behaving?" Dad asked UC.

"This is a fine son you have here," he told Dad.

"He'll be sixteen in a couple of months. Got your learner's license?" he asked.

"Yeah."

"You should have said something. Now you can drive me around."

"Yeah, now a gofer." Dad smiled.

"I got you more clothes," Dad said. "Not this week but next, your mom want you home for a week."

> Wo-Lee Bailie Lieutenant Smith Sha Lake Valley
> Sergeant Bailie Captain Lott
> Corporal Evans
> Wo-Lee

"Sounds good, Dad." It took all that day to lay those rafter logs then strip them with 2 x 6. The metal was almost finished. We had four more sheets, then all the caps. That wouldn't take long. I asked Dad, "Could I practice self-defense with Uncle Cho?"

"Fine with me, Son. Ask your mother. She will be calling soon."

"Thanks, Dad."

We were through with dinner now. I had dishes. I finished, then went to the porch and listened to Dad and UC; they like talking about Vietnam. Dad would get UC to tell about missions while he scouted for down pilots on special patrol. He went on. Dad asked UC what happened to Wo-Lee. UC sat a few minutes; then he started.

"We had a down pilot about the middle of Sha-lake-valley. We knew they would be lots VC there so we had an extra scout, Woo-Lee, with a Lieutenant Smith, a Sergeant Bailie, Corporal Evans, and me. We made it to the drop area OK. Then we moved south to our pickup point. We had come across three patrols. Wo-Lee wanted point. He was the oldest so I had to let him. Our signal kept moving so we know the pilot, Captain Lott, was in hot water. When we got to a large creek, we split up. I took Lieutenant Smith. Wo-Lee took Bailie and Evans. They had worked together before. As the signal was getting louder, all of a sudden gunfire started. Then two patrols move out of the thicket, not a rock's throw away from us. We moved behind them. I could hear them talking on their radio. We followed them maybe a mile. The shooting had stopped. It was our patrol with Wo-Lee. The pilot's locator signal was close.

Shot Captain Lott
Shot Sergeant Bailie
Shot Corporal Evans

"The VC set up an ambush. We went around them and found Wo-Lee and Bailie. Corporal Evans had been shot in the leg. They had to leave him. He couldn't walk. Our signal was close but VC were all over the place. We saw several patrols. Wo-Lee went across the stream and we both moved up the water. He was buried somewhere but we couldn't call out. Finally Wo-Lee had found Captain Lott. He had been shot in the shoulder. That side of the creek was hot with VC so Wo-Lee had Bailie bring Captain Lott over to us. He was setting up a fire patrol and he was drawing the VC away from us. When the shooting started, Bailie came across with Captain Lott. Wo-Lee was leading the VC away. He would meet us at the pickup spot where they left Evans as soon as we joined Captain Lott and Bailie and Evans. I took point. The shooting was still going on but getting farther away, about four clicks out. Shooting started. Behind the team was Lieutenant Smith. We moved south to our pickup zone. It was not far away. We ran across another patrol. We took our movement off the main path so it was a little harder to see us. Someone in back was alerted where the shooting started. I always use the AK. It sounds like their guns and confuses them. I had the entire patrol in front of me and Captain Lott. When we started firing, we got eight or ten before the VC saw they were in an ambush. Then it was too late. After the first fight, Lieutenant Smith had got one in the head. We had to leave him. We got some of his things, his gun, and all his bullets, then got out of there. We passed several patrols but when we got to the pickup zone, we got a surprise. The VC were there so we moved south. When the helicopter got in range of the radio, we told him to go to a second point tomorrow night, same time, for pickup. He didn't get close after he signed off with the starship. 'See you tomorrow night, good luck.'

Corporal Evans shot in leg
Captain Lott

"We moved all night. I was worried about Wo-Lee but he knew to go to second base. We had two men shot we were helping. I had Captain Lott. His shoulder wound was bad. He lost lots of blood and was very weak. We had shot him and the captain with morphine and I was almost carrying him. By daybreak I was exhausted. Sergeant Bailie said he couldn't go any farther. He was so tired so we rested. It was maybe a mile to the pickup point but we would have to do it tonight. There was too many patrols. We were in a good thicket and I moved out far enough to watch the main path. That day I saw six patrols and I was worried about tonight. It finally got dark and we moved to our pickup zone, when a squad of VC were coming our way. When I got the helicopter on the radio, I told him to fake a pickup nearby, then came back to us. We had a good clearing and knew it was a bad pickup place. The chopper moved out and down a little valley about a mile away, when we heard the shooting begin and then the VC went down there to help. When the starship said, 'Coming in, make it fast,' he landed a hundred yards away but I was so worried. I carried the captain on my back and so did Bailie carry Evans. Wo-Lee was never heard of again." Uncle Cho's eyes were misty. Wow, that was a bad time, I thought. Wo-Lee was staying with us when he lost his wife.

Dad said, "I'm making roast beef sandwiches and some home tea."

"Good," UC said. "I'm getting hungry."

We finished stripping the top, then the last of the metal. We were through before noon. UC thanked me and Dad for our help. We relaxed the rest of the day; then Dad went home. "See you next week," he told us and left.

Mom called. I told her dad had left. We talked a few minutes. "Come home with Dad next weekend."

"Yes, Mom, love you, bye."

She said, "Love you too, bye."

It was so quiet, just an occasional bird or cricket. I love it. "Mom said it was OK to learn self-defense from you, Uncle Cho."

"Good," he said. "I hope you will honor my rule. Never use what you know for any reason except for your safety or someone else ready to start."

"Yes," I said.

"Good. Get an axe and follow me." I got an axe, and we went to some trees. "You will need a training tree like mine," he said. "Pick out a straight tree with not many limbs." I walked around and selected an oak tree about as big around as a five-gallon bucket. "Cut it down," he said. So I started. I worked for fifteen minutes, then took off my shirt. After thirty more minutes, it fell, now the top out.

"How long?" I asked.

"As long as you want," he said. I picked a spot, then started. It was easier with it lying down. After finishing, I started cutting off all the limbs. I cut them close as I could. The tree was about fifteen feet long, and I started rolling and moving it to our training area. When I got it there, I was tired. "Get the bow saw. I'll get a chain and bolt." So I did.

UC came back with a chain about twenty-five feet long, and he told me to cut the top off straight. I used the bow saw and cut the end off straight. "Now cut the top off," and I did. We drilled a small hole in the end of the tree. UC had a long-threaded bolt. We put the bolt in and started screwing the bolt to it. After getting the chain connected to the bolt, he told me to get the tractor; I did. We used the tractor to hold the tree up off the ground a foot. UC went up the tree and bolted the chain to a large limb across from his. I was so tired, but when he came down, he started working out on his tree. I watched a little; then I did the same. He would side kick the tree. As it moved, he would turn and move and kick again until the tree was swinging way out. I could get my tree to swing but not way out. My legs got so tired, but I wouldn't quit; then I missed a kick. The tree hit me and knocked me down; it bruised my side. UC saw what happened and said, "You need to stop and rest." UC started back hitting and kicking; he was in great shape. After a while, he stopped and went to his rock to meditate. I sat and enjoyed the quiet. We had a roast on the smoker. We would have a salad, smoked corn on the cob, and cantaloupe for dessert.

After eating and I finished the few dishes we had, I went back to the porch. My bruises were a little bad, but I would never complain. Dad nor UC never spoke of anything wrong. I went to bed. The next morning, I woke early and decided to go for a run. I didn't feel good, but maybe a good workout would help. I made it down the driveway, but I was so sore and tired, I only ran halfway back up the mile drive. I had to walk, but near the top, I ran the last fifty way. I sat, out of breath, for a few minutes. After eating, we started picking rocks out of an area we would plant fruit trees in. We had a wagon we used behind the tractor. We filled it up four times before we had lunch; then we loaded five more loads before we stopped for the day. It was Monday, and I hoped we wouldn't do this all week. I was so sore and tired. My bruised side and leg were hurting, but after eating and

I finished in the kitchen, I went to the porch. UC was doing his workout. I got up and went to my tree and started kicking and hitting it. UC said, "Maybe you should let your wounds rest today."

"OK," I said and went to my swing. UC hit, kicked, and moved around, kicking the air, punching imaginary targets; then he stopped, went over to his rock, and meditated for an hour. I watched the birds and lizards, anything that move; it was nice.

The next morning, we started gathering rocks again. After three wagonloads, UC said, "Let's go fishing," looking at me. I grinned and put the last rock in the wagon, and we went for our gear. As always we got our spring lizards on the way down; then we got to our first fish hole. UC motioned for me to go first. I baited my hook, then eased up to the water's edge and cast upstream. The lizard floated back down, and at a big rock, a rainbow trout grabbed my bait and ran upstream. I pulled on it and got one. UC moved up and took my spot, while I took the fish off the line and moved down to the next fish hole. By the time we got to the bottom, we had our limit, and at the waterfall, Dorothy and the children were there. I spoke to Dorothy and went to the pool. Jeff and Albert started throwing water on me. I grabbed Sandy and got near them, and we started splashing also. Sandy was having fun. I got out of the pool and went to a mountain laurel and got Sandy a flower. I put it in her hair; then I asked, "Let's go get in the pool." She was for it. For an hour I played with the children. Finally Barbara came over and got in the pool with us; she helped me splash water on Jeff and Albert. I started talking to her. She likes school and staying with Dorothy, but she knew they would take her away and put her with another family that she didn't like. Well, maybe not at that time.

Jeff said, "Oh, I hope we make it past Christmas."

"Let's play," Albert said. "Don't be so sad. Let's enjoy it now," and they did. We splashed water on the whole area. All the children laughed. I felt good playing with them.

Finally Dorothy Bray said, "Time to go home."

We all got out of the water, and UC said, "It's time to start back."

"Let me drive you please."

"OK," UC said, and we all loaded up the wagon and came up the mountain. When we got home, she asked for the bathroom for Barbara. I showed her the way. Dorothy and UC talked. The boys got out and was looking around. We went to our training area and looked down the mountain to the trussell and valley. It was great.

Then Dorothy said, "Let's go to the children."

UC told Dorothy, "You're some kind of a special person."

She looked at UC and said, "That's the nicest thing you ever told me. Thank you, Cho."

The children were all looking out the windows, and Jeff said, "Chris, come play with us sometime."

I waved. "OK, I will," and they drove off.

We sat and talked a little; then UC went to his tree and started kicking it and hitting it while it swung around, so I went over to mine and started the same. I was getting better kicking. There was a technique to the position you should take before you kick. I worked at it until my legs were tired, and then I would climb the tree and up the chain to the limb, then climb on it and sit. The view was great up there. I sat a few minutes, then climbed back down. UC had gone to his rock to meditate after swinging and thinking about home. Dad would be coming up day after tomorrow, and I would go back home with him. We ate and went to the porch to sit. A jeep came up the mountain to our cabin. A well-dressed man got out, and UC greeted him. "How are you, Mr. Smith?"

"Fine, and you, Cho?"

"Well," he said.

"Cho, we have some work at the school if you have time."

"Sure," UC said.

Mr. Smith said, "In the dean's office we have some changes we want to make. Could you come Monday? Charley can help you if you like."

"Good," UC said. "I'll be there at nine Monday."

"Who is this?" he asked.

"My nephew Chris from Covington." We shook hands.

"See you Monday," and he left. UC explained he did work for Young Harris. That's a good college, I thought. We ate, then went to the porch and watched for shooting meteorites; the sky was so clear up here.

The next morning, I ran down the mountain and almost back to the top before I had to stop running and walk the rest of the way. Uncle Cho had breakfast ready; we ate, then walked on, moving rocks. The next morning, Dad came, and we went fishing and around our mountain for a good hike. Dad was carrying a backpack with our fish on some ice; it was after two before we got back and cooked the trout. It was around five, and Dad said it was time to go. "Thank you, Uncle Cho. If it's OK, I'll be back in a couple of weeks. Dad said he thought it would be OK with Mom."

The ride home was nice, and Mom was finishing our food. Brendon and Andrew were home, and we played video games until ten; then Mom said it was bedtime. The next morning, I had a good run; it was five miles, I thought. I went to town and around the square, then back home. After eating, Mom wanted us to go to church. David Paine, our preacher, was preaching on family values and how our fathers and mothers struggled to make life easier for us. I almost felt our preacher was preaching to me, but I knew how much he loved God. His father (Brother Paine) and mother, I like them very much. Brother Paine was our preacher before David, his son, took over the church; he was preaching to us all.

After church, we had lunch. Mom had a pot roast ready and corn, string beans, and mashed potatoes with biscuits. Mom is a great cook. Dad was working on his shop, so I helped. We talked about Uncle Cho and his family in Vietnam; he missed them, I knew. Dad was a quiet man, very intelligent. I got a great memory from him. Mom is a very smart redheaded schoolteacher. Education was a must, and all homework was done daily. My memory made it easy for me. I never had a C in school and only a few Bs. That got Mom and Dad easy on me. I enjoyed reading from second grade on. Mom could always find a good book I would like, but now sports was my main concern. I had joined the track team the past term, and next year I was going to set a school record, I hoped. Doug, my best friend, and I raced a lot; he was good, and on the two-mile run, he was the best, and I could almost catch him. He was the football kicker and one of the most popular people in school and definitely a little wild. I had called him the night before, and he said he might come by. We had the shop looking good. I started with the weed eater, and I did that for the next two hours. Tomorrow I would use the lawn mower, and it wouldn't take long to finish. After a good run and breakfast, I finished mowing. It was almost eleven and I was through, so I went to town; and as often, I stopped at the corner drugstore and got a Coke float. Before I finished, a man came in, sat down a couple seats from me, and ordered the same. "I've been addicted to Coke floats since the time of Noah," and laughed.

"Me too," I said. We talked about the history of Covington for the next few minutes. "You must be from here," I said. "You know our history good."

"Only the past few years," he said. "But this is a fine county. Newton has lots of history," and he left the question in mind. He looked like any one of a hundred men, white hair, beard, and mustache, a wiser Kenny Rogers, well kept. I felt I knew him. He introduced himself as Tom Quick.

"I'm Christopher Doan," and we shook hands.

"I'll see you around," he said. As he left, I sat looking around. How the store had changed. The counter waiter said the last owner died and it's in new hands now. We talked about school. It was his first year at Newton High, and he was hired to come work here. "Are you from India?" I asked.

"Yes," he said.

"I'm Chris," and reached out to shake hands. He smiled.

"I, Raj," he said.

"Nice to meet you. I have an uncle from Aligarh, near Delhi."

"I'm near Delhi, at Rohtak. I've been to Aligarh many times," he said. "And I've been to all the area around the Pink City. How is that Coke float?" he asked. "It looks good."

"It is," I said.

"I don't know how much to charge," he said.

"It was sixty cents last year."

"Sixty cents," and he smiled.

"I'll see you around, Raj," and I started home.

On the way, I saw a sign saying Help Wanted, and I sure needed a job, so I went in. It was a dojo. Men were working out with weights and kicking a hanging punch bag. I stopped for a few minutes, and I knew a couple of students there. I went to an office, and a fit man was working at his desk. I just waited. He saw me and asked, "Could I help?"

"Yes, the ad for a job."

He said, "I'm Mike Gill. What I need is someone to clean up my shop three times a week—after eight Tuesday night, eight on Thursday, and sometime after four Saturday or anytime Sunday. It takes about two hours to sweep and mop, put everything in its place. It pays seventy-five dollars a week."

"I'm Chris Doan. I live down the old AT&T Highway, about two miles from here." We shook hands. "I could do what you said. I need the work to buy a car."

"It will be a little while before I need you, October, about when school starts."

"That's fine with me. I'm working with my uncle in the mountains and that will give time to take care of that job."

"Fill out this application." I sat down and filled out the papers. I handed it to him. He read it and said, "OK, Chris, you got the job. Come by one Saturday around four and I'll go through what we do."

"Yes, sir, I'll see you this Saturday." We shook hands, and I went home.

That next week, I did garden and flower work for Mom. Monday afternoon, Douglas Nix (Red) came over. Red, our football kick, was a few months older than me and already had his driver's license. We rode together. He wanted to go to the varsity; some school friends were going there. Mom said to go; I knew what to do tomorrow. So I showered and got ready for town. Lots of our school friends were there, all the cheerleaders and lots of Rockdale, our worst rival. I figured a fight would start; I sure didn't want to. Red had parked at an easy place to get out of, beside a street curb. "Last time, I parked on top, and when the police came, they took my name and address," he said.

A three-man team was playing guitars, and the top parking lot was full. We walked up there and got with the cheerleaders. "Chris, this is Beverly, my gal," he said as he hugged a pretty cheerleader.

"Hi, Beverly, nice to meet you."

"Me too, Chris."

Some of the kids were dancing. Beverly couldn't stay; still she wanted to dance, so Red said, "Come on," and they went out, and they were good. I enjoyed watching.

One of the cheerleaders, Ashley, came over and started talking. I'm not shy, but I held back and didn't talk a lot, but Ashley was so lovely, and I didn't think I had a chance. She was so popular. "Want to dance?" she asked.

"I'm sorry, Ashley. I don't know how."

She stood up and said, "Come on. The way you run, you're bound to be good." She took my hand, and I had to get up, and I knew my friends would laugh, but Ashley insisted; so up and on the upper parking lot, where there were lots of the cheerleaders in their uniform and Rockdale, with at least twenty or more of them. I tried to move like her, and she counted, "One, two, three, skip. One, two, three, skip," and I finally was getting better, when they started playing fast music. That was something else. Ashley was like a beautiful ballerina, but I just kept trying. It got easier, but several of my classmates were ribbing me and laughing. I smiled and kept moving; it got easier to hold one of the finest girls in the school. Ashley said, "See, this isn't hard, is it?"

"Not with you," I said. We sat down, and Red had gone and got us a chili burger and orange drink. It had ice cream in it. We sat on the hood of a friend's car. Beverly and Ashley had been friends since grade school, and Beverly was falling for Red. He laughed and made jokes. I would listen and laughed.

Ashley asked lots of questions, making me talk more. "Want to dance?" she asked. She had already stood up, so if I didn't, I knew someone would. It got easier. Not only was she a good teacher, it was a pleasure to hold her. I was having fun. Some of my friends were still making fun of me, but I knew they wanted to take my place. Red was kidding me as much as anyone. We stayed until six, and Beverly had to go in. Red had already told me he was taking Ashley home, so I knew Red was sitting it up, and I was glad we talked about school, football, and what we would do the next month before school started back. We planned going out Friday night. I got her phone number and promised I'd call her. After we dropped the girls off, Red took me home and said he would call. Dad had come in from work, and Mom had cooked a pot roast, with biscuits. It was our special. After eating, I went to the living room. Dad was reading the paper. Brendon and Andrew were playing video games. When the news came on, everyone was watching the weather. Mom had promised the boys she would take them to a movie in Conyers. I decided after the news I would call Ashley. She had been on my mind since dancing at the varsity. I dialed the number, and Ashley answered.

"Hi, Chris." Then I asked her for a date next Friday night. "Let me tell my mom and dad," she said. "Call me back in ten minutes."

"OK," I said, and we hung up. I asked Mom if it was OK.

"Sure," she said. "Just be in by eleven, OK?" she said and looked at me.

"Yes, Mom, I will." I called her back.

"What time?" she asked.

"I'll see you around six. That OK?"

"Good," she replied. "See you Friday." I hung up and started on the yard in a good mood. The week went fast, and Red said he and Beverly would go with us.

That week went fast. I put a new flower garden in, planted a row of okra, squash, and ten tomato plants. I had the yards in good shape, and on Friday, I didn't have much to do. Tomorrow, Dad and I would go to the mountains. I ran five miles every day, and I would stop in the dojo and talk to Mike. I got ready for my date, and Red came at five thirty, and we went to pick up Ashley. Her father was a big football fan; he went to every game. Ashley looked great; she was wearing yellow and white, with a white scarf on her golden hair. Hal, her father, told us to have fun but be home by twelve. "Yes, sir," I told him, and we left. Red had an old Chevy. Everyone at school knew it, and most had ridden in it.

We went to the drive-in and saw a scary movie. The girls would scream every time the axe murderer would kill someone. I held Ashley close, and we kissed several times. She was wonderful. I told her I was going to the mountains tomorrow. She got sad. "When will I see you again?" she asked as we took her home.

"When I come back in a couple of weeks, but I'll call you."

"Can I call you?" she asked.

"Sure," I said. We kissed, and I took her to the door.

I had called Dad and asked if I could stay out until twelve. "OK," he said.

"Thanks, Dad."

The next morning, we started to the mountain around six; all my thoughts were on Ashley. The ride was nice. We saw several deer and a flock of turkey. Uncle Cho had breakfast ready. We ate and started on the side porch. I would use the tractor to pull logs UC had cut, to him and Dad. They would hew the corners to overlap, and we set them in place. By noon we had the floor ready. We ate sandwiches, then started back. That evening, we had the floor in and started the roof. At six, we stopped for the day. UC started working out with his tree, and I started kicking my tree. UC had a hanging duffel bag filled with sand. It was six feet high, and he would kick it. It was too high for me, so he said I needed to limber up, and I would stretch and do bending. I could touch my toes, but he said I would have to put my palms on the floor, so I would stretch more. The next day, we put the ceiling joist up, and we stripped the top with smooth lumber for the metal roofing. We stopped at three, and Dad went home. UC hugged Dad and told him how much he thanked him for all his help. Dad said he wanted UC to help him with some shelves for his shop. Uncle Cho said, "What about the coming weekend?"

"Good," Dad said and left.

I called Ashley and set up a date for Saturday night, and we talked for a while. On Monday we finished the side porch; it was early. Then UC put on a pair of stilts he had made and walked around. When he finished, I tried, and it wasn't hard; so he told me to make a pair, and I did. We would race, but I didn't have a chance, but it was fun. We worked all week on the garden and removing rocks from the fruit trees area. We had gone fishing one day, and UC smoked the trout to take to Mom and Dad. On Friday we went to the house. We got there around seven, and I called Ashley. "Can you come over?" she asked.

"I don't have a ride."

"I'll call Red and maybe he and Beverly will pick you up."

"OK," I said, and she called me back.

"They're on their way and we can go out with them if you like."

"Sure," and I got ready, except they picked her up first. I was glad she came in with Red and Beverly to meet Mom and Dad.

That evening was nice. We went riding looking for animals. We saw several deer. Ashley was so nice and sweet. We kissed a lot and held each other and planned to go to the zoo tomorrow. They had got a new gorilla. We went home early, but Red and Beverly were staying out later. I walked Ashley to her door, and we stood talking and had a small kiss before I left.

Red came to get me at two the next day, and we got the girls and went to Atlanta. The zoo was nice. We stayed until six, then went to eat. Red was trying to imitate the monkeys, and people were laughing. He was enjoying the reaction of the monkeys. I told him he was in his natural place. When the monkeys reacted to his carrying on, it was fun.

School would start in three weeks. Ashley was glad; I was also. I had run a lot that summer, and playing football was fun. On Sunday we went to church. David Paine, our preacher, always met us and the congregation at the door. He was so good and a great preacher; everyone liked him a lot. Mom had a pot roast and okra with squash and a fresh salad for lunch. Dad and UC had finished the work in the shop; it looked good. We left to go to the mountains early. Mom had said I could stay two more weeks, then come home; school would start the following week.

That day, UC started training me self-defense, how to stop someone in a fight. My legs were my best weapons. "Use them," he would say, and most of my training was how to kick and where. Also how to throw someone on the ground. We picked rocks all week, making a large terrace. We would move eight to ten trailer lands a day, and I was getting much stronger. Each day we would walk with stilts, work out with our tree, and more rocks to move. I talked to Ashley every day, and she was glad for school to start. I would be sixteen next week on Friday, and I would get my license then. That weekend, we went fishing, Friday and Saturday. On Sunday we lay around. I ran mornings and evenings now. I could run all the way up the driveway, and I tried to get faster each time.

We moved rocks and hauled dirt that week. We had a terrace twenty-five feet wide and over one hundred feet long. UC would plant fruit trees that winter. He was very pleased about it. On Thursday we went fishing and down to the falls. Dorothy and the children were just getting there. I got Sandra and had her ride on my back. She laughed, and then we got in the water and played with the Jeff and Albert. Barbara finally got in and started splashing water on everyone; it was so nice. Dorothy said for us to play. She and UC walked away from us and talked. After a couple of hours, they had to go. The children wanted to stay longer, but Dorothy said they needed some things from the store. They left, and I promised them I would see them the next time I came back. UC had cleaned the fish, and we started back up the mountain. That day we practiced with the stilts. We would race around the house, and UC would get behind me and kick me with his stilt, then get away from; we had fun. It was hard on my legs, but that was the training UC wanted me to have. My legs got much stronger.

On Friday Dad came up and spent the night. We sat on the porch and talked late. I promised UC I would come back when I could. He thanked me for all my help, and we came home early Saturday morning.

I planned a date with Ashley that evening. Red was coming over around four to get me. He picked Beverly and Ashley up before he got here, and we went to the varsity in Athens and hung out with the players in the parking lot until nine; then we went riding around. We came through Madison, an old town with lots of history. Grandpa knew Col. Dan Hickey and Mrs. Hickey, working for them in their old home, built in 1816, the Stokes-McHenry House and several others. He talked about them and what great people they are. In the country area, we saw several deer and coyotes, then went home. With the starting of school, on Sunday I had learned what to do cleaning up the dojo, and next week I would start work. Now with my driver's license, I got to drive to the store and more places.

School started, and football practice started; then every day except Friday, we practiced. I got up early and would run for four or five miles. Red joined me most days; then we went to school. Ashley and I had three classes together. She would go with me to clean up the dojo. It took about two hours. Mopping was the worst part. On Tuesdays, Thursdays, and Saturdays, I would be at the earliest eight o'clock getting home, but I was making seventy-five dollars a week.

It was the third week of school when we had our first football game; it was with Morgan City, the Falcons. I was second-string end, and in the second half, Coach Mead let me play. Red had kicked a field goal, and we had one touchdown. Our ten to the Falcons' thirteen. Bert, our quarterback, threw a long pass to me on the eleven yard line. I caught the pass, but I was hit hard and had to come out of the game; but after two plays, we got inside the goal for a TD. Red kicked the extra point, and we were seventeen to their thirteen. We beat the game twenty-four to twenty.

My leg was bruised, and I limped for a couple of days. As I cleaned the dojo, sometimes I would get there early and worked out with the weights. On one evening, Mike asked me if I wanted to join the club, but I didn't have enough time. Later I told him as soon as football was over, I might. I would kick the hanging ball around each night. I worked some, and I was getting better. Now I could kick six feet high. By the middle of football season, we had won four games and only lost one. I was playing more now, and I enjoyed the game. Red was doing good. His extra points were enough to help us win two of our games; he was a clown, and everyone liked him. Ashley was now coming to our house for dinner some, and we were very fond of each other. We went out every Friday night, and on Sunday after church, we would go somewhere. Just being together was great. I had saved nine hundred dollars and was looking for a small car, maybe a Honda. One day, Red told me about a car for sale near his house. We rode out to look at it. An old lady let us drive it around the area. Her name was Emma Dean. Her husband had just died three months earlier, and she didn't drive. "I hate to let it go," she said. They had bought the Honda new nine years ago, and it was the only car they had ever bought new. "I'll take a thousand dollars for it," she said.

"I only have nine hundred dollars, Mrs. Dean, but if you let me pay you that, I will get the car and pay you the rest in two weeks."

"You seem like a nice young man, Chris, and I will do that, but if you will take me to the store on Wednesdays for a while, I'll sell it to you for the nine hundred and you can take it now."

"Yes, ma'am, I will do that, but I play football and it might be seven or eight before I could come to get you."

"That will be OK," she said. "That is the only way I could go get groceries. Could you take me now to the store?" she asked.

"Yes, ma'am, I can." I told Red and Beverly, and they left. I took Mrs. Dean to Kroger, and we talked. She was so nice and very lonely.

"I'll be a little while," she said. But I didn't care. The car had been kept in good condition and ran great. I went into the store and pushed the buggy around for her. It took an hour.

"Old folks are slow," I told Mom as we talked. "She is so nice and very lonely," I said.

Mom said, "Maybe I can take her to the store for you. I buy groceries on Wednesday."

"She will talk your ears off," I said.

Dad liked the car. "You got a good deal," he said, "but you have to have insurance before you can drive it."

"I know."

Dad said, "I'll buy your insurance this time for you but you have to buy it next time."

I gave him a hug and Mom too. "You are the best dad and mom in the world." I had studying to do, and it was getting late now. "Books," I said.

The next morning, I went for a good run. Red caught up with me, and we did over five miles. He had breakfast with us, and we went to school. Mom would get my insurance after work. After football practice, I went by the house. Mom said she had got no falt for me but no coverage on my car. "Please be careful." I hugged her and went to the dojo to clean it. They were still practicing, so I watched, until Mike told me to join them. He was showing us how to throw a larger person. My turn came, and I threw a large boy, Lester. He didn't like it and got mad, but he would not do anything because Mike had a rule about getting mad. You could get thrown out of the club if you fought.

Friday came and we had a game. In the second half, I got to play. On our first play, I went downfield and caught a pass. We got within twenty yards of the finish line. On the first play, Bert threw a pass to the other end, but we only got a couple of yards. On the second play, it was a running play, and they stopped us. The third down, Bert threw to Charles, the left end, and he missed, so we had to kick, but Red kicked a forty-two-yard field goal. We were tied seventeen to seventeen. They got the kick and brought it back to our forty six, and we held them; but on our return, we only got back to our twenty-seven, and I was sent in. We were to do a down and out play, only one minute and a half left in the game. Bert threw the ball to me at the fifty yard line. I got it and went to their nineteen; then Bert threw to Charles and missed. He did a running play for five yards, and on the third down, he threw another pass, but it was incomplete. Only twenty-five seconds left, he told me and Charles to run to the end zone, and whoever was clear, he would pass to. I ran to the middle of the end zone, then ran as hard as I could to my right, and I saw the pass coming. I dove for the catch and got it for the touchdown with five seconds to play. We were twenty-three to seventeen. We beat them. I felt good.

There was a picture of me catching the ball in our local paper. I was diving for the ball, and I felt proud. We had won seven games and only lost one, but our next two games were our hardest. Rockdale was undefeated, and Morgan had only one loss also. The school dance lasted till eleven, and I waited till twelve before taking Ashley home. We were spending lots of our off time together. On Saturday I went to the dojo early and joined in the workout. Afterward we teamed up for a little one on one. Mike put me with Lester, and we were allowed to do some kicking. We had been warned not to strike the body above the shoulders, and Lester was kicking me hard. After the second time, I did a side spin and flat kick that knocked him down and took the breath out of him, and he got mad; and when he started getting wild, I threw him on the floor and got a neck hold on him. When he was getting real mad, I let him go. He came at me, swinging. I got his arm and threw him to the floor and got an arm bar on him. He settled down then, but I knew he had a lot of dislike for me. After everyone left, I cleaned up and went for Ashley. I went home for a shower and some clean clothes. We went to a movie and joined Red and Beverly. On Sunday Ashley was going with her family to see her grandparents. I got up late and went for a good run. After seven or eight miles, I stopped at the drugstore.

Raj was working. We started talking while he made me a Coke float; then the white-haired old man whom I had met before came in. "Hi, Raj, Coke float." Then he said, "Hi, Chris, good game you played, nice catch."

"I'm sorry, I forgot your name."

"Tom Quick," he said. We three talked. Mr. Quick had been to India and saw the Taj Mahal.

"Beautiful place," Raj said. "We would go there for a picnic."

Tom finished his Coke float and said, "I'll see you around," and left.

"I'll see you later," I told Raj and started running home.

The next week went fast, and Friday we went to Morgan City for our game. With only one loss for them and us, it was a tough game. In the third quarter, we were tied fourteen to fourteen, and both teams were hitting hard. The last quarter, we got the ball and got to their nine yard line. We couldn't get in to their end zone, so Red was sent in for a field goal attempt; it was good. They had four minutes left and started a good drive. They got to our eleven yard line and attempted a field goal and missed. We won seventeen to their fourteen.

The next week, we had our last game, and we also had our finals before the holidays. I studied all weekend and felt good about the tests. That week, Mom asked me to carry Mrs. Dean to the grocery store; she was very busy. So on Wednesday, I went to get her; she wanted to talk. "Your mother is so nice. She invited me to your Christmas dinner. It's such a lonely time for me, and how is your lessons doing?"

"Good," I said.

"Keep your grades up for that scholarship."

"Yes, ma'am, I do."

"I read the paper and I know you are good at football."

"Thank you," I told her as I took her groceries in. "I'll see you next week," I told her as I left. She wanted to talk, but I worked my way out. I knew it was a lonely time for her. She had no children, with Bill, her husband, gone. Mom spent what time she could with her, and I was glad Mom invited her for Christmas dinner. We practiced every day that week. The game would be played at home, and on Friday, at the start of the game, we lost the kick, and they elected to receive the ball. Red kicked high and long. They got by our rushing guards and ran the ball back to our forty-two yard line, and after three first downs, they went in for a TD. We received the ball, and after five first downs were stopped, we kicked to them; and they took the ball on their sixteen and moved it back to our twenty-two, and we got the ball on our twelve and went back to their forty-two and were stopped again. The half ended with the score seven to zero, and second half, we received the ball; and after six first downs, we were at their seventeen. Coach Mead sent in a play with me, and it was a pass play to me. I caught the ball in the end zone for a touchdown, and the game ended with a score of seven to seven.

Football was over, and the holidays were here. I promised Uncle Cho I would come to the mountains and stay till Saturday. Christmas was on Monday, and UC would come back to Covington then for the holidays with us. On Monday we got rocks up for the terrace wall and that evening worked out on our trees. My stretching had increased to where I'm able to put the palms of my hand flat on the floor, and I could straddle wider and kick six feet high now. UC was watching, I thought, seeing if I had improved or not. When we finished, he went to his meditating rock. I sat on the porch and swung; it was cold enough now for me to wear a small coat. On Tuesday we hauled rocks and in the evening got our stilts and walked and ran with them. He had fun kicking my rear and moving away while I tried to catch him. By Friday we had the nice terrace. That was the third terrace, and he was very pleased. "I'll put fruit trees in next month," he said and then we did some training together. How to fall properly, how to kick someone behind you. "You're improving good," he said, "but never use your skill for pleasure or fighting. That was a promise I made to McCoo, my priest."

"I won't," I promised. Friday evening we went home for the holidays; eating started Saturday.

CHAPTER II

The holidays were over, and school started back. I had made four As and two Bs on my report card. That pleased Mom, and Ashley and I spent lots of time together. I would run each morning and some evenings. Track would start in February, and Red and I would try to break the school record and maybe go to state competition. Coach Mead had told us to keep running every day, and we did, always timing ourselves. I enjoyed working at the dojo. I was saving my money, and the training was good.

In February, track and field started. On our first trial run, Red was seven seconds from the record and I was nine on the two-mile run, and now Red and I raced every day. By March we were three seconds from the record. Our school had the regional record set three years earlier. The middle of March, we had our first competition, with Morgan City and Rockdale City. Red and I had a plan not to start so fast and hold back till the last mile, then turn it on. Rockdale had four men, and Morgan had three. We only had me and Red. At the start Rockdale started fast. We held back but not far. On the second mile, we started. Red gave it all he had, and I did too. We passed the two leading men and didn't look back. We knew we were close to the record, and as we passed the finish line, the people started hollering. We were wide open, and we had to run slowing down; then we walked back to Coach Mead. Everyone was excited. Red said, "We did it."

We could hear our friends telling us we did it, and Coach Mead said, "Red, you and Chris just set a school record by four seconds."

We were very happy and took the girls to Red Lobs. Ashley had the most loving ways that night as we sat watching the Yellow River. I started playing with Ashley's breast, and she stopped me. "Chris, I think the world of you but I promised myself and my mom I would stay a virgin until I got married. Please help me honor that." At first I was a little mad, but I knew that took a lot of devotion to one's self and willpower. "Please don't be mad," as she held me close to her and kissed me. I was disappointed, but I knew I had a special gal.

The next month was great. We went to region for our next match. We came in second and third. A runner from DeKalb City beat us by two seconds, but Coach Mead was very pleased. He was a senior; we had two years to improve.

Uncle Cho asked me to come to the mountains when I could, and I went every chance I could, and we practiced with our stilts and also different ways to disable an opponent. On one Tuesday at Mike's dojo, Mike was gone, and while practicing with Lester, he got mad and started swinging at me. I grabbed his arm and went under it, twisting it behind him. He was furious. I had one arm pinned, with the other around his neck. "I'm tired of you swinging madly at me and your kicking me," I told him. "You're going to stop, do you hear me?" I said.

"Yes," he replied, but when I let him go, he swung at me, and it caught my face. I tackled him, throwing him to the floor, and I got a leg lock on him. He started hollering, "Let me go." The whole dojo was watching; everyone was glad I had him. He was always a bully, and no one liked the way he practiced.

"I'll let you go this time, but if you ever hit me again, I'll break your arm or leg."

"OK," he pleaded. "I won't," and when I let him up, he went to the restroom, and from that time on, we were good friends.

School was about out, and I was going to spend the summer with Uncle Cho. We made plans to walk on the Appalachian Trail for three weeks. We were going on a survival trip. No food, except what we could find on the way. We would carry a poncho and blanket, our knife and a machete, flint to start a fire, and a change of clothing.

"Are you worried?" UC asked me.

"No," I said. "If you can do it, I can," I said. He laughed.

"We will see."

The first week I was with him, we worked on his driveway. We got all the large rocks from it and built a terrace. That winter, UC put six apple trees out and two chestnuts trees. He already had muscadine vines. He had plenty of muscadine and a few strawberries. We went fishing twice and several hikes around the mountains, and on Monday, we planned to leave. On Sunday we hiked down to the falls and met Dorothy and the children.

Sandra was more outgoing now. Jeff, Albert, and Barbara were doing good in school. They had all passed with good grades. We played in the water until it was time to go. "We will see you when we come back," UC told Dorothy, and we started up the mountain. On Monday we started out. It was about seven miles where we got on the trail, and we walked another ten miles or so before we made camp for the night. I was very hungry, but I was determined not to complain. If UC could do it, then I could. The next morning, my stomach was hurting. I was so hungry. UC had dug up some sassafras roots, and we chewed on them. We walked all morning. At noon we stopped at a ridge looking down a long valley. It was beautiful. After a good rest, we started back walking. I had cut a staff and used it to help me on some steep spots. That evening my stomach was really hurting, but I didn't complain. We made camp by a creek, and we caught several spring lizards and cooked them over the fire. They didn't have much meat on them, but I was surprised they tasted OK, and I went to sleep hungry again.

While going down a long winding hill, UC said, "Look," and we went to a chestnut tree. The nuts were small like a pecan, but we picked all we could, and I had maybe a gallon plus what UC had. "We have dinner," he said. I ate several while walking. UC said they would be good roasted.

That evening, we made camp, and after building a fire, we put some chestnuts at the edge of the fire by some coals and roasted the chestnuts. We turned them several times and took them and got the shells off and ate. They were so good. I was so hungry, I ate a double handful. UC ate about half what I did. I went to sleep for the first time satisfied. I still had lots of them left. The next morning, we were up early, and on our way, UC told me we would try to make it to a lake and that evening might catch us some fish. We had fishhooks and line with us.

I started walking a little faster. I was so hungry, all I could think of was a meal. Around noon we stopped for a rest. I asked, "Are we making good time?"

"Very good. We should make it to the lake by night or before," he said.

"I'm ready if you are."

"Let's go," he said, and we started. By four he said, "See that mountaintop? At the bottom is a lake." It looked so far away, I thought, but we kept going. By the time we reached the top, it was only an hour before dark. We came by a wet spring, and UC said, "Let's get some bait." So we looked for spring lizards and found several; then we picked up the pace. By the time we reached the lake, it was almost dark. I started gathering woods for a fire, and UC started fishing. I built a fire by the water, and UC hung a nice fish and lost it. "I need a pole," he said, so I found a long limb. He started again. Within thirty minutes, he caught a nice three-pound, maybe four, bass. He gutted it and took out some aluminum foil and wrapped it and laid it by the coals and started fishing again.

"Turn the fish over," he said. "Be careful not to puncture the foil." I carefully rolled the fish over, and then he caught another fish. This one about two pounds. I was so hungry, my mouth was watering. UC looked so patient and never spoke of being hungry. With a full stomach and three extra fish for our trip, I went to sleep. So satisfied, I slept like a baby. A little after daybreak, we were on our way.

We made good miles. The next week, we would eat crawfish, chestnuts, spring lizards, and fish when we could. Most days had something but not enough. I lost weight. My pants were loose, and the scenery was great. I was feeling good. All the good air and mountain water, UC said it was cleaning out the poisons from our body. I missed the food, but I was not hurting like I had been. Starting the third week, it began to rain. We found a good cliff with a big hangover near a lake and stopped for a day and two nights before it cleared. We caught several fish and ate good.

On the second morning, it had stopped raining. As we started around a mountain, the trail was muddy; and I had stopped to clean the mud off my boots, when I thought I heard a baby cry. As I listened, I could barely hear something like a cry. UC noticed I had stopped and was waiting. When I motioned for him, he came back to me, and I told him I thought I heard a crying. We listened; then we heard it and started going around and up the mountain, and then we could see a truck turned over, and it was a child crying. We hurried to the truck, and inside was a small baby in a child's seat. A man and a woman were unconscious, with blood showing on the man's head.

The truck was lying on its side, with a small tree holding it from rolling on down the mountain. We were afraid to touch the truck until we could do something. Uncle Cho said we need two strong poles to wedge the truck first. "Let's get a big rock under the tires to start." I found a big rock, but I needed help to get it. We got it to the truck, and UC took his machete and dug a spot under the side of the rear tire. When we were satisfied it would help, we got another rock. It was smaller, but it made a good base for another rock to rest on. While I find a good one, Uncle Cho was cutting down a small tree about six inches around. I got the rocks under the front tires, and Uncle Cho started on a second small tree.

The baby was crying a lot now. When we got the trees wedged, holding the truck, we hoped, I got on the truck's side and opened the door and crawled in. The baby was in the backseat, and I cut the seat belt off and lifted the baby out to UC. The lady was lying on the man, and she had blood on the ear and mouth. I cut the seat belt off her, but I could not get her lifted to get her out. UC said, "Knock out the windshield." He handed me a good rock to knock it away from the truck. It took four hard hits before it broke out; then I got her handed through the windshield. UC got the woman above the truck with the baby. As I busted the air bag and cut the seat belt away from the man, his hand was caught in the door, pinned, and I could not see how to get it loose. A drizzle had started now. We need to get a pole under the cab of the truck and lift it off his hand, but if we moved it, it might break loose and tumble down the mountain. UC reached through the windshield and took his knife and stuck him in the side of the leg slightly to see if his body reflexed; it did. "Good," he said. "Maybe there is no spinal injury. Find the tire jack. Maybe that will work to wedge the door enough to get his hand loose." UC found a jack and dug a place to get the jack between the truck and door and said, "This is dangerous. If the truck breaks loose, it will tumble on me with you caught inside. We have to try if you are willing." I was scared; he was nervous. It was the first time I saw a sign of fear in him. "Are you ready?" he asked.

"Yes, let's do it."

I was standing on the door. It was the only place I could get to pull on his arm. The truck moved, and my heart started pounding. He was still caught. UC had to wedge more. He pushed down on the jack, and the truck moved again. I was sweating now, but the hand came loose, and UC slowly let the truck loose. He came to the window, and we got the man passed through. I got out as fast as I could. I was shaking. We got the man away from the truck, and UC told me I would have to go for help. The man was bleeding down his hand now, and UC put a compression bandage on it. He had his shirt tied around tight. "Go to the road, put some brush in the way, then go down the road for help."

The baby was crying now, and I said, "I'll run."

"Don't overdo it. You have a long way to the highway." UC was holding the baby now, and I started.

I made it to the road and got some limbs lying to block anyone that might try to come by. I didn't know which way to go. I just started to my right at a good jog.

I ran down the road for over an hour. I knew I had come at least five or six miles. I could hear cars on a highway. I started faster. When I got to the highway, I was out of breath, and I was going to stop the first person for help. About two minutes went by when I saw a pickup truck coming. I was in the middle of the road, waving my arms, and the truck pulled over. "What's wrong?" he asked. I was so excited that I had a hard time telling him. "Get in," he said. He took off. "We have to go to a phone," he said.

We stopped at a house, and he hollered. Inside a woman came to the door. "Martha," he said, "an accident on the mountain, people hurt." She got the phone, and he call 911. "Ron," he said, "this is Pop John. We have a bad accident with a child and man and woman on Mountain Road, Elk Park, maybe six to ten miles up, need help. I'm going back up now. Thanks," and we left, heading back. I had calmed down a lot now. "What's your name?" he asked.

"Chris," I said, and I told him my uncle and I was hiking the trail, when we heard the baby, and we went to investigate, and I described what we found.

"They were mighty lucky you heard them." I told John what we had to do to get them out. He just listened.

After fifteen minutes or so, we got there. I hollered down, "Help is coming!" We got to UC, and he had the woman in his arms with the baby. She was moaning; the baby was crying a little.

Pop John said, "Elda, this is Pop, you're going to be OK. Hi, young man, I'm Pop John."

"I'm Charles Doan," UC told him. "She is in shock." It was raining lightly now. UC had his poncho over her and the baby. Pop went over to Mark, her husband; he was still unconscious. UC had my poncho over Mark, except his face.

Pop said, "This is terrible. These people live on the other side of Elk Park, good people." Pop felt the pulse of Mark. He has a weak pulse, but he is alive. With his messed-up hand and the tourniquet, blood was on the ground and all on his arm.

UC said, "The hand was caught under the door."

Pop got up and walked to the bottom of the truck, staying well away from it; then he went above the truck and down to the back, looking at the small tree holding the truck, the two poles wedging it, and the rocks the rocks were placed under the tires. He asked, "How did you get them out?" looking at me. I started telling Pop John what we did. "You had to get in the truck and cut them loose and pass them out?"

"Yes, sir," I said.

He looked at UC and said, "You had to go below the truck and wedge the door to get Mark out." UC just nodded at him. "My God, man, you sure took an awful chance. That truck was only being held by a prayer." Then I could hear a siren down in the valley. "Sound like help," Pop said. Pop had put his coat over Mark and was trying to talk to Elda. Uncle Cho was rocking the baby in his arms. Now the baby was not crying. I was wet and now realized I was very tired, and with all the worry, a chill went over me as I looked at Mark. The ambulance was first, and a fire and rescue truck and more were coming.

Men started down toward us, bringing armfuls of things. A woman saw Cho with the lady and the baby. She started there. Two men were working with Mark. By now there were ten or more people. They were asking Uncle Cho all kinds of questions. They gave Mark and Elda shots and started a transfusion on Mark. They got both of them on stretchers, and now Uncle Cho was standing. Men were looking at how we wedged the truck to do what we had done. One said we did more than they thought could be done with poles and rocks. They had got a statement from UC and now were asking me questions. One paramedic put a blanket over my shoulders and handed one to UC; they wanted to know all kinds of things. It took thirty minutes standing on the road.

I started talking to UC. The first ambulance had left with Mark, and the other one was leaving with the baby and Elda. We wanted to know how they would be, so we decided to go to the hospital with Pop John. He said he would help us get strengthened out. "What you want to eat?" he asked me. I realized how hungry I was. I looked at UC. He smiled at me.

"Let's treat ourselves," he said. "A steak would be good."

Pop said, "After the hospital, a steak it would be." We got to the hospital, and they had Mark, Elda, and the baby in the emergency room. The sheriff department was there, and an Officer Lily was wanting to take more information. A newsman wanted to talk to us, and Officer Lily made him wait in another room with some friends of Mark and Elda. After an hour, we had got word both of them would probably be OK. The baby was doing good. He was very hungry, and now Elda's mom and dad were there holding him. Pop told Officer Lily, "These men need food and dry clothes. Could we go and come back later?"

"Sure," he said.

We went to a motel and checked in. Pop had insisted on taking our clothes, both changes, and said, "I'll be back in a few minutes." We showered and shaved. Pop had our things back in an hour, and we went to the restaurant clean and dry. Several people came by and said how much they thanked us and what a great job we had done. I had a salad potato and nice steak. UC had steak and salad. When we finished eating, we went back to the hospital.

We kept getting people wanting to talk about what happened and thanking us. I was getting tired of telling. UC would excuse himself and go walking around the hospital or anywhere. Later that evening, a doctor came out and talked to us. Mark had surgery on his hand and now was unconscious. He had two broken ribs, a shoulder that would have to have surgery, and a concussion. Elda was heavily sedated but would probably be OK. The little boy was doing good; his grandmother had him. I called Mom and told her what had happened and where we were at. We went to the motel satisfied. We could do no more. Pop said he was coming back to town in the morning. Maybe we could have breakfast with him. "Sure," I told him and thanked him for so much help.

"My pleasure," he told us and left.

Uncle Cho had called a friend, Bill, and he was coming after us around noon tomorrow. We asked him to pick us up at the hospital, so that would be a good way to get away from here. Pop got to the motel around nine, and we went to breakfast with him, then went to the hospital. We were told Elda had broken ribs, her right leg was heavily bruised, and she had began to come out of the shock but was still sedated. We went in and spoke to Mark. He was looking much better and thanked us. We wished him luck and went to the front of the hospital. Bill had come. "Good-bye," Pop John told us and said he would call us if it was OK and keep us in touch about Mark and Elda and the baby.

CHAPTER III

Bill came back home on I-20 and brought me home first. I thanked him and said good-bye to UC. They were talking to Mom and Dad while I went in for a shower and a change of clothes. I promised UC I would come back to the mountains for two more weeks. I called Red, and he was coming over later with the girls. Ashley was excited. I promised to take her out to dinner when I got back, and she and Beverly were ready. Uncle Cho had left, and while I waited for Red and the girls, Dad wanted to hear from me what happened; and when I finished telling the story, from the start of the trail till the accident, he said, "You and Cho took lots of chances, sounds like." Then he smiled. "But that's your Uncle Cho and you. You're my kind of people," and he smiled.

We went to the Red Lobster, then rode around. I had told Red already I was sick of talking about the accident. He or the girls never asked anything. It was so nice holding Ashley and kissing her. "I'll be glad when school starts," Ashley said.

"Why?" I asked. She blushed away, which makes her look so loving, and we kissed more. We went out every night until Friday. That's when I went back to Uncle Cho.

I had talked to Coach Mead and told him how much I was running and jogging. "Great," he said, "but be back for football training in two weeks or sooner." He was great, letting me off while some of the players couldn't.

Saturday morning, while I ran down to the highway, UC fixed breakfast. It took twenty-five minutes without stopping. Good start, I thought. UC wanted to build a separate terrace for the next fruit trees, fifteen feet wide, one hundred and fifty feet long, so we started digging and moving rocks. We dug every day, loaded rocks, pulled them to the wall, and kept pilling rocks. On Friday we were almost finished, so UC said, "Let's go fishing," and we did. We had made sandwiches from a roast that had been cooking and left with our poles for fishing.

We found plenty of spring lizards in weed leaves, and as we got to the creek, I stopped and motioned UC to go first, and he did, easing up to a casting spot first. Quietly he let the lizard float down. As it went by a large rock, a trout jumped and grabbed the lizard and started up the creek. UC was smiling; then he set his line and pulled in a fifteen-inch brook trout. I moved up to the edge and cast just like UC, but nothing; then again after five casts, I went by UC. He had caught two. I finally got a small rainbow; then I got another bigger one. By the time we got to the bottom, we had eight. That would feed us two meals. I should have known Dorothy had the kids swimming. I was glad we played, splashing water on each other until we were tired. Everyone was laughing, even little Sandra. UC and Dorothy sat by themselves talking. I knew he liked her, but to get him to say more would take a pry bar. Finally they came over and asked the kids if they want to go to the mountain with us. "Yes, yes, let's go," so we rode up the mountain with them and made sandwiches. After eating, we walked to the new area where we were working. They were figuring how much horse manure it would take to fertilize new ground. We came up with three trucks and trailer loads. Dorothy had been saving droppings, and there was more if we needed. She boarded horses. They had four now, but most springs, she had six to eight. We played pitch and Frisbee chase, and when it got almost dark, we would play hide-and-seek. Those kinds were so loved. Everyone was a friend; it was nice. Finally Dorothy said it was time to go. I promised the boys I would see them tomorrow.

"Me too?" Sandra asked while riding on my shoulders.

"You too," I said as I hugged her bye.

We were up and eating at daybreak. I washed dishes and cleaned up the kitchen, then went to help UC load the trailer. By nine we were at Dorothy's house. They came out to help us. Jeff got the Bobcat, and we went to work at ten. He could drive a Bobcat good. I was proud of him, and he just grinned. After we loaded, he and Albert wanted to help us unload, so we took them with us. We had a pallet tied to the tractor, and we pulled the pallet with all the horse manure off on the ground; then I had the tractor putting piles where they could be spread out. After that load, we went back for three more before we stopped. We had a foot thick all over the new area. It would take two to three weeks to dry out good; then UC would plow it into the ground to sit till winter. It would be ten apple trees, four plumb trees, and four pears. He had already made a scupperdine orchard. That was his way. Grow anything you could; he loved it, any gardening.

On Sunday we went on a picnic. We hitched the wagon to two horses and loaded our things and went riding out a dirt road by Dorothy's farm. It was a dead end, so there wasn't any traffic for three miles. Barbara was eleven and drove the wagon. Dorothy rode with Sandra, and Uncle Cho rode another horse. The boys and I would get off and run a ways, then wait on everyone to catch us. We swam in the creek. We made a little dam, and everyone helped with rocks and dirt. After five hours eating and playing, we started back. That was a wonderful day. Sandra was so happy, and everyone was pleased with the day.

Monday came, and we started one more side porch. It would be twenty-eight feet long and ten feet wide. We sat all the logs first for the floor and foundation, which took two days; then we decked the floor with pressure-treated lumber. We finished the flooring late that Wednesday. On Thursday we started the ceiling rafters and joist with legs; then on Friday we stripped the logs and got ready for the metal roof. Saturday, Dad came up and helped us. By five we finished the metal. Now we had finished, and it looked great. We planned to go fishing. Dad loved it, and he and UC talked a lot while fishing together. Near dark, Dad left to go back home. I had one more week. Monday morning, after running to the highway, UC said, "It's time to get your training started," and we started on the stilts. We raced around the yard; then he started across the creek on a log. He crossed easy, but I started and fell. I tried it again and fell, getting wet. He laughed. "Isn't easy," he said. I didn't know if I would ever be able to cross on a log. That day we worked on our tree, hitting it, kicking and moving, and kicking. By noon I was worn out. Now my legs were feeling the pain, but after eating, we started again. UC said, "Now is when you are creating muscle." We kept training all day. On Tuesday we worked out more, then went back to our stilts. By that evening my legs were aching. I knew all this legwork was good, but it sure hurt. By the end of the week, I was getting over my hurt and felt good. Mom and Dad came after me on Friday evening, spent the night, and we came home on Saturday. Uncle Cho thanked me and Mom and Dad. "It's been a good summer. Chris has done a great job helping me." I really felt good looking at our progress, and we went home.

Mom wanted to stop in Helen while we were so close. We looked around and stopped for a special ice cream. At one place, a jeweler was making jewelry from gold mined from these mountains. Another place was making glassware, blowing the glass, twisting shapes very good. There was also a blacksmith that was working and two men shoeing horses, making things, selling all types of metalwork they had. Walking down the Chattahoochee, it was a fun place for a variety of things. We got home around dark. Mom had called Brendon and Andrew and told them to be home by six. She had plans. I searched my mind to think why it was a special day; then I remembered it was Andrew's birthday. Mom made a birthday cake, and we ate pizza and had cake and ice cream. I had called Ashley and Red. He picked up the girls and got here at seven. We went riding around, and it felt good. I had spoken to Mike at the dojo, and I would start cleaning it tomorrow. School would start in one week. I had football practice on Monday. We rode around Covington, then went to Atlanta to the varsity and hung out until ten, then started home. Sunday morning, I went to church with the family, and after eating, I went to the dojo. Mike was working on his paperwork, and I started cleaning. I put up all the weights, then straightened up the gym, then swept. I started mopping, and Mike was through and said, "Lock up when you finish." I had my own key now, and Mike left. I finished, and it only took me two hours.

On Monday I went to football practice. We practiced for six hours. The coach said we looked like an accident looking for a place to happen. Me and Red outran everyone on the two-mile run. The coach timed everyone and said we have to do better if we expected to win any games. I went home and cut grass and started reading my computer book. On Tuesday I went to the dojo early. It was six, and I started working out with the weights and watching Mike teach his students. I knew most of them. When he finished, I cleaned up and left. That week went fast; then school started.

First football game
Jasper City Bulls vs. 21-7

We only had two weeks before our first football game with Jasper County Bulls. We won it twenty-one to seven on Tuesday. That week I went to clean up the dojo early. Mike had asked me if I want to join. I had told him, "Maybe later."

"Don't worry about paying," he said. "I'll let you do some extra work for it."

After exercising, we teamed up with an opponent and did one-on-one training. Mike had me working with Lester. He was the oldest student. He had been a student for three years and acted like he was our instructor.

We did an arm bar, with flipping our opponent. Lester didn't like being thrown, and on my time to throw him, he sidestepped me and threw me down, then said, "I'll show you how to do that." I got up, and when he attempted, I reversed the move and threw him. He got mad and came at me with fist swinging. I grabbed him and did a side throw, and he went down. Mike had come out of his office and saw what was happening and came over. Mike had a rule that if you got mad or fought, you would be kicked out. Lester calmed down and when he had a chance said he would get me for that. "If you must," I said, "I'll be around."

CHAPTER IV

School had started, and football practice was four times a week. We had won our first three games. When we were through with practice, cleaning the dojo, and studying, I had a full schedule. Friday nights after football, Red, the girls, and I would hang out with the other football players and cheerleaders. It was good times. I ran every morning for three to seven miles. I enjoyed running and looked forward to track. I knew I would be in the finals, at least I thought I would. Red always ran with me on Saturdays. I had got where I could run as fast as Red and maybe a little faster. By the end of football season, we had only lost two games, but I was glad football was over. Track would start in the spring, and now all I had to do was work at the dojo and run.

Christmas came and went, and every day I went to the dojo and worked out. Mike had four classes—yoga, meditation, weight lifting, and karate. On one Sunday while running, I stopped in Covington at the drugstore to see Raj and have a Coke float. While I was talking to Raj, the elderly man I had spoke to before came in and ordered a Coke float also. "How are you doing, Chris?" he asked.

"Good," I said, surprised he knew my name. He spoke in Arabic to Raj. They talked a little, and I heard Raj call him Mr. T. "What does the *T* stand for?" I asked.

"Tom," he said. "Tom Quick." I shook hands with him. "You had a good football season," he said.

"Thank you."

"Going to college?" Tom asked.

"Yes," I said. "I hope to get a scholarship in track at Young Harris."

When Tom started to leave, he gave me a business card. "If you ever need my services, call me." The card read Advisor Tom Quick.

"What do you do?" I asked him.

"I fix problems," he said.

"Any problems?" I asked.

"Most," he said and left. Tom was very distinguished, black hair with enough gray to look good.

"Nice person," I said to Raj.

"Oh yes. He is a regular customer, always a Coke float. Coke with two scoops vanilla ice cream and he speaks good Arabic."

I went to the dojo. Mike was doing his paperwork. I started working out with weights. Mike finished and said, "See you later," and left. The dojo was clean. I had cleaned it the night before, and now I wanted a good weight workout. When I finished, I weighed, and now I was one seventy-five. I could press two hundred pounds three times. I changed back to my street clothes and ran home. Mom had a roast for lunch; then I picked Ashley up and went for a ride. We had ridden to Madison looking at the old homes and talking about the summer. We would have our first track meet in three weeks. I was ready.

Finally, track started. I ran every day, five miles in the morning and five miles at school. When our first competition was held at Morgan City School, it was for the two-mile race. There were ten of us.

I won it by seven seconds. That would mean we would be in the quarter finals in three weeks. We had two months before school was out, and our last race would be in five weeks. At the second meet, all the racers were good. The coach had told me not to lead but to hold back until the last mile, then to turn it on; so as we started out, I lay back and was in fourth place. At the start of the second mile, I felt good and passed everyone, except the leading runner, so I got even with him. He turned it on also. I didn't realize he was told the same thing. Now we had a race. He was the best runner Rock City had. We stayed shoulder to shoulder for half a mile; then I gave it all I had. His nick name was Cheetah. Now I knew why. That fellow could run. I beat him but only by two seconds, and I had given it all I had, but I felt great. All my running had paid off. Coach Mead was happy. We won division for the first time. Now maybe I could get a scholarship. I had my application in for Young Harris. My goal was to become a newsman. I had watched reporters for the past three years, and I like the idea of traveling and announcing. Computers were the key to reporting, and I wanted a degree in computer science. They had a great program at Young Harris.

On Saturday Red came over, and we planned to run a long way. We started by the river and ran down by it for five miles to the dam at Porterdale and noticed people in the lower section. It was Raj and Lenny. Four students from Rockdale were there harassing them. We went down. "What's going on?" I asked.

One of the bigger boys said, "We're going to kick these Moslems' ass unless you want part of it."

Red spoke up first. "Whose ass you going to kick?" he asked.

Then the loudmouth pushed Raj back. Red started toward them, and I followed. As Red got to him, one of the other fellows tried to trip Red; then they started swinging. I hit one in the mouth. His teeth cut my knuckles, but he went down. Red had kicked one, and he was also down. Another fellow hit me from the side. I spun and elbowed him in the head. The last one standing was saying, "I don't want no trouble." They all had Rockdale High jackets on.

Raj said, "Thank you, Chris and Red." We told the boys to get out of there and not come back.

Then Red asked, "Whose ass you want to kick now?" They left. We walked back to Covington with Raj and Lenny, talking about the summer. Raj was going to India for two months.

"Who will make me Coke floats?" I asked jokingly.

Lenny said, "Thank you both. You're fine people."

"You are too," I said.

We stopped at the dojo. Red was going to clean it for me while I worked with my Uncle Cho over the summer. Mike said it was OK with him, and after they finished, Red and I cleaned up. He could do it easy I knew.

School ended, and I went to the mountains and helped Uncle Cho. We started with building a barn to keep his equipment in. We finished the first week and on Saturday went to see Dorothy and the children. It was early Saturday morning. Her stables needed new metal on it. We started taking all the old metal off. Jeff and Albert were good help for eleven-year-olds. They would pick up the old metal and stack it on her trailer. We had all the metal off by two and went to the waterfalls, swimming. Sandra was growing, and I spent time with her. Barbara was still a sad girl, so we played, splashing water on the boys. She liked that and would laugh a little. She was always afraid of being sent to live with someone else. I felt sorry for such children, who had no parents and were raised in foster homes. Even though Dorothy, I knew, treated her children better than most. When we started home, UC told Dorothy we would be back Monday. The new roofing would be there then. She thanked us, and we came on up the mountain to our cabin. "Good person," UC said. "That Dorothy is a special person."

"Yes, she is. Does that mean she is your girlfriend?" I asked.

"Of course she is my friend," he said and changed the subject. On Sunday we worked out. We had practiced with the stilts every day, and that evening we had a little race. Of course he beat me. We started going through the rough area, then across the creek on the log I fell in, and then up the hill and down the other side. It was fun. UC would kid me about being so slow. He knew how well I had done in the competition, but I hadn't said anything. He knew this was building my legs up, and I wanted to go to Young Harris. I would stay with him while I was in school if I made it.

On Monday we went back to Dorothy's house and on Tuesday finished the top. All that week, we trained. UC showed me different ways to disable someone. We practiced and practiced more.

I ran up and down the road every day and would time myself. My legs were improving a lot. Sometimes UC would run with me, and we went fishing every couple of days. We worked on the driveway, lining big rocks on each side and small rocks in the middle all the spare time. We had three terraces almost around the yard. Two had fruit trees. The garden area was clean and irrigated. We let water flow through it every few days. Uncle Cho would pick up the dirt and squeeze it. Maybe tomorrow we will water it. He had squash, okra, tomatoes, lettuce, corn, and peas. We had been eating most of the things, but the corn and okra were slower to grow.

That weekend, Dad came up, and we went fishing. "Looks great," he told UC. "You keep a nice place." That evening, me and UC had a good workout. He would show me different ways to strike with my elbow in close, or a spinning strike, different spinning moves, and flat kicking for power. After we stopped, I worked on my tree, kicking and hitting it. I had an army duffel bag hanging five feet high, and it was filled with wood chips to kick high, and sometimes I would do a jump kick, anything for exercise. Dad and UC sat on the porch and talked all that evening. It was nice to see them together. Dad needed his attachment back to Vietnam and the days while he was young.

"We are going to Panama City on vacation," Dad told me. "In another week."

"Great," I said. I sure like camping at Saint Andrew's State Park. The beach is so nice, and jetty fishing. The park had good roads to run on and bicycle riding. I enjoyed the swamp alligators. At night they would be easy to see. We would drive to the pier and fish. They had several deer, and they would run all around. Lots of raccoon and birds. It was going to be nice. "I'll come home Wednesday," I told Dad, "to help get things ready."

"Good," he said. "Want to join us, Cho?" he asked.

"No," UC said. "I have some plans. I'm going with Dorothy to see some horses she plans to board, but it sounds fun. Maybe next time."

Dad went home early Sunday morning, and I did some leg workout. UC worked on some fancy woodwork; he was making a cabinet. That evening, we had a race with the stilts, then a good workout. Monday and Tuesday, more rock digging and moving. On Wednesday I went home and promised UC to be back in a few days. "Anytime," he said. "I enjoy the help. Thank you so much."

"Thank you," I told him with a hug. I got home, and it was early, and I started cutting grass. Andrew joined me with the weed eater.

"You must enjoy working," he said. I laughed.

"Better than on that computer playing games." Brendon had a job, and that evening we ate and played a four-man game on the computer with Dad. I had promised to work on a flower bed tomorrow. Mom was enjoying the summer vacation. She had some special classes she was doing, but in her spare time, she enjoyed working with flowers. On Friday we got the truck ready with the camper.

On Saturday we left for Florida. Granddad and Grandma would meet us there. We were there by three and got our camp set up in an hour. Brendon stayed home, but Dad, Andrew, and I finished, then went bicycle riding. Mom just lay around sunning and watching the bay.

After eating hot dogs and fries, I got my rod out and started fishing with Dad and Grandpa. The bay had lots of boats going from the marina. This was great, but after an hour not catching anything, I decided to ride around the park on my bicycle. The park was full—people setting up their campers and lots of people walking. I spoke to most of them, and when I got to the alligator lookout, I went down the walkway to watch. People were there, but no alligators were in sight. I sat and looked around. It was so peaceful. After a few minutes, I decided to go for a swim and went to the beach. It was almost seven now, and a nice breeze was blowing. I walked to a good spot at the lagoon and took off my shorts and shirt and went in. It was a pleasant cool, and I swam, then floated for a few minutes. Lots of people were going now, and I felt good. The water was right, and the beach was nice.

After a good swim, I went back to camp. Dad had caught a nice redfish. It was thirty-four inches long, big enough to keep. One more like it, and we would have a fish fry. Grandpa was still trying, but Dad had to stop and clean his. Andrew was playing with another boy, and I was glad he had found a friend. Grandmother was fixing a salad for tonight, and Mom was fixing fried chicken. I tried to help Dad, but he was almost finished, so I got my rod and started fishing with Grandpa.

I went to bed around ten and got up early for a good run. As I started to leave our camp area, I noticed a girl leaving out to run. I watched her for a minute; then I left out. She was going around the camping area. I did too, and I could see her every once in a while in front of me. I wasn't going fast. I wanted a long run, maybe twice around the park. That would be at least seven, maybe eight, miles. After halfway around the beach area, she stopped to fix her shoes, and I caught up with her. "Nice day," I said.

"Yes, it is," and we were running together.

"From around here?" I asked her.

"No," she said. "Georgia, Conyers area."

I said, "Me too. I'm from Covington."

"I'm Maria," she said.

"Chris Doan, pleased to meet you." I realized she was Spanish. I was telling her we had come down to Saint Andrew's Park since I was very young. "My granddad came here in the early fifties and we all came here most years since then."

"This is our second time," Maria said, "and I hope we keep coming back." About then she said, "Look out." In the undergrowth was three deer, a doe and two fawns. We stopped to watch them.

"Look," I told her. It was another one by itself. A car came by, and they moved away. We started running again. "You run every day?" I asked.

"Most days," she said. "I'm a cheerleader and I like the exercise."

"Rockdale High?" I asked.

"Yes," she said. When we got back to the camping area, she said, "That's enough for me," and I told her I would be seeing her and kept going. One more time around but this time a little faster. I had noticed no one was up at camp when I went by, and I picked up my pace. This time it didn't take as long to run all the park, but I was getting tired; and when I got back near our area, I started walking down. That was a good run. Maybe again tomorrow, I thought. At camp I got the bucket and throw net and went catching fish bait. After several throws, I had a dozen or more minnows. Now I would fish until breakfast was ready.

After breakfast, Dad and I started fishing. Grandpa wasn't up yet. He was a late sleeper and joined us around nine. "No luck?" he asked.

"No luck," Dad said. We all put fresh minnows on our lines and started again. I noticed a young boy watching us, holding his fishing rod.

"Want to join us?" I asked him.

"Nothing biting," he said, and I noticed something was wrong with him.

"You never know," I said, "when they will start."

Grandpa said, "Sit over in that chair, it's OK," and he did.

His rod was lightweight, not big enough for the reds, so I asked, "Want to use a big outfit?"

"Yeah," he replied, so I got my spare rod and put a fresh minnow on it and threw it out for him. We had holders stuck in the ground for the rods, and I set his.

"Now if that rod gets something on it, you bring it in, OK?"

"I will," he said. "I can catch them." He was Spanish. I wondered if he was with Maria.

I asked, "What is your name?"

"Pedro," he said.

"I'm Chris. This is my dad and my grandpa."

"You caught any?" he asked.

"No," I said, "but Dad got a big one yesterday." He couldn't talk good, but he tried to ask how big.

Dad showed him. "This long."

"Wow," he said.

Maria came walking up. "Pedro, here you are."

"Hi," I said. "He is fishing with us." About then a fish hit Grandpa's line. "Got one," I said.

"Let him run," Grandpa said excitedly. Pedro was out of his chair watching; then Grandpa picked up the rod and pulled back on it. "Got him." I think everyone was watching. It was a big fish. I brought my line in so it wouldn't get tangled up. Dad did too. Grandpa played the fish. "Woo," he said. "It's a good one." Then Maria's father came up and was watching. Mom and Grandma were there. As he brought it near, I got the dip net, and when I could, I netted him. He was big.

"Wow," Pedro was saying. I held it up and got the hook out. We measured it, and it was thirty-three inches long.

"Good," Dad said. "Now we have a fish fry."

Maria's father asked about fishing. "Got a license?" Grandpa asked.

"No," he said.

"Get one and join us," Grandpa said. "This little fisherman wants one, don't you?"

Pedro said, "Can I have this one?"

Grandpa said, "We'll eat this one but I'll help you. Maybe you can get one too."

I took the fish to clean. Pedro followed me, and Maria watched. Wow, was she lovely. I talked while I cleaned the fish and filleted it. Pedro went back fishing. Maria said, "Pedro has Down syndrome. I guess you noticed."

"He is nice," I told her; then she told me about being there with her dad and Pedro. "My mother, we don't know, and I take care of Pedro."

"I'm sorry," I said. "I know it's hard on you but you are doing a great job. I know your father is proud of you."

"Thank you," she said. We stayed away from everyone, talking about school and Panama City. Brendon had got up with Andrew and joined us, but he wasn't into fishing. He'd rather go swimming. Maria said, "I think I'll go swimming." She told her father.

"Let's go to town and get a fishing license," their father told Pedro. Dad had told him Pedro didn't need a license, but Mr. Malone said, "I'll take him with me and if I can join you, maybe you can show me how to catch one like that."

"Sure," Grandpa said. "Don't get any bait. You need live minnows and we will catch them."

Mr. Malone said, "Thanks," and left.

Granddad, Dad, and Grandma went back fishing. Mr. Malone took Pedro to the store. I had changed to swimming trunks; then Maria came back with a towel around her waist. I got my bike, and we went toward the boat ramp, toward the beach, her black hair blowing back, a beautiful smile on her face. What a beautiful gal at the beach. I had a little cooler with my drinks in it and a big truck tube to float on. We started down the sand toward the curve, an area bordered from the bay and a small inlet, letting boats in at the edge of the water. I laid a towel down with our drinks and the big tube. I started blowing the tube up.

Maria took the towel off and started putting suntan lotion on. After blowing the tube up, I started with the lotion, and Maria asked me to put it on her back, and I started. She said, "Rub it in. You are barely touching me." Then I rubbed it in and all over her back as she lay on the blanket, and I put lotion on her legs and feet. She began to laugh. "That tickles," and we both laughed. And I kept rubbing the lotion until she said, "That's enough. That's all I can stand," and got up and dove into the water. I followed. We swam out with the tube past most people and got on the tube and just floated. After swimming and holding on to the tube, Maria lay beside me, and we talked about the world's problems. She said, "I'm not going to mention anyone's problem. I'm having fun."

"Good," I said. "I'm lucky most of the time. I think of college."

"Where?" she asked.

"Young Harris," I said.

"A good school. I've had friends that was there. What are you majoring in?" she asked.

"Journal newsman. I want to travel to report what really happens around the world. And you?" I asked.

"I would like to be a cheerleader at UG. The teams travel everywhere. Lots of new friends and get a good education while having fun."

"Then what?" I said.

"I don't know," she replied. "Depends on Dad and Pedro." We talked about school nicely, and we laughed.

"Lying with the enemy," I said. She punched me in the side, and I threw her off the tube, and we started playing. It was lots of fun.

Near noon, I knew Mom would have fish. "About ready to go?" I asked.

"No," she said. "I'm staying forever."

"No eating?" I asked.

"Well, under those conditions," and laughed. I deflated the tube, got my pack, put the blanket and towel with my cooler minus two drinks, and we went toward the bikes. At the shower, Maria asked, "Do you see any red places?"

"Looks good. I'll pass it." The shower was good and cold; then we went back. Maria took off, and I had to hurry to catch her. "We were speeding," I told her.

"Feels good," she said.

At camp, Mom told Maria they were having fish with us. "Great," Maria said. "What can I do?"

Grandma said, "You just enjoy yourself. Me and Danita have things under control."

"Just holler," Maria said. We went over to her dad, Grandpa, Dad, and Pedro.

"Any luck?" I asked.

"Not yet," Dad said.

We set down and watched the water while Dad and Mr. Malone talked. Grandpa would talk with authority, and they would comment. It was about growing food. Mr. Malone was into hydroponics, Dad in genetics, and Grandpa natural sun and rain; then Dad got a hit. Pedro was excited. Dad said, "Let it run," and Pedro grabbed the pole. Dad pulled back on it, and it set the hook.

"Get him," Grandpa said. Pedro was fighting the pole. Dad was ready to grab it, but Pedro kept reeling in. Dad had the drag set so it would run, and it did. It started going out. Pedro was so excited, he held on like life or death, and then it started coming in again.

Dad asked, "Need any help?"

"No," he said. After a good tussle, it came closer, and Mr. Malone had the dip net. After a few minutes of glory for Pedro, he was red in the face. We all congratulated him. It was a thirty-two-inch red, just big enough to keep. Pedro was talking so excitedly. He had a hard time talking.

"You're a fisherman now," Grandpa said. "You're a member of the big ones."

Mom said, "Wash up, it's almost ready." I was. It smelled so good. Mr. Malone put the fish on a stringer till after we eat. It was so good. I like grits, and Mom had onion rings and hush puppies and slaw. Everyone commented on how good it was. We sat around the table talking about going to the game park tonight, so we planned to go at six, play goofy golf, and ride the cars. It was almost three, so I started fishing. I would shower at five. Maria went back to their camp with Mr. Malone, and Pedro wanted to fish.

We stopped fishing, but Pedro wasn't ready. We told him we would fish tonight when we came back. He finally agreed and went to their campsite, while Dad watched till he saw Mr. Malone. I drove our car, with Grandpa and Grandma in the front seat. Dad, Mom, and Andrew were in the back. Mr. Malone followed; he was nice, and Grandpa liked him. Me too.

At the goofy golf place, we played two groups. I played with Maria, Pedro, and Andrew. After that hour, we walked to the car races—Dad, Mr. Malone, me, Maria, Andrew, and Pedro. Pedro rode with his dad. We had a group race and stayed for a second race around the track.

We let Pedro win, and he really enjoyed the evening. After a candy apple and popcorn, we watched him ride some little cars. After a good evening with Maria and the family, we went back to camp. Maria said it was nice of us to take up time with them, and she thanked us and went to her camp.

Next morning, same thing, a good run, but this time without Maria. On my second time around the park, I could see her cooking on the outside stove. I waved as I went by. She hollered back, "Hi." I picked up the pace on the second trip, not wide open but faster, and my legs felt the stress. I kept going. When I got near the camping area, I slowed down; then I walked some. It felt good. Grandpa was fishing with Dad. I sat down, and we talked about swimming. Mom was ready to go to the beach. After breakfast we got ready to go. Maria had come up with Pedro. He wanted to fish with Grandpa, and his papa said it was fine for Pedro to fish with him, so Mr. Malone went to the beach with us.

Dad and I had a cooler with drinks, and we had chairs with umbrellas. We had everything for a good time. Maria was wearing a white bikini, and with her dark skin, she was something. I had already told her, and she laughed. Most of the swimmers had nice suits on. I got my eyes full.

Around one, everyone was getting hungry, so we decided to come in and eat hot dogs and chips. Pedro had caught another red and was eager to show it off. It was big, thirty-five inches, and Grandpa was just as happy watching Pedro land it. Dad and Jim joined in fishing. Maria wanted to go on the nature trail, so we talked Pedro and Andrew to go exploring with us. We rode our bikes to the sand at the boat ramp and then started around the two-mile trail. We went by the back side of the alligator swamp but didn't see anything. Maria was spending lots of time talking. She had a white scarf around her hair, with a yellow blouse and white shorts. "Like to go out sometime?" she asked.

I smiled. "Sure, love to."

We had stopped while the boys were looking for shells. We were standing close. She moved closer to me, and I reached around her and pulled her next to me, and we kissed. After two more kisses, she said, "I was beginning to wonder if you liked me."

"Sure I do. I'm not a fast mover," I said, and we kissed again. The boys started laughing, and we did too. As we went around the trail, things were different. Maria talked about herself and asked me lots of questions about what I liked to do and places to go. My mind thought about Ashley and how she would be hurt to know I was dating someone else, but Maria was so special in her different way. Sometimes she would talk about Mexico and going back to see her family there. She had been in the United States since she was ten, and her dad had gone to Southern California before going to work with AIS, a company for food research. It was a good hike. When we got back to our bicycles, I was ready for some water.

The week went fast, and on Friday, we started getting things ready to go home tomorrow. Mr. Malone wasn't going in until Sunday. Maria and I spent most of the day together. Pedro fished all the time. He had caught two big fish. Jim had caught one, Grandpa two, and Dad one. I didn't do any good, but it didn't matter. I had a great time meeting Maria and Pedro. Jim thanked us for spending time with them. He knew Maria and Pedro enjoyed all the good times. He and Grandpa took phone numbers and said they would stay in touch.

Saturday we started packing. After we got our camper ready, we helped Grandpa. When we were all ready, I told Maria bye and I would call her. "I'll be looking for your call," she said. We had a small kiss and started home. It is a seven-hour drive, and we stopped at a Golden Corral for lunch and were home by five. Brendon had been with a friend all that week, and Mom had called before we got home and told him to be there, and he was. "Next trip, don't ask not to go," Mom said to Brendon. "I missed you too much." He told about going to the mountains and stopping by to see Uncle Cho and going swimming at the waterfalls with Dorothy and the children. They had gone to the movies and to the zoo in Atlanta. He had a good time with Raymond, his best friend. "Good," Mom said. "We did too."

Red called. He had Beverly, and Ashley and wanted to go out. "Sure," I said. "Give me an hour to finish unpacking and get ready," but they were there before I finished.

Red said, "Go bathe and I'll help finish with your dad."

Dad said, "Go on, we're almost finished." Brendon and Andrew had the rest, so I did. Mom was talking to Ashley and Beverly about school. Mom taught, and her thoughts were on school most of the time.

As we drove to Atlanta, Ashley had snuggled close to me. "Did you miss me?" she asked.

I kissed her and told her, "Every time I think of you, I miss you."

Beverly was so close to Red, it looked like she was in his lap. "Did you miss me?" she asked Red.

"I didn't even know you were gone," he said, and she hit him lovingly. We went to the varsity and hung out for a couple of hours, then drove south by the farmers' market, looking for a watermelon. We found what we wanted and then headed to Covington to the river to eat the watermelon and watch the river go by.

Sunday came, and we went to church. David Paine, our preacher, had a special sermon, and Mom wanted all of us to go. We had a pot roast for lunch and fresh okra, squash, and tomatoes. It was good, and I got my things ready to go back to the mountains for a couple of weeks. I worked on the grass and a good cleanup around the house on Monday; then Tuesday morning I left out for the mountains. I got there early. It wasn't nine yet, but UC was working with moving rocks. I joined in and had a great workout.

We ate at noon and started back digging rocks and lining the driveway. UC said he wanted one more big terrace twelve feet wide, and on Wednesday we started. We put up a string to show where to dig and where to stop. We had three terraces now plus the garden area. "What are you putting in here?" I asked.

"Nothing now, just grass and maybe a swing over there," pointing to a spot, "a covered sitting area with roses and a flower garden around the edge, but all that next week." We kept digging rocks and loading them on the trailer. Some of the big rocks would be our border, but there were plenty of both.

By Saturday UC said, "Let's go fishing." We were working out on our tree. I had it on my mind already.

I said, "Let's go."

As we went down the mountain, we stopped, as always, for spring lizards at damp places where water was showing, and after getting around twenty, UC said, "We have plenty," and when we got to our first fishing hole, I waited back as UC got near the edge. He cast way upstream, letting the lizard drift back down. Sure enough, a trout dashed out, grabbed the lizard, and headed upstream. UC let him swallow the lizard, and UC set the hook and pulled him in. It was a thirteen-inch brook trout; then I changed places and cast. Nothing as my lizard floated downstream. I drew it back and cast again. After three casts and I didn't even have a strike, I moved to the next hole and cast. This time I got a small ten-inch brook trout. By the time we got to the bottom, we had our eighth trout and stopped. I went in swimming, and ten minutes later, Dorothy and the kids came in. I grinned, knowing UC had this planned for at least a day. That rascal, I thought.

I got Sandra on my shoulders and ran from Jeff and Albert; then after a good chase, I said, "Let's go swimming now," and they raced me back to the falls, and we went in, splashing and playing. "Come on in," I hollered to Barbara. She was not in a happy mood. She just walked around looking. I told the boys I would be back, so me and Sandra went to her. UC and

Dorothy were sitting on a rock talking. I went to Barbara. "Are you mad at me?" I asked.

"No, you know I would never be mad at you."

Then Sandra asked, "Are you mad at me?" Then Barbara took Sandra in her arms and hugged her. I knew then Dorothy may have a letter from Family & Children's Services. They must have let Dorothy know they would be taking the children soon.

"Let's go swimming," I said, then we went to the falls and played splash for a while. UC and Dorothy had gone below us to a good place and cleaned the fish. He gave the trout to her. He had picked three big bags of vegetables for her. He called to me, and I knew he was ready to go. I hugged them and said I would see them on Tuesday.

"You promise?" Jeff asked. Then I asked Dorothy if she would meet us there Tuesday at noon.

"I think so," she said.

"Good," and we drove off. "Did Dorothy get a letter from the state?" I asked.

"Yes," UC said. "First of next month they will change them." My heart sank. I know how hard it was, for these two years I knew them, to adjust. Why do they do this? I was mad and hurt. Also this was the eleventh, and first of next month was only two and a half weeks away.

"Are there nothing we can do to keep them?" I asked.

"Not unless Dorothy adopts them and they would cut off all the money she gets to raise them and she can't afford to do that, and if she went to work, she wouldn't be eligible to keep them."

Ashley had asked me to go out with her mom and dad on Sunday, so I planned to go home for a couple of days. I had promised I would go back to the waterfalls on Tuesday, so early Sunday morning, I went home. I had a couple of hours till I went to see Ashley, and I went for a run. Coming back through town, I stopped at the drugstore to see Raj. The old man Tom was there and spoke to me. "How are you, Chris?"

"Good," I said. "And you?"

"Very good." Raj was already making me a Coke float. Tom was already eating his.

Remembering Tom's card—"We fix problems"—I asked Tom, "Do you fix domestic problems?"

"Sometimes," he said. "What kind?" he asked. Then I told him about Dorothy and the kids. "Something might be done," he said. "Write down all the information—Dorothy's last name, all the children's name, and their address."

I got my cell phone and called UC. "Why do you want to know?" he asked.

"I'll tell you when I know more," I said.

He gave me Dorothy's last name. "Bray," he said. "At 70922 Mountain Creek Road, Toccoa, Georgia."

"Thank you and I'll see you Tuesday morning," I told him. I gave the information to Mr. Quick.

"I'll be in touch." My phone number and name were on the paper I gave him. Tom left. I told Raj I would see him in a couple of weeks.

"By the way, how was India?" I asked.

"Very good. I enjoyed the trip."

On my way home, I wondered if Tom Quick was all talk, and I wasn't going to say anything until I knew. *But what could he do?* I thought. If the government had rules, you had to do them. I got to Uncle Cho's around nine thirty. UC was busy with rocks, so I joined in. We loaded two before it was time to go meet Dorothy and the kids. I showered and put my swimming trunks on under my pants, and we drove down to the falls. We were fifteen minutes late, and the kids were playing. I joined in, and we played chase. Sandra, on my shoulders, was laughing. Jeff and Albert were living it up. UC and Dorothy were talking. After getting tired of chasing, I asked the boys if they were ready for a swim. Each time we got together, I tried to teach them how to swim, and this time was the same. We all held the edge of the rocks and kicked our feet. I would take one at a time, hold their hands, and let them kick as we walked around the pool, sometimes letting them go and move back. "Come to me now," and moving farther each time. Albert was doing good, but Jeff was a little slower. We went and got Barbara, but she didn't want to come in. We all coached her, and finally she came with us to splash water on the boys. It was a sad time for her. I knew she knew what was happening, but Jeff and Albert didn't. We played until three, and everyone was hungry and tired. Dorothy and UC had come over with us as we played. The sadness on Dorothy's face told everything. I felt the pain myself. What would happen to those children? On the way back to the cabin, I asked UC if there were any changes.

"No," he said. "They will pick up the children the second of next month."

The rest of the day, we worked out on our trees. I was doing stretches and high kicks. After two hours of kicking, we got on the stilts and started racing up the mountain, through the underbrush, over the creek, up the hill, then down the other side. I would never be able to catch UC. He was too good. That evening, after eating and while UC was meditating, I swung and enjoyed the quietness; then the train came through the valley. That whistle was so far away and lonesome. It could make you sad.

CHAPTER V

On my phone I had a message: "Call T at noon tomorrow." My heart beat faster. *Why tomorrow?* I thought. I didn't like all this waiting. The next morning, I had a good run down the mountain and back. After eating, we started moving dirt and rocks. At fifteen till twelve, I asked UC, "Let's stop." I had a couple of calls to make, so we stopped. He fixed two large sandwiches and a salad for us. I went outside and called the number on Tom's card.

"Hi, Chris, I may have some news. Where are you?" he asked.

"In Toccoa, at my uncle's cabin," I said.

"I need to see you. When will you be back at Covington?"

"I can come now. Is it good news?"

"Maybe," he said. "I need to see you."

"I'm coming home. I can meet you at four at the drugstore. Is that OK?"

"Yes," he said. "At four. And say nothing to anyone, you understand? No one."

"Yes," I said. "I understand." *Why all the secrets?* I asked myself. Unless he is a swindler, now wanting money. I told UC I was going home and would be back in the morning.

"Everything OK?" he asked.

"Yes, just something I need to do." I showered and ate my salad and took my sandwiches with me and headed home.

I got home at two thirty and spent some time with Mom and Dad, then went to the dojo to kill a few minutes. I walked the three blocks to the drugstore. I got there five till four and was talking to Raj when T came in. He was so distinguished looking. He sat at the booth. I ordered a Coke float for T and sat down with him. "Chris, to keep any children over two years makes it hard to put them in another home."

"I know. It's hard now to move them. Now they are so sad."

"I might be able to help but it will require a lot," he said.

"How much?" I asked.

"My time is important," he replied. "Can you afford a couple thousand dollars?" So that was it. He wanted me to pay him. It was a scam, I thought.

"No, I don't have that kind of money," I said.

"If I could arrange this, would you do some computer research for me?"

"Are you serious?" I said. "I would do about anything to help those children leagle of course."

"Good," he said. "I'll be in touch and from this time on, no one can know about you working with me or any of our business, understood? No one."

"I understand." He finished his float and spoke to Raj and left.

I felt good. Was I getting my hopes up for nothing? *Well, I didn't pay him anything, so what could I lose?* I thought. I went back by the dojo and talked to Mike, then went home. Mom had dinner ready, and we ate; then Dad and the boys and I played video games till ten. Mom had washed my clothes, and I left for UC early. He was working in the garden hoeing out the grass. I got a hoe and started also. We had all the garden cleaned by four; then we let the water flow through it for three hours. It was plenty. The corn would be ready in a couple of weeks. We had picked squash and beans and tomatoes. We had a bushel of tomatoes, almost that of squash and beans. "I'll take these to town in the morning," UC said. Then we started working on my self-defense, how to immobilize someone and how to fight two people at a time. Then UC started his meditating. I worked on my stretching and high kicks. Next morning, I had a good run down the mountain and back, breakfast, then back to the rocks and dirt. We stopped to eat lunch, when UC got a call from Dorothy. She was worried; she had got a call from Family & Children's Services. They were having a hearing that Friday at one o'clock, and she was to bring the children with her.

"I'm scared," she said. "They have been telling me that now there must be two parents in the home where the children stay. I think this is it. Ten years watching sixteen different children, now this," and she started crying.

UC said, "Don't give up yet." He told her, "Maybe it's something else."

"What could it be?" she asked.

"I'm coming to town. I'll see you in a couple of hours," and he looked at me. He was worried, I could tell.

We drove to the barbershop where Don, a friend, worked and left tomatoes and squash; then by the bank UC left two sackfuls, and I waited. After he came out, we went to see Dorothy. After she and UC went for a walk, I played Frisbee with Barbara, Jeff, and Albert. I carried Sandra while we played. It made me feel bad for these children, but I laughed and tried to make them happy; but in a week, they would probably be gone. Tomorrow was Friday and the hearing. What could it be? But maybe they would take the children tomorrow. I began to feel bad. After an hour, Barbara asked me to go with her and talk, so we went for a little walk. Dorothy and UC were watching us. "You know we are leaving, don't you?" she asked.

"I heard," I said. Then she burst out crying. I held her close to me. Tears were in my eyes. *This is awful. Why do they do this?* I thought.

Barbara had gone into the house, and Dorothy went after her. I started playing with the children. UC came to me. "It's time to go," he said. I told everyone bye, and we left. I felt awful.

Back at the cabin, UC started cooking. I went on the porch, and I thought about Tom, and I took out his business card and called him. "Hi, Chris," he answered.

"I just came from Dorothy's house and saw her and the children. This is terrible. Is there nothing you could do?" I asked.

"They have a hearing tomorrow at one, don't they?"

"Yes," I said.

"Well, let's see." Then I knew he must know something. "Call me tomorrow evening," he said. "Good-bye."

"Good-bye," and I felt better. He must know something, but how, I wondered.

That evening, we had a good workout, then a race up the mountain on our stilts. After that, UC started meditating. I sat and swung, thinking about Dorothy and the children. The next morning, we went back to our terrace. We knew the hearing would be at one, and we both were very concerned.

On Tuesday, two days before, Judge Henry Baker received a phone call from Judge Alex Barthem. "Henry, how are you?" he asked.

"Fine," Judge Baker said. "This is a pleasant surprise."

"You have a Dorothy Bray in your town that keeps children for Family & Children's Services. She has four now and it's time for them to change. I would consider it a favor to look into this case and see if we could leave these children in her care."

Judge Baker said, "Give me her name again?"

"Dorothy Bray. The children are Jeff, eleven, Albert, eleven, Barbara, twelve, and a baby, Sandra, four."

"I will look into it, Alex. When are you coming down to do some trout fishing?"

"I'm mighty busy for the next month but I would like to come down in October if I can get away."

"Do, Alex, I would love to see you."

"I'll try," he said. "Thanks, Henry. I'm sure you will do your best for this lady."

"I will," he said, and they hung up.

Judge Baker called the director of Family Services, Nora Hicks, and told her he was going to have a hearing on the case to see if this Dorothy Bray might be better to keep these children.

At the hearing, Judge Baker had the analyst for the state, Bill Wooten, along with a member from Family & Children's Services to attend the hearing. They interviewed all the children separately; then they had a talk about how it would be too much on these children to move them from their existing home. Barbara had a bad case of xenophobia, and the strain on her was in a bad time; and the young girl, Sandra, also was not a good idea. The two boys, Jeff and Albert, were the best help for Barbara and Sandra, so it was recommended by the court not to move these children, and Barbara would need counseling once a month. An increase of three hundred dollars a month should cover their new expenses. Then Dorothy and the children were brought in and told of the court's findings. Dorothy started crying; the children were all so happy and excited. Court's dismissed. As soon as Dorothy left the courthouse, she called UC. He was so happy telling Chris the good news. "Let's go see them," and we both cleaned up to go. I couldn't believe it. Tom had done it. Who was this man, with all his connections? I wanted to tell UC, but I had given my word, and I just felt great for Uncle Cho and the children.

We got to their house, and the children were playing a video game. Dorothy was holding Sandra. We asked, "Want to go get an ice cream?"

"Yes!" they hollered.

Dorothy said, "That would be nice," so we headed to Toccoa to the Dairy Queen. We went inside and ate.

That evening, after taking them home, we went back to the cabin, talking. "It's like Dorothy has a special angel looking over her," he said. "She gets to keep the children, plus they are giving her extra money. It's a good time for us. What a wonderful country America is."

"Yes," I said. "It is a wonderful country." It was dark when we got back, but we had baked potato and salad before we went to bed.

We took the Saturday off and went fishing and worked out all evening. On Sunday UC worked on the cabinet he was making. I had a good run and worked on my tree, kicking and climbing, hitting it, then stretching. It was an easy day, relaxing and good eating. Monday came, and after my running down the mountain and back, we ate and started moving rocks and dirt something all week, and we were getting close to finishing the terrace. It hadn't rained in two weeks, so we watered the garden, and the corn was almost ready. "Another week," UC said, but I would be going home that weekend. It was three weeks until school started back, and Mom had some yard work she wanted help with. We finished the terrace, and on Friday I left. I told UC I would try to come back before school started. He thanked me for all my help.

I called Ashley and Red. He wanted to pick up the girls and come over. Good. I would see them this afternoon. I called Tom and told him I was back in town. "Can you meet me at twelve?" he asked.

"Yes," I said. I had a good run, and at twelve I stopped by the drugstore. Tom came in at twelve, and we sat and talked. I thanked him for what he had helped me with, how happy the children and Dorothy were.

"You're welcome. Now about the work I want you to do. I want a listing of all ships in the Persian Gulf region listed. Also their last trips for a year, all ships and their owners and when they were purchased."

"OK," I said.

"Chris, no one is to know what you are doing and that includes your family, you understand?"

"Yes, sir, I'd do good."

And he said, "You will be paid for your work." We drank our Coke float, and Tom talked to Raj a little, then left. I talked to Raj and went by the dojo. Mike was there and asked if I wanted to work out.

"Sure," I said, and we had a good training session at home. After eating an early dinner, Doug and the girls came, and we went to Madison, then to Athens at the varsity. We talked to some football players and sat around as if we were students also.

On Saturday I worked on mom's flowers. We started another flower garden, mostly roses. I cut the grass, and Brendon and Andrew helped. Sunday, we went to church. Afterward we went to a Chinese restaurant. It was good, but I always eat too much. That afternoon I lay around and played games with Dad and Andrew. Brendon went to a friend for the night. It was good.

All that week, we worked in the yard's new flower beds, repaired the fence, and painted it. Things looked good. The new flower beds were extra nice. I asked Mom if she needed me next week. "No, not really," she said. "You going back to the mountains?"

"Yeah," I said. "We're getting a lot accomplished."

"Yeah, but come home for church next Sunday."

"Yes, Mom," I said and packed a few things for the morning. We watched a movie Mom had got. We ate popcorn and drank lemonade that evening. At UC's house, it was like always. Saturday, he would take some vegetables to town and go by and see Dorothy. They were working on cleaning out the stables. I drove the tractor. UC dumped the fresh droppings, scattering them around the field. Jeff and Albert worked the shovels. Dorothy and Barbara were helping, but they stopped to fix lunch. We had it finished in three hours and had new straw put on the floor. Dorothy had fixed meat on the smoker, and we had barbecue with slaw and baked beans. The children and Dorothy looked so happy. I felt a little proud. After eating, the kids wanted to go swimming and then get a Dairy Queen coming back. Dorothy had promised this if they finished the stables. We drove to the falls, and two more families were there—one with two girls, one with two boys and one girl. With our four, that was a good group. They played for another hour, then left. We had our water battle then.

After getting an ice cream and coming home, we left with the promise of seeing them at the falls on Wednesday. That evening we had roasted corn, salad, and baked potato. Next morning, after my run and eating breakfast, we went fishing. I knew by heart what and how to fish like UC wanted. Bait your line, cast up to a spot. You can cast upstream. Let your line with a lizard on it float by a trout hole. It worked over half the time, but only with a spring lizard. We had our limit halfway down, so we came on back and put them smoking.

CHAPTER VI

We planted a few roses and camellia trees, built an eight-foot swing, and practiced a lot and most days used the stilts. It was a good week, and I enjoyed seeing the children and playing with them. I went home on Saturday morning. Maria Malone called, and I had been thinking about her and wanted to get out that weekend. "Would you?" she asked.

"Sure," I said. "Tomorrow after church?" I asked.

"Yes," I told her. "I would be there at two." Red and Ashley and Beverly came over that afternoon. We went to a movie in Covington, then out to eat. Ashley was so nice and extra polite. It was her upbringing. She has a great mom and dad. I didn't want to hurt Ashley, telling her, but she knew I must be seeing someone else; but nothing was said, and we had a good time. I don't know why I felt guilty. I liked them both, but Maria was a little more exciting, I thought. We went to Shoney's to eat, then bowling in Conyers. After that we rode to the river and sat watching the stars, kissing and holding each other. It began to get hot. The kisses were getting too overwhelming. Finally I had her blouse open and her bra unsnapped. Her breasts were so large, and we both began to get too excited. Oh how I wanted her, and then a car pulled up. She buttoned her blouse up. Then a policeman came over and asked what we were doing. "Just watching the river," I told him. He asked for our names and checked my driver's license. Then after a few minutes, he left. That ended our moment of passion. After taking her home and promising her to call her more, I went home and took a cold shower.

On Monday, after a good run, I went to school. Coach Mead wanted every player there. After running around the field twice, the coach had a good idea what shape we were in. I ran at a heavy pace with Red, and the coach was timing us real good. He told us we had several extra new men, and one, Allen, was pretty fast. He came in behind me and Red. "Be back at nine in the morning," he told us. He wanted a good workout. All that week, we practiced. There was only one week before school started and three weeks till our first game.

I had worked on logging every ship I found that was registered in the Persian Gulf area. I was working on who owned the ships now. I logged them by how large they were, their weight, and now the countries they were registered in. One evening while working on it, Tom called and wanted to meet me tomorrow at ten. "I'll be there," I told him. After a good run, I got to the drugstore ten minutes early. I talked to Raj. He was glad school was about to start. Tom came in and sat at a booth. He talked to Raj in Arabic; he was good. I already had my Coke float when he ordered his. Then we went to a booth, and he asked me several questions. Where did I want to go to college at? "Young Harris if I could get a scholarship or U Georgia."

"I like the work you are doing on logging the ships," he said.

"Thank you. I was wondering how you liked it."

After some small talk, Tom left, and I went by the dojo. Mike said, "I'm going to fight in the ultimate fighting competition." I knew there was good money in competing, but I also knew there were some tough people in it. Doug came in to clean up the dojo. Mike asked if I was going to give it up.

"Is Doug doing a good job for you?"

"Yes," he said. "He comes regularly and he does good."

"That is good," I said. "As long as he is doing good, I'll let him do it. I have football, track, and also a side job with my computer." Mike asked if I wanted to keep training. "Yes, I would like to."

"Good. Could you keep classes going sometimes when I am gone."

"Sure, if I'm not busy."

"Let's do some workout," he said, so I changed to my gym shorts and put on my head protector. "Don't hold back on your kicks," he said. "Or your punches." Doug was watching us. Mike asked about Cho and my training.

"We train all the time I am there," I said. Then Mike grabbed me and took me to the floor. He had a choke hold on me, but I didn't let him get a good hold under my chin. Finally I got one hand and bent it backward until he let go; then with his feet locked around my waist, I stood up while he held on, and I dropped back on him, and he turned loose. We were both tired.

He said, "You're the only person that has ever stood up with me on their back. You have great legs. Use them. They are your weapons."

The next week went fast; then school started, and every day I was busy. At the end of the second week, we had a football game with the Cubs. We won twenty-one to seven. After the game, we had a dance in the gym. I had finally got comfortable dancing. I wasn't good, but I was OK. Ashley likes slow dancing. I learned the two steps, and that was good enough. We held each other close, and I like dancing with her. She was always so loving. I felt a little bad when I went out with Maria, but she was just as loving, and she sure was proud of her beautiful body. On Sunday I picked her up, and we went out to eat, then a movie in Covington. It wasn't dark yet, so we drove to the Yellow River and watched the river go by while we kissed and played around. Finally I got so hot, and she too. We drove to a good place where we wouldn't be seen, and there we undressed each other and made love. She said, "I thought you just didn't want me. We have been out all these times."

"Oh, I wanted you," I said. "From the first time I saw you in a bathing suit, my blood pressure rose."

"Maybe now I'll see more of you," she said, and I knew she would. We beat our next three football games and lost one to Rockdale, our biggest rival, by one point. We still had five games to go, and Coach Mead made us practice harder. That was the only game we lost that season, but we still didn't win region, which we were hoping for. Then one month later, track started. Red wasn't playing football. The last two games, he had been tackled, and his ankle had twisted, so he said to me the dojo was mine again for a couple of months. I had a full schedule now, and I wasn't getting much done on registering ships. Now I was logging their trips by dates. I was looking for ships that were losing time, not scheduled to be gone. Red had come in to help cleaning the dojo now, but he needed some help, and for two weeks we worked together.

Finally we had our first track meet. We had it at Rockdale City. Ashley came with her dad, and Maria was there cheering me on. I came in first on the two hundred meters. I had to speak to Maria, and Ashley was watching me. Maria kissed me, and I told her I would call her; then I went to Ashley, and I kissed her. Her dad had seen me with Maria, and I felt guilty. "Great run," he said.

"Thank you." I told Ashley I would take her home, and she said OK, and her dad left after the meet.

We left, and when we were alone, Ashley asked, "Was that one of your friends?"

"Yes," I said.

"She is pretty."

"Thank you," I said.

"Are you serious about her?" she asked.

"No, just a good friend." Nothing else was said about her.

We went to eat; then we joined Red and Beverly and went riding. Ashley held me very close and was very quiet when I took her home. She said, "I'm going with Mom and Dad to Florida next week. I'll miss you."

"I'll miss you too," I said, and we kissed, and she went in. I drove home feeling a little bad, but I liked them both; but Ashley was a special person, and I felt closer to her.

I went to the dojo and started cleaning it, when Red came in and helped a little. I told him about Maria kissing me and Ashley seeing it. "Well, at least you won't have to hide it," he said. "Plus that Maria is some hot chick," and we both laughed. Red told me he had a letter from Georgia University to come and talk to the athletic department, a Coach Thompson. "I am being considered for a kicking position." That made me feel good. I knew how much he wanted to play for them. I had submitted my application to Young Harris, but I haven't heard anything. "You have plenty of time," Red said.

That week went fast, and on Friday, Tom e-mailed me. "Can you meet me at noon on Saturday?" he asked.

I answered, "Yes."

"Good. I'll see you then," and I kept on working on my logging of ships.

On Saturday I took a good run and stopped at the drugstore a little before noon. Raj was there, and we talked about school. He was going to Young Harris and hoped I got a scholarship. Tom came in, and I went to a booth. Raj was making Tom a Coke float. Tom asked about my going to college. I had told him before that I wanted to go to Young Harris but I hadn't heard from them or Georgia State. "Chris, would you like to work with one of my people next Saturday? It will pay extra," he said.

"Yes, I could do that."

"Good. I'll pick you up here at seven Saturday morning."

"OK, see you then," and he left.

That next week went fast. We had exams that week, and I felt good about my tests. I had to have at least a B average to get a scholarship. I was earning A in four subjects and a B in one. On Saturday morning, I went to the drugstore, and at seven Tom came. "So you want to be a newsman?" he asked.

"Yes, I have wanted to be one for all my high school years."

"Good," Tom said. "No word from Young Harris yet?"

"No, I haven't."

"I might be able to help you if you are interested in working for me," he said. "Doing what I ask, computer research, and some fieldwork."

"But I want to be a newsman," I told him.

We drove to a building in Buckhead and went in. Only one man was there. Tom introduced him. "Chris, this is the professor." We shook hands. "Chris, the professor will show you what we want and I'll leave you with him. He will take you home this evening."

"Yes, sir," I said.

"Chris, you have been logging ships in the Persian Gulf and working on the owners of those ships. What I want to do is check each trip they log and see if they have sometimes been missing from being where they are supposed to be. One day doesn't matter, but three days or more, I want a list of." We had walked over to a desk. "This is your office," he said, "and I'll be in the next room doing the same thing. I'll be working backward. When you find a late ship, let me know and I'll work with that one." By ten I had found one ship, the *Monarch* out of Syria. It belonged to a Mohamad Attoche Inc. The professor had come to my desk as I researched the *Monarch*. He watched. "Good," he said. "Five days late, with no mention where he was at." He sat down beside me and watched. "Chris," he said, "try this." He put in some words, then got new information. All ships must be recorded in the country it is from by the owner, the cargo of the ship, when it is leaving, from bay to destination. "That's what you are doing."

"Yes, sir, I know what I am doing. I just wonder about who I am working for."

"Yes, Chris. Let me say this. I love my country. I have been in departments that need this information to help keep our country informed of smuggling weapons cargo that is illegal, and Tom is a high-ranking officer that loves America as much as any man. He is honest, caring, and a devoted man. I've known him for over thirty years and call him my friend."

"Thank you, sir. That's what I care about too."

I looked up the cargo on the *Monarch*'s first trip and logged it; then we did the same with his second trip, the third, and through his present trip. He had two trips, from Abadan and Kuwait to Taizz, Yemen, same cargo; then he started looking over the cargo listed. He was looking for boxes three feet by three feet to four feet long. There were forty; then we pulled up those particular sizes, and they were exact to the cargo listed on two other trips, so I flagged it. The professor said, "Good, Chris. You keep looking and I will work on something else," so I did. That day we found three ships with six and seven days not logged, and then the professor said, "Let's call it a day." It was six, and I had a sandwich for lunch, but that was gone. "Let me take us out for dinner," he said.

"OK, sounds good." We went around the corner to a little restaurant and had a good meal.

On the way home, he gave me an envelope. I opened it, and there were two one hundred dollar bills. "It's yours." Tom also pays good. Great, I thought. We talked about the weather, other countries the professor had been in, most countries. That's what I want, to travel or tell the news. We got to the drugstore, and the professor asked, "Next week?"

"Sure," I said. "I could use the money toward college."

"I'll pick you up here at seven next Saturday."

"Yes, sir," I said as he pulled off. He was the smartest man with the computer I had ever met. I walked to the dojo, half a mile away. Red was there cleaning up. I sure was glad. We were through in an hour; then he followed me home, and we played video games with Dad and Andrew. Mom made fudge, and we had popcorn and hot dogs. Red finally at eleven said he would go home at the end of the game, and I showered and went to bed.

The next week, my grades came back, and I had made all As. That was good. It looked good for scholarships, and Mom was very pleased. "You work hard and do so good on everything. I'm proud of you," and then hugged me. I felt proud.

On that Saturday, I was at the drugstore at seven when the professor pulled up for me, and we started to work. We did the same thing with each ship, checked it and listed its cargo. The professor had put his desk beside mine and showed me several tips. Wow, he was smart, I thought. That day we listed four more ships that were suspicious and again went next door to the restaurant; then he brought me back, this time to the dojo.

"Would you mind picking me up here instead of the drugstore?"

"No trouble," he said. "I'll be glad to. Same time next week?"

"Yes, sir." He had already given me an envelope with two hundred dollars again, and I went into the dojo, and red was cleaning up.

"They had a late class," he said. "Only been working thirty minutes." So we got busy. I was hoping he would play video games with Dad and Andrew, and he said, "Sure." He was looking forward to whipping me.

I smiled. "You wish." We were through, and he followed me home again. It was almost nine, and Dad and Andrew were for it. We were racing in the Grand Prix when Red left. I had a little talk with Dad. I didn't talk about work. I talked about school. I was concerned about a scholarship. It was so late, but I still wanted to go to Young Harris. They offered Arabic language and computer science.

It was nine the next morning when Tom called me. "Can you meet at twelve?" he asked.

"Yes," I told him.

When I got to the drugstore, he met me outside. "Let's go for a ride," he said, and we walked around the corner to his car and drove around town; then he asked me if I could get a scholarship to Young Harris, would I be willing to work for him evenings and that summer go to the army for two months' basic training?

"Yes, I would and would love to."

"Chris, from this time on, I don't want anyone to know anything about what I do."

"I understand and I have never spoken to anyone about my work."

"Good," he said, and on Monday I started back on registering and logging their trips.

On Wednesday I got a letter from Young Harris to come and talk to Coach Bryan. "Call for an appointment." I was elated. That Tom had more connections than I could believe. I called Coach Bryan's secretary and made an appointment a week from Wednesday. When Mom came home, I showed her my letter; then Dad came in. "I'm so happy for you, Son," Dad said. "Let's hope it's a scholarship.

"Yes," I said. "Now it's just an appointment."

That Saturday the professor picked me up, and I told him the good news; then I asked, "Why do they call you *the professor*?"

"Well, I am," he said. "I teach a semester every year at Cornell University." I was amazed. Now I realized how smart he is. We got to the office and started. The professor had his computer set up by mine. We found two ships before noon, and he was working on them. By the end of that day, we had found another ship. In all we have found twelve. "This is good," the professor said. "Chris, do you remember the first ship you found?"

"Yes, sir, it was the *Monarch* out of Syria."

"That's good. You remember any more?" I called off every ship we found, their base, and their destination. "That is very good, Chris. You have a great memory." I wondered if he was testing me or was just inquisitive.

On Wednesday I drove to Young Harris in North Georgia and went to the athletic department. There I met Coach Bryan. He was an older fellow but very fine. "Good to meet you, Chris." He pulled my record and asked me several questions. Would I like to attend Young Harris and run track?

"I would love to," I told him.

"Good. I'll put you down and school starts the fifth of September."

"I'll be here."

"Chris, go see Martha Hays, a counselor, and get your subjects cleared with her." I shook hands with him and walked to the main building to see Martha Hays. She was there, and I set my schedule with her. She had already placed me with Arabic language and computer programming and computer science, and the last subject was mathematics. I was so happy. I left, thanking her, and drove back home that evening. There were six more weeks left in school. I wondered why Tom wanted me to take basic training in the army, but I would be glad to get a scholarship. The next weeks went fast. After I graduated, I had a week before my orders to report to Fort Jackson, South Carolina. I rode the bus, and there were a lot of men reporting for active duty.

The first day, we went to induction; then they assigned us out to various companies. I met one man from Georgia named Carl. He was nice but a little fat. The first sergeant informed us if we were caught with a gun or any liquor, we were in the brig. I was in the first platoon, and since I had ROTC training, I was made squad leader. The first week was late training, and we were pushed hard. The second week was lots of bayonet and self-defense training. I got the opportunity to work with the instructor. He was impressed with my training and made me his guinea pig, but on one occasion, he allowed me to try to throw him. Each of us had a knife. I moved to him. He was expecting me to use the normal way. Instead I faked a side kick, but as he grabbed at my leg, I quickly grabbed his arm and turned and brought him to me, and I gave him an easy landing. He was surprised. "You want to try that again?" he said.

"Not really, sir," I said.

"But you will," and made me try it again, and I did, the normal way. I grabbed his arm and pulled him to me while I dropped to the ground and brought my feet up to his stomach and threw him over me; then I was up fast. "You're good," he said. I was surprised for the compliment, but I gained respect from the men. Every morning we fall out in our underwear and do exercise for almost an hour; then we were allowed thirty minutes to shower, dress, and clean up our area. After reveille, we loaded a truck with our gear and went to the rifle range for two weeks. We had our three changes of clothing, normal gear rifle equipment, and knapsack. Two weeks of rifle training and target shooting to qualify or do it again. Everyone has to qualify or will be put back in another company and start again. I had no trouble on the long marches or any of the physical training, and it helped me a lot. When I could, I joined the karate club. It was free, and the matches were every week. I liked them best. I could learn from everyone. We were rated by our wins, and after four weeks' basic, I had joined. The self-defense instructor was Sergeant Moss. He was tough, and he was good. He was forty-two and a lifer, with ten years to retire. I liked him a lot. He took special time to work with me. He liked the power I had in my legs. He was a leg man and used them a lot. After reading my 201 file, he knew I was being specially trained to have basic in the middle of starting college. He had been to Iraq, Afghanistan, and had two tours to each. He knew it would be a long war. Those Moslems are dedicated, religious people, and when they are hungry and need money, the Al-Qaeda is the place to be, they think.

Time went by fast, and I had two weeks left and three weeks till school starts. After being released, I went home and put my uniform up. I got home on Friday, and Red came over with the girls. Ashley was beautiful, and we spent most of that week together, but Maria had called Mom three times, and I had to see her some.

Tom met me that Sunday, and we went for a ride, talking about Fort Jackson. He had been stationed there one time, and he preferred the western part. He always changed the subject when talking about himself, so I never inquired much. I was stopping at the dojo. Mike was always there, and we worked out a couple of times. My first day at Young Harris was all introductions. I found out where each subject was. Arabic was first, with an older lady. She preferred to be called Professor Tate, and my second subject was computer technology. My third class was math, with Mr. Duff, and my last subject was computer science. These were some of the subjects to become a newsman. I figured I would work for Tom, but I didn't know yet how long.

The night before, I had moved some things to live with Uncle Cho, and I had a bedroom and dresser, two nightstands, and a light by my bed. The closet had a long mirror on the door. I had a stool and a rug over the hardwood floors, which shined like it was freshly painted. The room was very clean, and UC wanted it kept like that. Good. I preferred to keep good quarters myself.

My first class, with Professor Tate, Raj from home was there. He was working with learning English better, and in computer science, we sat by each other. After class I would go to the field and run. Coach Bryan was always timing us. One good runner, Sammy Gill, was a fast country runner. He had lived all his life in Meansville, Georgia, near Zebulon. He had two older brothers, and when they went to town on Friday nights, they got the horses, and if he wanted to go, he had to run, so he did and got the experience. I laughed. "Sounds good," and he laughed too, but that man could run on the two-mile run. He was a little faster than me, but not much, and we ran together a lot. On weekends we would run on the mountain roads through the country. That was great. On one trip we had covered fifteen miles one day. Now I think I am as fast as Sammy, but we would see.

On Saturdays we would go to see Dorothy and the children. On Sundays I ran a lot and helped UC do chores. We split wood, we gathered firewood for winter, we worked on his garden, anything and everything. I loved it. At the end of every month, I would go home and stay the weekend. Andrew and Brendon were growing. Not seeing them every day, I could tell. Dad was always helping other people. They always had something to do, or he would find some project. Mom was always doing something for us boys. I always wondered what would it be like if we had a sister. I believe Mom would have loved it.

We will have our first competition match in three weeks. That would be our test week for the semester, and then we'd have a week off.

It was held here at Young Harris on a Friday and started at four. There were four teams. We had three people entered—Sammy, me, and Leroy. At the start, Sammy and I took the lead, and at the one-mile run, everyone started putting pressure on us. There were twelve of us, and three people moved up with us. It was a tight race, but Sammy kept the lead, and at the quarter-mile line, I gave all I had and caught Sammy at the finish line and beat him by a nose. "That was close," he said.

"Yes, I gave it everything I had," I said. Leroy came in sixth place. Coach Bryan was very pleased, and after the race, I went home for a week.

Tom had contacted me through the computer once. I answered. I would see him on Sunday noon. After the race, UC, Mom, and Dad were there, and I didn't know it. I was very pleased. We went to eat in Helen, about twenty miles from us, but the ride through the mountains was so fine. The restaurant was serving fish, but they had steak or most things you might want. The cooking was great. "I'm having steak. It smells so good." Dad and UC also had steak, but Mom had a salad and baked potato. Since I was only going home for three days, Dad had talked UC to come down for the weekend. UC agreed, so we went to Covington that night from Helen.

CHAPTER VII

Next morning, Dad and Uncle Cho went somewhere. I called Ashley and made plans for that afternoon. That morning, after a good run at daylight, I started weeding Mom's flower beds and worked on Mom's favorite hobby, flowers and more flowers, and they were so sweet smelling. It was in my blood. I didn't mind either.

That afternoon, Red came with the girls. I was glad Beverly and Ashley were very close. We drove to Athens at the varsity. We talked to several friends we had on the football team with Red. It was a good day, and Red and me split up that evening so he and Beverly could be alone. Ashley enjoyed walking, so we went to Covington Square and looked around town and stopped for dinner. That evening I promised her I would see her on Tuesday night and we'd go to a movie; then I went home feeling good. It was only nine, and Dad, Andrew, and I played war games and ate popcorn.

Sunday morning, I had a good run, then cleaned up for my meeting with Tom. At noon I was waiting when he came into the drugstore. We sat in a booth and talked about school. "Chris, I wonder if you have time to do some computer work, maybe an hour a day."

"Yes," I said. "I think so." He used his laptop to show me what he wanted. I was to do a time trace on three different men. If any other code names were connected, I would log them and note all areas they were in. That wouldn't be hard, I figured.

"Everything else doing good?" he asked.

"Yes, sir, things are good."

"I'll stay in touch," he said as he left.

I had walked to town, and I went back by the dojo to see Mike. He was there practicing for a match. "Care to work out?" he asked. Good, I thought. I needed one. I changed, and we started. "Don't hold back," he had said. "I need the punishment," so I hit hard and kicked hard. After stopping twice as we went, we finally stopped after an hour, and I was exhausted. He was too. "That was good," he said. "You are still the best kicker I know."

"Thanks," I said.

"Work on those hits and you will be the terror of the ring."

I laughed. "I doubt that," I said.

Mom had our favorite dinner—roast, rutabaga, potato salad, and eggplant. It was delicious, and I ate too much. I spent the rest of the day with the family. Brendon had stayed home with us. He would chase the girls tomorrow, he said, and we laughed. I talked to Maria and would take her out on Monday to dinner, and it was nice. She is so pretty, and what a figure. She set me on fire every time we were alone. And I loved it. As I took her home, I had promised her to take her out that weekend. I went back to the mountain with Uncle Cho on Wednesday, and we worked on firewood three days. We had five cords put up for the winter. He was very pleased, and we went fishing before I came back home for the weekend. On Saturday me and Ashley went to Atlanta, shopping with her mom. On Sunday I spent the afternoon with Maria, then that evening went back to Uncle Cho for school.

That next month went fast—run in the mornings, school, then track. We had our final meet. Track was fun. I enjoyed running, and with a competition, man, it was even better. Our main competition would start in a week, and for the next month, every weekend if we stayed in competition. Our first match was on Saturday. I ran every day with Sammy at least six miles a day. We were doing good, and Coach Bryan said we could win if we stayed together and pushed hard, and we did. On the first mile, a long-legged boy took a fast lead. Sammy and I stayed on his heels. For the first mile, we were out front of nine others, but at the end of that mile, everyone turned it on. Zulu, we called the lead man, had pushed hard, and we began to catch him. He was on the inside, then Sammy and I on the outside, with two runners coming up on us at the half mile. Zulu got a little lead, and a good runner passed me on the outside just by a nose; then Sammy gave all he had, and I did too. We caught Zulu and passed him. The other runner, they called Cougar, was barely leading, when Sammy came even with him; then I caught Sammy. We were all out of the finish. I could not tell who was first. I thought I was. Sammy thought he was, but it was decided Sammy was, only by a fraction, then me, then Cougar. After a cool off and back at the finish line, Coach Bryan said that was the finest race he ever saw and was very pleased. We were now in the finals.

The next week, Uncle Cho had me on the stilts, working. We climbed the mountain twice that weekend on stilts. My legs were aching. Every morning, a five-mile run, and every evening, another five-mile run. Five weeks till school was out and Tom had asked me if I would take another course at Fort Bragg for six weeks. I knew to say I would, but I was getting tired of school and training, but I would have five weeks for myself. Our next competition was being held at Georgia Tech in Atlanta on Friday night. There were ten of us. Sammy said this race, he and I were getting out front and going to stay there, so at the go, we were in lane 3 and 4. We were even for the first quarter mile; then we took first and second place. We had a good lead at the one mile, and everyone started their move up. We had four of us neck and neck for the half mile, with half mile to go, and everyone was all out, when a man fell behind us, taking out two runners. Sammy barely had the lead as I caught him at the finish line. I beat him by a nose. Now we had our division won, and it was great.

That weekend, Uncle Cho gave me big workout stilts. Stilts and more stilts. My legs were tight, so the rest of the week, we just ran and ran but rested on Thursday, except a small two-mile run in the regional race. It was held at Young Harris. There was twelve of us, and we used our strategy at the last match. Get out front and don't hold back, and we did. We had lane 3 and 5; I had lane 3. Coming out of the turn, I was second. A dark-skinned runner called Greyhound had the lead. My nickname was Jet, and Sammy was Roadrunner. At the one-mile line, Greyhound had a small lead. Sammy had come up next to me in second. We stayed on the heels of Greyhound to the half-mile line, and we gave everything, but we couldn't pass him. We finished second and third. I was second, but that was the fastest man I had ever run against. Coach Bryan said we had done better than he had expected. "That black man can run like the wind," he said, and I was proud of doing this good. We were out of the competition for the year, but we were not ashamed, for we had won our division. Now there was finals for two weeks; then school was out.

Our first week out, I went to Panama City with the family. Maria's family—her dad and her brother—was also going. Pedro was fishing when we got there, with Mr. Malone. After we set up camp, I helped Grandma and Grandpa set up their camp. Maria was at the beach, so I rode my bicycle. There she lay on a beach towel, reading a book, *Great Travels*. I stopped behind her and asked for a date, changing my voice. She said,

"I don't think so," then turned and looked my direction and laughed. I reached down and kissed her. "It's about time," she said. "I thought I was losing my sex appeal."

I looked over her beautiful body and said, "Never." I took my shorts off and started in the water. It was cool and pleasant; then Maria joined me. We played in the water holding each other and enjoying each kiss like it was our first time. After a couple of hours, we went to camp hungry and thirsty. Mom had hamburgers ready, and I ate three, then joined Mr. Malone and Granddad. Pedro had caught two small fish, and we used one for bait but had no luck. It was getting dark when I went bike riding with Pedro, Andrew, and Brendon. Maria had things to do at camp, and we were going later swimming. We rode for an hour, stopping at the alligator pond, looking around. We saw two, then returned to camp. Grandpa had caught a fish, a large red, and now they were excited about fishing. After eating and talking, Maria and I went riding to the beach. I had a large towel and my bathing suit on. It was late enough. No one was on that side of the cove, a quiet area surrounded by a long jetty. We walked to the end. It was our beach. I laid the towel down and got on it. While talking, Maria undressed and put her bathing suit on. My heart was pounding. She lay down beside me, talking about school's out and what she was doing that summer. There was a nice breeze, and after a few minutes, we started kissing, then made love. I knew how tender and lonely she was, not having a mother around for her teen years. She wanted to be loved, and I felt a great fondness for her; then we went swimming. The water was cold enough to be good to the body and mind; then we went back to camp. Maria's dad liked Grandpa, and they talked a lot about Mexico and the life there. Dad joined in but listened mostly. The next day, we went out to eat lunch. Everyone went to the beach with coolers, umbrellas, and tan lotion. We stayed most of the afternoon, then went back to camp and did some serious fishing. We caught three reds and planned a fish fry on Tuesday.

I woke early and went for a run around the park. When I got back, people were just getting up. Mom and Dad lay in unusually late. It was almost eight. Grandpa was already fishing. Mom fixed the fish; Grandma made slaw and potatoes. Maria had a Mexican bean dish that was great, very spicy, and hush puppies. It was the best fish fry I ever had, and after eating, I joined the men, fishing all afternoon; then that evening, we all went walking to the alligator pond. After we came back, Maria and I went swimming. It was late, but how nice it was to hold her and caress her.

That was a good week, but it had to end, and Fort Bragg was now my new duty.

On Sunday I met Tom at the drugstore, and we talked about my new duties. He gave me a credit card and told me to use it. It was part of my reward for all my help. I wanted to ask how much I could use it for, but I didn't. I would not abuse it. On Monday I reported to camp. I was in uniform, still a private. I was put in a company that was ordnance. My duty was light weapons for the first two weeks. The second two weeks were mortar and handheld rockets launchers. I enjoyed the fieldwork, trying out the different weapons. There were thirty men in our company getting special training. Most of the men were noncommissioned officers. It was just me and another man that didn't have any stripes, but we were treated like everyone else. Our training was very involved. We would disassemble the weapons and learn how to use each one; then we would take it to the weapons range and fire it. I liked the training, and firing the weapons made it fun. At the end of our course, we went back to the field, and with each weapon, we disassembled them, then assembled them back, then fired them for our qualification. We were dismissed on a Friday, and I flew back home.

I met Tom on Sunday, and we went for a ride. He gave me a new assignment, some names to research. They all were Americans—some congressmen, three senators, and one governor. I was surprised what I found out about each one. They had all been charged with embezzlement, taking bribes, or money laundering. There were eleven of them, and knowing each state they were from, I used their local paper for most of my information.

It was two weeks until school started, and I was running every day at least five miles, and on Monday I went to visit Uncle Cho. He was almost finished with the last terrace, and we worked on it. In the evenings we practiced and trained on my self-defense; then we raced on our stilts. I could walk across the creek now without falling in, but I couldn't catch him as we raced up and down the hill. My legs were much stronger, and I could run down the road and back up the driveway in eighteen minutes. We would go fishing and join Dorothy and the children. I enjoyed playing with Jeff and Albert, with Sandra on my back. Barbara was much happier now that she knew she would not be changing homes anytime soon, and Dorothy was much different, more playing and smiling and laughing. Things were good for them. They were boarding four horses, and they had two. After playing in the water, they came back to the cabin with us. We went for a hike. I carried Sandra. Now she was four and always hugging me. I was her sweetheart, she would say. I felt very close to all of them, and each time I went away, I would bring back gifts. I had got Jeff and Albert a hunting knife; Barbara, a dress. I had Dorothy to get an outfit for Sandra, and they were happy. After our long hike, we got back to a good meal UC and Dorothy had fixed. After eating, Barbara and I did the dishes. The next two weeks went fast, and school started. I ran every morning, then went to classes, then track for two hours. I worked on logging all information about the corrupt senators and governors, but I had all the information I could find. As each one had a hearing or court, I would compile the file on them. I had added three more names to my file. Now I had fourteen.

On one Sunday, I met Tom, and he said the file was good and asked about my school. "Everything is good," I told him; then he told me my credit card wasn't used much. "Not many things I need," I told him.

"Use it more," he said. "You work hard on the files and I want you to feel it's there for you."

"I will," I told him. Then he asked about school break, if I could work a week with him. The Christmas break would be in three weeks. "Yes, sir," I said.

"Good. Anything you need?"

"No, sir," I told him.

After meeting Tom, I went to the dojo to see Mike. He smiled. As I went in he, had a trainer working out with him. Mike was hitting hard, but the trainer wasn't. "Hit harder if you can," he told the trainer, but Mike was too fast. After Mike threw him down, he wanted to rest. Mike came over to me, and we talked. His trainer asked if he could leave. "Yes," Mike said, and Mike asked me to work out with him. "I have a match in two weeks with a mean ass," he said.

"What is your record?" I asked.

"Four and two." I changed to my trunks and headgear; then Mike put his headgear on. "Don't hold back," he said, and we started. We jabbed, and then Mike tried to throw me. I got loose and started using my legs, and my first kick surprised him. It got him on the side; then he started with his feet. I did two jabs, then one head kick. I knocked him down. "Wow," he commented. "I'm glad I put my headgear on." Then he grabbed me, and we went to the floor. He had a leg hold, but I had his, and we both twisted as much as we could. I didn't have to, but I gave up. I didn't want to twist his foot any more. I was afraid to hurt him. We rested a couple of minutes, then started back. He was enjoying the hard workout. We kept at it for ten minutes; then we rested. As we started back, I did my turn and kicked backward. It barely got him, but it was enough to hurt. "Wow," he said. "I didn't see that coming." I did lots of side kicks and leg kicks; then I went high and caught his head. He went down. "I've had enough," he said. "That's thirty minutes with you and twenty-five with Louis. You have some bad feet, Chris. Those are your best weapons."

"Thanks," I told him. We talked for a few minutes; then I ran home. Mom had dinner cooked, and Dad had got in, and we ate. All the men played video games. Andrew and I played Dad and Brendon; it was fun.

I drove back to the mountains to Uncle Cho late, and after driving to school, I missed my running that morning. Competition with track would start after the holidays, and I was looking forward to it. Sammy was running that afternoon when I got to the field. We ran five miles. I was a little faster than Sammy. I guess it was the stilts making me stronger, and I was glad.

That weekend I stayed in the mountains working out. We raced on the stilts twice a day. Now I was giving UC lots of competition. I could not beat him, but now I was close behind. Each time we got back, we would have leg battles with our stilts. We stood on one leg and tried to make the other one fall. We hit each other. We laughed as each one fell. I could take him every once in a while.

On Sunday we met Dorothy and the kids. We played games until we ate; then we went horseback riding. I rode with Sandra, and it was a good ride through the hills. We got home around dark and then sat on the porch. It was cold now. I put a heavy coat on and swung as UC did his meditation.

The next week, we had test before the holidays. I was ready for them and found them not hard. As the last week finished, I went home. On Sunday I met Tom and was to work with the professor the next week. I would meet him at the same place I had worked with him before.

The next week, the professor had me working with taking a name with a specific location and following the name to every place a phone call was made and listing each place through GPS on a map and getting any names or other places and listing them. I followed Mohamad Aldoo all the first day and had him listed at thirty-three different places on the map. The second day, I completed Mohamad Aldoo, with forty-six locations. I also had his code name as Tonica. He had been at a base house, twenty-one calls. The professor went over the list with me, and he also spoke Arabic. Mine wasn't as good yet. "Good," he said and took my listings to work with. I started a new file, an Al-Hilliah Omar. I worked on his file all day Wednesday and Thursday. I followed him through forty-eight locations, with nine calls to an area near Baghdad. On Friday I worked with the professor. I enjoyed that he was great. He showed me many things. I liked him a lot. He asked if I could work the weekend. I was reluctant, but I said yes. We worked together on each location and made a file on each name we had that called, then started a file on each one. We began to have a lot of same places. The professor showed me many shortcuts and new things. He was the smartest computer person I had ever known. Now I knew why they called him the professor. Early on Sunday he said, "Let's call it a day. We have had a very good week," and thanked me for my help. "You did very good," he told me. Christmas came on Tuesday, and we all celebrated. Dad gave gifts. Uncle Cho had come to join us, and we enjoyed his cooking with Mom's.

Ashley came over several times, and we went out to the movie and dinner twice. This weekend Maria came over, and we went out to Stone Mountain, then to dinner. I spent all day and most of the night with her. She was so loving. She told me she loved me, and I felt bad about that. I told her not to let it go that far. I had so many plans after graduating and getting on with some newspeople. I wanted to travel to get that experience first. It would help me get a name established.

"I won't hold you back. Just see me as much as you can, will you?"

"I will," I told her and held her tighter as we sat watching the Yellow River.

I went back to the cabin on Sunday and got ready for school. I got my grades for the first semester, and they were very good. In Arabic I made a B+; computer science, A; computer programming, A; mathematics, A. I felt good about my grades, but I did a lot of studying.

Track started, and our first meet would be in two weeks, with Morris Brown College. I heard they had some good runners. Sammy and I ran every morning and every evening. We pushed each other to our limits and felt good about our chances to win.

We had our track meet at Morris Brown. We had another man on our team, Johnny. There would be twelve runners. I started in lane 4. Sammy was in lane 6, and Johnny was in lane 8. On the start we started fast by the first half mile. There were four of us at the front. Sammy was next to me, barely behind first place. At the one mile, a runner passed us and moved to first place, and Sammy and I moved to second and third place. When Sammy moved beside me, we made our move and caught first place. We both tried to pass him, but he stayed with us. At the last quarter mile, I gave it all I had and moved up to first place; then the other runner tried to catch me and pass, but Sammy caught me, and as we got to the finish, it was me and Sammy in first and second place.

"That was a great run," Coach Bryan said when we made it back to him. I felt proud. We had beat region and set a school record by two seconds.

For the next month, I worked Saturdays with the professor. We would have our last competition Friday, three weeks later, and school would be out in five weeks. Sammy and I ran as much as we could every day and evening. When the next match came, it would be at Young Harris on Friday. It was there, and I was ready. This was state competition, and the best runners in Georgia were there. I got lane 2 to start; Sammy had lane 5. The gun fired, and we were off. After the first half mile, I was in third place, Sammy back farther. They had some good runners. We were all pushing it at the one mile. I was still in third place. First and second place had changed. A runner pulled up beside me; it was Sammy. He winked at me, and I knew it was time to go, and we caught the runner in second and started gaining on the lead runner; then another runner came beside me and Sammy. We had less than a quarter mile to go. I was all out. Sammy started falling back a little. Now it was me and another runner gaining on first place. We caught him at the finish line, and I didn't know who won. The people were all standing and cheering us on. I was exhausted, and after sitting down when I had walked a little, Coach Bryan came to me. "You won!" he said. "You won!" I was almost in tears. I was so happy. By now I was OK and walked up to the officials. I was given the ribbon and award. I felt very proud. They announced the results. Sammy was in fourth place and was disappointed but proud for me.

As I went over to Mom and Dad, I saw Tom and the professor in the back. Now I really felt proud. Mom and Dad were smiling. Mom hugged me. "I'm so proud of you," she said with tears in her eyes.

"Thank you, Mom and Dad, for being here."

I went back to Covington that evening, and Maria had called and asked if she could come over. "I'll meet you," I told her and set a time.

I got home, then went to Wendy's to meet her. "I heard," she said. "I know you won state," and hugged me.

"That's all?" I asked.

She smiled. "No, no, no," she said, and we both held each other and kissed. We stayed out till two, and she said, "Will I see you before you go back to school?"

"We will talk and see."

"OK, OK," she said as she drove off.

Tom called me and asked to meet me, and we did. We drove around Conyers and Covington for over an hour, when he asked, "You still want to be a reporter?"

"Oh yes," I said.

"How would you like to work with our team and be a freelance reporter also?" My heart began to beat faster.

"I'd love it," I said.

"Good," he replied. "I think I can get you started with a couple of papers. Also how would you like to start after school's out with your master's degree?"

"How could that be?" I asked.

"It's all legal and approved," he said. "Can you work tomorrow with the professor half a day?"

"Yes," I said.

"Good, he will call you." I spent that afternoon with Ashley. We went to a movie, then out to dinner. We went riding around Covington for a while; then I took her home.

The professor called. "Chris," he said, "could you meet me tomorrow around ten?"

"Yes, sir."

"Good. Meet me at the office then."

"Yes, sir," I said and hung up. I drove to the office, and the professor was there. I went in.

"Sit here," he said, and I pulled a chair closer to him. "Chris, do you know what we do?"

"Not exactly," I said.

"We help the government with their problems." He was looking in my eyes. "It takes a very patriotic person to do our work. We work longer hours and sometimes dangerous places. Tom says you want to be a reporter. Is that right?"

"Yes, sir, I do."

"Good. With us you would be the first to know many things and some you could print. Does that sound interesting?"

"Very," I said. At that time, Tom came in and sat down.

"That was a good race you were in."

"Thank you, sir," I said.

"Do you want to give our team a try?" Tom asked.

"Yes, sir."

"Good. Can you do a two-month tour at Maryland APG Base? You are now a second lieutenant."

"What would I do?"

"You will study different types of electronic surveillances and how to detect them with electronic devices and how to make your own. Then when you come back, you would start with our team."

"Yes, sir, I would like to give it a try."

"Good," he said and shook my hand.

The professor said, "Welcome aboard," and grinned. I went home happy. I knew what they had said was true, and to work with such intelligent men also, I had firsthand information to write about.

I had two weeks of school and tests left before graduating, and I enjoyed it. I worked every evening with Raj. He was struggling with computer science. We studied every spare minute we could. Raj was so grateful and thanking me continually. Finally we took our tests. I found them easy and was the first to leave after taking the tests. I waited; Raj was one of the last. "I don't know how I did," he said nervously.

"I think you will be OK," and we went for a drive.

For the next three days, we had our tests, and I felt good about them; and on Friday after our last test in mathematics, I went home. Next week we had graduation. I had made an A in everything except Arabic, and I made eighty-nine B+, and I felt good about it. On Friday we graduated. Mom and the family were there, including Uncle Cho. It was good. I was mentioned about winning state track for the school, and I really felt good about that. That evening I went home for a week's vacation in Panama City at Saint Andrew's. Mr. Malone was there with Maria and Pedro.

CHAPTER VIII

What a nice week, lying around, fishing, riding bicycle, swimming, and no studying or running. Maria and I just walked a lot, talked about school being out, and doing whatever we wanted. Of course I had to go to camp and then to work, but I liked that idea. I knew I would be traveling; it was good times. The week went fast, and I only had one day off before reporting to APG, Maryland. My flight would leave at noon on Monday. Tom had asked me to come to the office, and he would drive me to the airport. I knew he wanted to talk.

Tom had me four new uniforms with my lieutenant bar, new shoes, and special orders to report to a Major Duncan in personnel. "Chris, I'm proud to have you with us after your training. You have an appointment with a couple of news organization for work." My heart raced. "Also now you are on our payroll. You have a charge card. Use it. You have a savings and checking account with you local bank in Covington. After you complete this training, you will work with my special group at home. Any questions?"

"No, sir," I said. "Thank you for all you have done for me. I'll do my best."

"I know you will, Chris," and he let me out at the entrance to the airport.

The flight took two and a half hours, and I took a cab to the base from Baltimore. At personnel, I found Major Duncan and gave him my orders. "Fresh out of school?" he said. I was at attention.

"Yes, sir."

"At ease," he said. "Lieutenant Doan, this is a security base. Here we do our secret experiment. You will forget everything when you leave these gates. Is that understood?"

"Yes, sir."

"Good." He looked at my 201 file. "I see you have had training at Fort Jackson."

"Yes, sir."

"I dislike that base" he said. "I started there eighteen years ago and have had duty there twice at Columbia. Here is a list of things. Your room and building, the courses you will take and their location, a map of the base, and where everything is at. If you need any help with something, you will come to me. You will talk to no one about your courses, who you are, or where you are from. Is that clear?"

"Yes, sir."

"A Hummer is parked in the side of this building. Here is the key. That's all, lieutenant." I saluted him and left. At the side of the building were several Hummers. I found number 7 and sat in it while I looked up building three thousand one seven, my new home. I drove there and went in with my things. It was the first door on the left, number 2. I had a window looking out and one looking on.

"We will start with basic locksmith," Sergeant Hillery said, and he passed out nine books. They were small, only eighty-two pages. I will leave you to read for the next hour; then he left the room. I opened my book and began to read. I didn't learn much from the book except that any lock can be opened with the right tools.

Sergeant Hillery came in, and on a table he had several locks disassembled and lying with pieces together. We were given a lock like the one opened. The sergeant started explaining about keyways inside the locks that had to be matched usually with a grove inside the object being used; it was simple. Then we used the flat, slim objects to open the locks. We played with the locks a few minutes; then we started with other locks. We ate at noon, then started back.

At the end of the day, Sergeant Hillery dismissed us. The officers that he had told to stay kept seated. I went to my room, wondering what I was going to do; then I went to the PX. I got several things, including some tapes of Barbra Streisand; then I went to the officers club. It was located on the edge of the bay, and I sat outside and had a cold glass of buttermilk and watched the water and a few boats. A pair of binoculars were on the table, and I watched the fishermen. One boat caught several fish; then I ordered dinner. Another lieutenant was at the table beside me. She asked if I wanted some company.

"Sure," I said, and Lieutenant Banner joined me.

"You new here?" she asked. Knowing I couldn't say much, I told her yes and kept from saying as much as I could. She was in intelligence and knew not to ask too many questions. We made small talk. She told me her first name; it was Elizabeth. We talked about fishing. She had started watching the boat that was catching fish and commented on it. "My father took me fishing a lot when I was young and he was alive. Those were the good days." She asked several questions I couldn't answer—where I was from, my first name, and which schools I attended. Realizing I didn't answer the questions she wanted, she said, "You're on restricted security, I see. That's OK. I'm just nosey. You look fit." Then she said, "You go to the gym?"

"I am wanting to," I said.

"Good," she replied. "I'll see you around. Nice talking to you, Lieutenant Doan," and she left. I sat for a few more minutes, then went to my Hummer and back to my room.

I lay listening to my tapes, when Sergeant Hillery knocked at my door. "Come in," I told him.

"Want to go to the gym?" he asked. "I am going."

"Sure," I said and got up and got my shorts.

We rode to the gym. He talked about hunting and fishing. "I'm from upstate NY. We have good hunting there." And then he said, "I know you are from Georgia and I have read your 201 file. It doesn't give lots of information but you are able to talk to me if I already know those things."

"Thank you, Sergeant. We have great hunting at home—deer, bear, hogs, turkey, and duck."

"Sounds great," he said. "You hunt much?"

"No," I replied, "but maybe later I can take it up."

"You're only twenty-one?" he asked. I smiled. "Making a career out of the army?"

"I'm not sure," I said. We got to the gym and went in.

The sarge started with the weights. I followed; he had me some twenty pounds. I am one eighty-five; he was a good two hundred plus but in excellent form. The sarge looked like he was maybe thirty, and after we did some presses and leg lifts, we ran around the indoor track a few times. I noticed people gathering. I asked what was happening. "Ultimate fight," he said. "Want to watch?"

"Yeah, looks like fun," I said, so we went over.

The marines had four men there, and our base had scheduled the matches. Several officers had come in to watch. There were some bleachers to sit at, but people were all around the ring. I sat in the upper section and watched. The match was three five minutes with one-minute breaks. The announcer called out the names. The army had Sergeant Kipper, and the marines had a Sergeant Linnard. It started. The first round was a lot of jabs, and in the second round, it started more vigorously. The marine's Sergeant Linnard knocked down Sergeant Kipper. Everyone was excited. Then Sergeant Kipper took Sergeant Linnard to the ground and did some elbows to his head; he was cut and bleeding. The round ended, and in the last round, Sergeant Kipper knocked Sergeant Linnard out. The second fight was middleweight Corporal Tiss and Sergeant Miles for the army. Sergeant Miles started with a head kick. Corporal Tiss never recovered from it, and late in the first round, Sergeant Miles knocked Corporal Tiss out. I got very excited watching. I enjoyed martial arts, and these men were warriors. Sergeant Hillery asked, "Like these matches?"

"Oh yes," I commented.

"You do any fighting?" he asked.

"My uncle is very good and he showed me a few things." The last match started, Sergeant Banner and Sergeant Lacy for the army. The fight only lasted two minutes. Sergeant Lacy took Sergeant Banner down with a headlock, and Sergeant Banner tapped out.

The next weeks went fast. We studied all types of locks and how to open them. It got easy. The trick was to feel the lugs and turn them. I e-mailed everyone almost every day, especially Ashley and Mom. I would call Dad and Uncle Cho. I liked hearing their voices and encouragement. The third week, we started studying electronic surveillances and electronic detection. Some eyeglasses could see the different light waves, there was sound detection motion sensors—many ways to have security. We learned how to disable and render the units helpless, and we studied motion cameras. There were many ways to have security. I enjoyed those two weeks best. On our second month, we studied booby traps and how to make our own.

At the sixth week, we had a test. We had a building to go into, and we were graded by our efforts. At my time, I got through the gate easy. When I got to my building, I decided to try the top. I found a strong gutter, and I climbed it to the top. They had motion sensors there. I didn't see any way through them, so I went back down. They had windows with alarms on them. It had two doors. It also had a roll-up door. My best way was to go through a window. I went around the building; it was very secure. They had a walk-around guard. I timed him at eleven minutes to make his rounds. I looked through a window and saw a security signal going to the side door; that was it. I estimated the signal to be four feet high, in the middle of the door. Now I needed a deflector to return the signal. I had brought a rope and a twenty-foot string. Now all I needed was to open the door, slightly lower a deflector to the signal, and some way to hold it in place. It was a concrete block building with a metal door; that was it. I would slide my pocket knife and a plastic credit card behind the top of the metal frame to hold my deflector in place. Now I needed a deflector I didn't have. There was a truck parked on the side of the building. The tag would do, so I moved to the truck and waited for the guard to come by. When he was gone, I used my knife to get the tag off. I estimated that the distance down to the signal was two inches above the door handle in the middle. Now I had my deflector, and I went to the side door and waited. I hid behind the truck until the guard went by. I moved to the side door. I made my deflector. First it hung down to the right place. I had seven minutes left. I used my burglar tools to open the door. That took two minutes. I had my deflector hanging. I eased the door open two inches and lowered the deflector in place. I opened the door and crawled in and shut the door behind me. Now with my glasses, I could see all the security signals, and I moved around them. There was a table in the middle of the room with a buildfole on it. I took the buildfole and went back to the door and waited till the guard went by; then I went out, shutting the door almost close. I removed my deflector and took my knife and credit card from the top and went to the fence. I had three minutes till the guard would be back. I unlocked the gate and went outside; then I locked the lock back and went over to Sergeant Hillery and gave the buildfole to him. He looked at his watch, thirty-eight minutes. "Very good," he said. I was the fourth person to be tested and the first to make it.

    The next two weeks went fast since I passed the test. Sergeant Hillery said I could go back to my company; the other men had to have more training. I thanked him and went to my room, packed my things, and then went to see Major Duncan. I knocked at his door. "Come in." I stood at attention. He said, "At ease."

    "Sir, I finished my training and Sergeant Hillery has let me go."

    "You're finished?" he said. "You are two weeks early. That's good," he said. "Tell Colonel Quick to come see me sometime."

    "Yes, sir, I will." He saluted me. I gave him the key to the Hummer, and he called a sergeant to come in.

    "Take Lieutenant Doan to the airport."

    "Yes, sir," he said, and I left to come home.

CHAPTER IX

It was seven thirty when I got to the Atlanta Airport. I was very surprised to see Tom. "How did you know I was coming?" I asked.

"Major Duncan called me and said you were on your way and I called the airport, you were on this flight."

"Thank you, sir. I'm glad to see you." We walked to his car and started home.

"Take a couple weeks off," he told me. "Then we can start to work." I wanted to ask about my news career, but I was sure he was aware, so I just let it hang. We talked about my training and my working with the professor, and he told me I would be on army payroll, but I would also receive money from our special group.

"How many people are in our group?" I asked.

"You are number seven," he said, "but we have many at our disposal." Tom took me straight to my house. I knew he had never been there, and I was surprised he knew where to bring me. "Keep in touch," he said. After I thanked him for the ride, I went in and surprised everyone.

"You're early," Mom said. "We weren't expecting you for a couple of weeks."

"Finished early," I said. I had my duffel bag, and I went to my room to unpack. Dad followed me.

"How are things?" he asked.

"Great," I said. We did small talk. Andrew had come in and wanted to know about my training. "Just the usual," I said. "Just soldiering."

"You look good in uniform," he said. "How long are you home?"

"I don't know," I replied.

"I thought you worked by orders," he said.

"I do. I'll work in an office in Atlanta until they give me an assignment."

Mom asked, "You hungry?"

"A little."

"how about a sandwich?" she asked.

"Sounds good."

"Want to play a war game?" Andrew asked.

"Yeah, we can do that."

The next week went fast. On Friday I went to the mountains. Cho was working in his garden; I started helping. We removed the grass from around the plants. When we finished, Cho asked if I wanted to walk on the stilts. "Sure," I said, knowing he wanted a race, and we did—over the creek, up the hill, and down. At least I didn't fall; then we worked out on our tree. I kicked my tree and punched until I was tired; then I sat in the swing and watched him. He kept going, kicking and punching. The duffel bag we had hanging was a good punching bag, and after a short rest, I started on it. Cho had hung a kicking bag up; it was six feet from the ground. I liked the high kicks and had a good workout.

On Saturday we went fishing. When we got to the road and waterfall, Dorothy and the children were there swimming. We had our limit of trout, and UC started cleaning, while I played with the boys. I carried Sandra on my back. Barbara had a water pistol. We would splash water on each other. I enjoyed the playing. After a couple of hours, Cho and Dorothy went to the cabin. I walked with the kids. I carried Sandra on my back; she was so sweet. I had got them a present. I had two Australian hats for Jeff and Albert. I had a pair of Western boots for Barbara, and Sandra, a dress, with a bonnet. She loved it. I gave each one twenty dollars. Dorothy said, "I don't know what I would do without you and Cho," and gave me a kiss. They had started hamburgers, and we played Frisbee until it was ready.

On Sunday we went to Dorothy's house. The boys and I repaired the fence. We had to put three posts up and a new fence. It took half the day, and Dorothy had fixed lunch for us. After eating, Cho and I came back to the cabin. After a race on our stilts, we started training. Cho showed me some moves. He would stand behind me and hold a gun. I would turn and knock the gun away. If the person was holding the gun in his right hand, I would pivot to my left, grabbing the hand; if he was left-handed, I would turn to my right. You have to tell how close he was by his voice; if not, you would get shot. We practiced this for two hours, until Cho thought I had it down. On Monday we trained most of the day. Cho had smoked the trout, and we had a salad, baked potato, and smoked squash; it was great. I had e-mailed Tom, and he asked me to meet him on Wednesday, and I did. "Are you ready for an assignment?" he asked.

"Oh Yes," I said.

"Good. Tomorrow I want you to go to Washington and see the editor of the *Washington Post*, Mr. Albert. He is expecting you." My heart was pounding. "You will be a freelance reporter and also work with us," he said.

I was smiling and I told Tom, "Thank you."

Thursday morning I took a flight to Washington, then a cab to the *Post*. A lovely secretary met me at the office. "Can I help you?" she asked.

"I'm here to see Mr. Albert. He is expecting me."

She called Mr. Albert. "Mr. Doan is here, sir."

"Send him in," he said, so I went in. We shook hands. "I understand you're new in the business."

"Yes, sir."

"What makes you want to be a newsman?"

"My dream for a long time, sir."

"Well, you're not newsman till you have some news," he said. "You come with some good recommendation." He called his secretary. "Mr. Doan is starting as a freelance newsman. Sign him up." We shook hands, and he said, "Sylvia will take care of you." After getting my newsman's badge and all the information, I thanked Sylvia and left. It was late when I got back home. Brendon met me at the airport and drove me.

Next morning I e-mailed Tom. He asked me to come to Atlanta and meet him at twelve. I did; we ate lunch and went back to the office. We went into an insurance building and took the elevator to the bottom floor. We went to a door; Tom used a key to get into a hallway. At that spot, two cameras were looking at us. Tom put his eye to a spot, and the door unlocked. We went in. Several doors were closed. At the third door, Tom knocked. "Come in," someone said. It was the professor. We shook hands. "So you are starting with us," he said. "Welcome aboard."

"Thank you, sir."

"The professor will show you around, Chris," and he left.

The professor got up from his computer, and we went to the next door. He knocked. "Come in," a voice said, and we went in and met an elderly lady, maybe in her late fifties.

"Sarah, this is Chris Doan." We shook hands. "Chris will be in with us."

"Very good," she said, and we went to the next door. The professor opened the door.

"John, this is Chris Doan. He will be working with us." We shook hands.

"I've heard about you, Chris. You're a bright man that can run like a deer."

I grinned. "Pleased to meet you, John."

We went to the next door. The professor knocked, then opened the door. "Alex, this is Chris Doan, a new member of our group." We shook hands.

"Pleased to meet you, Alex." I noticed he had a hand with wires leading to a computer.

"My toys," he said, and we went to another door. The professor knocked, and we went in.

"Ann, this is Chris Doan." We shook hands. She was well built, around thirty, dressed to show off her beautiful body. "Chris will be working with us, Ann."

"Nice to meet you, Chris."

"Nice to meet you, Ann."

I followed the professor to a room. "Chris, this will be your office. We're setting it up for you. It will be ready on Monday when you start." Then we went to the door, which was locked. The professor took the cover off the lock section and mashed a couple of buttons. "Put your eye to this eyepiece," he said, and I did. After a little while, a light came on. "Got it. Chris, now you can get in." He put the cover back on. He had a special key to use on the lockbox. We went back to his office. He gave me a key. "Don't lose it," he said.

"Yes, sir," I said.

"I think Tom wants you to start Monday."

"What time?" I asked.

"Well, we don't have a clock to work by. I start around seven. Everyone sets their own schedule. Anything else?" he asked.

"No, sir," and I left. I noticed inside the main entrance there were lots of people. The directory said Max Insurance Co., 396 Peachtree Street. Good cover, I thought. Tom was outside the building, smoking a cigar.

"What do you think of our outfit?" he asked.

"Good cover," I said.

"Chris, you will work two weeks with each member of our group. I'll see you Monday."

"Yes, sir," and he left. I went to the parking lot and got my Honda and went home.

Ashley came over Friday, and we went to a movie and out to dinner. She was going out of town with her parents in the weekend. It was her second year of college, and she wanted to be a teacher. I carried her home Friday night. We sat in the car talking. "I'll miss you," she said. "Will you miss me?"

"Yes, I will. We can go out Thursday when you come, if it isn't too late," I told her. We kissed, and she went in. I cut grass and did yard work that weekend. Andrew helped, but Brendon lay around the house. His job was very hard. He worked at the local airport. He did gas fill-up, washed the planes, and assisted in mechanical work.

Monday working, I left for work at six. I wanted to beat the traffic; it's terrible on I-20. I got there at ten till seven, and no one was there. I went to the room that was to be my office. A computer was there and a file cabinet. It was a nice desk, with a middle drawer and five drawers on the sides. A printer was set up, also a cell phone, an atlas of the world, several ink pins in a round glass, a dictionary, and a Bible. I turned the computer on. My chair was very nice and comfortable. I heard a machine say the professor has entered. My door was open, and the professor came through it. "Good morning," he said. "An early bird."

I smiled and said, "Good morning."

"When Sarah comes in, you will work with her for a couple weeks."

"Yes, sir." He left me to explore. I noticed he went down the hall.

I heard a voice say, "Want some coffee?"

"Yes, sir." I went to the room. It had a microwave, a refrigerator, boxes of cereal, coffeemaker, and a good stock of drinks—with milk and orange juice—cans of different soups, and a good stock of lunch items. He poured my coffee and said, "Sugar?"

"Three and cream mate." I got both. There were chairs and a table. He sat down and started drinking, so I did too. Then the machine said Ann has entered. She came to the rec room.

"Morning," she said.

We both said, "Good morning." She fixed herself a coffee and drank it black. She left for her office.

The professor got up and went to his office, so I went to mine. Shortly after, the machine said John has entered. My door was open, and John said, "Morning, Chris."

"Good morning, John," at fifteen till eight.

At eight thirty Sarah came in. She said, "Hello, Chris."

"Morning," I answered. She went to the rec room and got a bowl with cereal and milk, then went to her office. Her door was open, so I went in.

"So I have you this week."

"Yes, ma'am."

"Don't 'yes, ma'am' me," she said. "I'm not that old," with a smile.

"OK, Sarah."

"Good. Pull up a chair." she had an extra chair in her office. "Chris, I work with building computers, repairing, and we all do research here. Me and you are going to have a crash course in building computers."

"That sounds interesting," I said.

She got a box from the top of her file cabinet and took a blank, flat panel from it. She had a book on her desk and said, "Look at this book while I eat breakfast," so I did. It had every kind of computer you could imagine, with a directory for each computer, what each component did, and each microchip in it. When she finished, she got a tray with hundreds of microchips. She turned to a page, and it was a Dell computer. "Start with this one," she said. I started and found every microchip was in alphabetical order, with each number progressing, so I placed all the microchips listed. Sarah had another box of diodes and components. After I located and placed each part, she got a soldering iron and told me to solder them. That was tedious. On several occasions, I had to clip away the microchip and redo it. It took most of the day. We stopped for lunch and ate soup from the kitchen. At five Sarah said, "We would work on finishing," and she left. I went to each door that was open and talked. John was a real talker. Tom didn't come in that day, and the professor had spoken to us twice. He was a very nice man. I had spoken to everybody. Ann was so lovely; she dressed in a way to show off her beautiful body, nice breasts, lovely behind, shapely legs, and long blond hair.

I went home at six. Mom and the family had already eaten, so I sat at the table with Dad and Mom and did small talk. Mom asked what kind of work did I do. I told her, "Computer work." She asked me all kinds of questions. I told her, "Mom, my work is very special but I couldn't talk about it."

"Is it with the government?" she asked. Then she got up and handed me an envelope with my government check. It was obviously a check.

"Yes, ma'am," I said, "but please don't say anything about it or ask me any more questions."

Dad just looked at me. "I'm proud of you, Son. You are a very wonderful person," and gave me a hug. They got up and started doing dishes.

We worked all week on making computers and learning how to repair them to find a weak microchip. We would send a signal through it, then locate the bad or weak one, then replace it. Sarah showed me how to use our special unit to find or see what was wrong. She was good, and the second week, on Thursday, she gave me a test. I took a flat panel and made a computer. She timed me, and when I finished, we used it; it worked. The professor was watching me; then he took the mouse and did a little test. It did what he wanted. "Very good," he said.

Sarah said, "It is neat and it works. Good work." She said, "Now you can work in your office tomorrow. Next week you are to work with Johnny."

"Thank you, Sarah."

"You're welcome." On Friday Tom came in and called a meeting at noon. At the meeting, he gave us our assignment. He gave a folder to each person; mine said, "Work with John for next two weeks."

That weekend I had a good six-mile run and worked out at Mike's dojo. Mike was in Vegas for a fight with the warrior Charlie Noble; he had a record of eighteen and four. Mike's record was four and one. I used the barbell first, then the bench, then gave an hour kicking the high bar. Laddy, Mike's helper, told me Mike would be back Tuesday. "When he calls in, tell him I came by."

"I will," he said as I left.

On Monday I was at work early. John didn't get in till nine; then I followed him to his office. "Come on, Chris. Look over my pet projects." There was a hand with movable fingers and a dozen or more wires going to the hand, which had an adapter to go in the computer. There was a duck hanging near his desk, also with a connection to go to the computer, one computer outside its case, with different ways to plug in to the computer. He looked at me and said, "I make things work from my brain impulse to the computer." I was amazed. He turned on his computer and put a headband on with wires going to the computer. He plugged the hand electro in, and shortly after that, the hand with the fingers startled crawling toward us, down the desk. He could make each finger move separately.

"That's something," I said.

Then he said, "This is your week to learn how to make your brain send impulses." He turned to the computer. A game was still on. With the headband, he controlled a submarine on the computer. It was going underwater, dodging big rocks and corals. Fish were coming and going. The sub would dive in some places and climb up steep ridges, and I watched while we went through a section of the ocean."

"What a game," I told John.

"Yeah," he said. "It's lots of fun but when we have work to do, our pet projects wait till we have time."

"What type of work?" I asked.

"Different things to research. You will see." That day we worked on putting different microchips into our computer. It required lots of different connecting and disconnecting; it was very interesting.

The next day, John checked my impulses with a microphone made specially for detecting static, electric, and microscopic wavelengths. I had about an hour and a half of sitting, with John moving over my head with this detector. "I have ten wires to connect, so now I want you to watch this show." He turned a computer on, and a beautiful girl started stripping her clothes off. She looked like Marilyn Monroe. When she took off her panties, John started a little laugh. "Strong signal there," he said, and I laughed myself. Finally he said, "I have it," and logged them in his notes. By Wednesday he had me moving his sub all around. What a game. We studied his computer, and he showed me what he had done, each microchip added, and what they did.

The next week, on Thursday morning, he gave me a computer with all the things I needed to convert it to do what I wanted and said, "OK, Chris, take your notes and this computer. Use any of my supplies. Make me a moving game."

"Good," I said. I had tried to memorize most of the additions, and I took notes. I set up on a table beside John and started assembling my computer. I had to add seven microchips and report other chips. I worked late that Thursday. John stayed with me, and Friday noon, I had my computer able to fly my eagle around the mountains. While I was flying my eagle, the professor came in; then Tom came in. They were both impressed.

"Good job," the professor said. "How long did it take for the test?"

"Twelve hours."

"That's a record, isn't it?" he asked.

"Yes," John said.

That evening, we had a meeting. Next week we all start on these names I have. He passed to each one of us a folder. Mine was to look for Al-Babaned with the given coordinates and list all people that associate with him and their coordinates. I was glad to do something productive. On

Monday I started early. I listed the coordinates of Al-Babaned and followed him from Baghdad all through Iraq and listed four new names and their coordinates. The second week, Tom called me to his office. "Chris, I have an assignment for you."

"Great," I said.

"I want you to help locate a problem. The Covington General Hospital is losing lots of medicine and the medicine is making it to the streets. I want you to find out what is happening with it. A Dr. Hugh Hampton, a friend of mine, will be at the hospital and help you with the information. You can start on it now." I drove home and called for an appointment. His secretary told me he would not be back that day. I decided to go to the hospital and look around. I stopped by Dr. Hampton's office. The secretary said that Dr. Hampton was in surgery and might be back, but she didn't know for sure.

"I'm Chris Doan. If he comes back, page me please."

"I will," she said. I went to the cafeteria and got a turkey sandwich. I sat there for over an hour, thinking about the missing medicine. I had no idea how I could help. About three thirty, I was paged over the intercom. I went to the office, and Dr. Hampton had finished in surgery and was there. We shook hands.

"Come into my office," he said, and we went in.

"Mr. Quick asked me to come over and talk to you."

"I don't know how you can help." He looked like he was in his early thirties. The perfect doctor, looked smart and dedicated.

"Tell me, Doctor. How often do you receive your medicine?"

"We have three suppliers. They come when we need the medicine."

"And what is missing?"

"Valium, oxycodone, and Vicodin. That we know of."

"Do these come from the same supplier?"

"Yes," he said. "They do."

"When will you order them again?" I asked.

"We just placed an order yesterday. They should come tomorrow," he said.

"Not to alert anyone we are looking, who could I get to help me in the medicine department."

He thought a moment. "Lisa Stready is a nurse and also assists when they need help. Let me page her and she knows when the medicine comes in."

"You trust her then?" I said.

"Oh yes. She is a dedicated and religious nurse. I wish I had her in my practice. I'm not the director. I have my own practice. I help when the hospital director needs me."

"Oh," I said. He had paged Lisa, and she called on the phone.

"Yes, Lisa," he told her. "Could you come to my office?" he asked.

"Yes," she replied, and they hung up.

"What kind of doctor are you?" I asked.

"General practitioner. Do you have an idea how you are going to help?"

"No, I don't, not yet anyhow."

Lisa knocked, and Dr. Hampton said, "Come in," and it was her. Dr. Hampton said, "Chris Doan, this is Lisa Stready." We shook hands. "Lisa, Chris is here to see if we can find out where the missing medicine is going, so no one but me, you, and Chris."

"I see," she said. "I'll do whatever he asks, related to the medicine. It is empty anytime, so I could look over the pharmacy without drawing attention. I relieve Dr. Hester every day, usually in the afternoon."

"Have you relieved him today?"

"No, I haven't. I could call him and tell him I'm available now and see what he says."

"I understand. Call him and see," I asked. Lisa used the phone on Dr. Hampton's desk and called. "Dr. Hester, I am a little slow if you need me. I'll be down in fifteen minutes," she said. She hung the phone up.

"That's good. I'll come down in twenty minutes. I thank you for your help."

"You're welcome," she said. "We need to know," she said. Lisa left, and I had timed myself. I need to go to my car. I told Dr. Hampton I have brought a couple of cameras with me.

"Thank you, Mr. Doan, for your help."

"You're welcome," I told him and headed for my car.

I had looked at the directory when I came in, and I knew it was in the basement. I took the elevator down, and as I got off, I saw a sign saying Pharmacy, with an arrow pointing to my left, so I went that way. It had been twenty-five minutes since Lisa had called, so I should be in good time; but at a window for the pharmacy, I looked in, and I could see Lisa. It looked like she was alone. She pointed to my right, so I went to a door that opened for me. "Is there another door beside this one?"

"No," she said, "and this is the only window, also for the pickups."

"What about when the medicine comes?" I asked.

"To this window," and we checked off the boxes by verifying them with the purchases and their order number.

"Does the deliveryman ever come in the pharmacy area?"

"Yes," she said. "If we are very busy, he will bring the medicine in and we check off each box by its number, and if he takes any back, its checked off."

"Taken back?" I asked.

"Oh yes. If the medicine isn't fresh, we send it back."

"How old is fresh?" I asked.

"Usually two or three months for some. Its effectiveness isn't as strong and we return any that's old."

"I see," I said. "Where do you store the medicine?" She took me to the storage area, a strong door with a good lock system. "Can we go in?" I asked.

"Yes," she said and produced a key and unlocked the storage area. It was cold inside. "Yes," she said. "Some medicine has to be kept in forty-degree temperature."

"I see," I said. I looked around the large room with many boxes on each side. I had an idea. "Can I put a camera in here?" I asked.

"Yes," she said, "but I don't see how that can help." In the back was the cooling system, and I set the camera in the back. It only took pictures when something triggered it to go off. It was a good place.

"Well," I said, "let's see what happens. Let the deliveryman come in here if you are on duty."

"I will be," she said. Dr. Hester calls for help when they came.

"Do you have any medicine that needs returning?" I asked.

"I don't know. The deliveryman checks that for us." We went out, and I thanked her for the time.

"I'll be back after your delivery has been made." I gave Lisa my phone number and asked her to call me when they got there.

"I will," she said. I left. Forty-five minutes after I left, she called. "Mr. Doan, the medicine is being brought in now." I had just got home and sat down. I was up and on my way. I parked where I could see the delivery truck and waited thirty minutes, and the driver was back with his hand truck and several boxes on it. After loading up, he pulled out and drove toward Madison. I followed way back, and he turned off Highway 278, and on Tillman Road, he stopped at a house and took two boxes in, then came out and left, coming back to Covington. He went to a building, backed up to a loading ramp, and unloaded. I left and went back to the hospital. I walked by the pharmacy, and Lisa was there with a man. I presumed it was Dr. Hester. I went back to my car and went home. It was six thirty when Lisa called. "Chris, this is Lisa. Dr. Hester is gone for the day and if you want to come, I will wait for you. My shift ends at seven."

"Yes, Lisa, I'm on my way," and when I got there, I told Lisa about the deliveryman taking boxes to some home. I got the camera and went home; then I put the chip in my setup and watched on my TV. On delivering all the medicine, the driver looked through the medicine and took some boxes and placed them on the table, then took one box and slid it off another box, then slid it into a box. He did the same again; then he put all seven boxes on a hand truck and left. At that time, he stopped in the pharmacy, and Lisa wrote down all the numbers and names of the medicine being returned because of the age; then he left. Lisa had checked all the medicine off by the order number, and she knew that was right. Now I knew how they stole the medicine, but how did they distribute it?

That night I lay thinking about how I would do it. Now my best chance to find out would be to follow the medicine. I would go tomorrow and follow where the boxes were left. I called Tom and let him know what I found out. He told me to make a copy of the film and send it to him. "Come in tomorrow," he told me, "and bring the film," so the next morning, I was there at eight. Tom got there shortly. After that we watched the film; then he said, "Yes, follow the medicine. I want you to take this pistol and go see Sergeant Thompson at this address downtown and get registered to carry the pistol. Don't talk to anyone else about registering." After talking to everyone, I went to the courthouse, and when I asked for Sergeant Thompson, I was directed to his location. When I got there, Sergeant Thompson had his name on his shirt, and I told him who I was.

"Yes," he said. "Fill out this form," so I did, and on it, it had a place for the serial number of the .357 Mag I would be carrying. When I finished, I came out and drove off. I followed. They went to Lake Jackson, and I had to drive by when they got out and went in. There wasn't a good place to watch, but I found some woods with a dirt road in it. I drove a little ways, turned around, and come back to a place where I could use my binoculars to watch. Later a car pulled up, and two men went inside the house. An old Nova in great condition pulled up. A man got out and went inside the house. I waited for two hours before the man in the Nova came out with a sack and left. It looked like a black '65 Nova. I could see it and tell any time. A few minutes later, the two men from Tillman Road got in a Yukon and left. I followed, and then the man at the housing project got out at a store and came out with a sack; then they went to Tillman Road and got out.

I drove home. I called Tom and gave him the tag number of the Yukon and asked if he had a good listening device and tape recorder. "Yes," he said. "Come by in the morning and get a few things."

At six thirty, after a good run, I went to Atlanta to the office. Tom got there a little later. I had talked to everyone that was there. Ann and John came in before I left, but Tom opened a room that had everything you could imagine—pistols, handcuffs, all types of surveillance equipment. He got two recorders and listening devices. They have new batteries; they should be ready. He also gave me a hard hat with sunglasses. "I don't need that," I said.

"This is night vision glasses."

I looked at the hat. "That is neat," I said.

Tom said, "The best made." I was impressed. "Keep in touch."

"Yes, sir," and I left. I gave Tom the addresses where the men had been, Tillman Road, the housing project, and the one on Lake Jackson, Harper Landing Road.

I went back to the house by the lawn, parked in the woods, and watched until dark. There was one car there, and at eleven I took the night vision helmet and walked to the house. A car pulled in our road, and I hid behind a tree. It went on down the road. The night vision worked great. Their porch light was on, so I stayed outside the lit area. I went to the back of the house. It was on a hill, and it had a full basement. I went all around the house. The lights were off in the lower part, but lights were on in the house upstairs. I got to the front and tried to look in a window. The hill was too steep. It was too chancy to look in the front. I went back to my Honda and went home.

CHAPTER X

That night I thought about how I could get a bug in the house to hear what was going on. It was eight fifteen. I called Tom and told him what I was doing. "Good," he said. "Those addresses you gave me, the black Nova is Al Carson's. He has a drug record and one conviction of burglary and the man that live on Tillman Road is Terry Wood, no record, and Bill Scott on Harper Landing Road served two years for dealing drugs." That was fast, I thought. "Chris, you need a better car. Have you thought about one?"

"Yes, I think I'll get a Dodge truck with a Cummins diesel motor, four-wheel drive, and passenger backseat."

"What color?" he asked.

"Black, I think."

"I have a good contact. Let me check for you."

"Yes, sir," I said.

"Keep up the good work."

"Thank you, sir," and I hung up.

I woke early and had a good run; then I stopped by the dojo. It was early, but Mike's truck was there. He was cleaning, and I started helping. In one hour we were finished. "I need a good workout," he said. "When can you oblige me?"

"How about Wednesday noon?"

"That's a good time," he said. "I'll see you then," and I went home.

It was Saturday, and I hadn't realized it. We ate breakfast. Then Dad said, "I have something for you," and he went to his room and came back with two metal poles about thirty inches long. He handed one to me; it had a lever that came down around three inches. On top was a button. "Don't mash that button," he said. "Let's go outside." Outside he handed me the other pole, and he said, "Open up the bottom piece to stand up." I opened the little lever. "Can you stand on the two levers?" So I stood on the two levers. "Now mash the button on top one at a time," and I did. It raised me up two foot. "Now the other one." I mashed the button, and that one raised like stilts. "Now the first one again," and it raised me two more feet; then I brought the other leg up. I had a grin on my face that would make an opossum smile. I did this six times, and I was eight feet high. "Can you walk on them?" he asked, and I took a step, then another. I was afraid I was going to fall, but I didn't. I walked around the yard. I couldn't believe it.

"Dad, this is great."

He smiled. "You like them?" he asked.

"I love them," I said. "How do I get down?" I asked.

"You don't. You have to live up there," and laughed. "OK, twist the gas button counterclockwise both at the same time. One half turn." I needed some way to strap them to my feet and legs. I had a hard time twisting them at the same time, but I made it, but one leg was up more than the other one.

"I need two Velcro straps for my legs and two for my feet," I told him. He got his tape measure and measured.

"You got big legs," he said.

I hugged him. "Thanks, Dad. I really like them."

"By the way, if you mash the button on top, that metal bottom will shoot out like an arrow, be careful." He unscrewed the cap and took out the gas cylinder, which looks like a paintball gas cylinder.

I said, "It is. You can get three extensions with each cylinder. If I had a way to carry these on my back."

He smiled. "I'll see what I can do," he said.

"Thanks, Dad."

I left for Lake Jackson to sit and watch for a while. I sat looking from the woods till eleven; then Bill came out and got in his truck and left. I waited fifteen minutes, then drove to his house. I went to the door and knocked; no one came. I knocked hard, and nothing. I took out my lock kit. It only took less than two minutes. I shut the door and went to the next room. It had beer cans lying, also snacks and their boxes; it was a mess. There was a bookcase there on top. It would be a good place. I moved a chain to stand on and key it back just enough not to be seen. I replaced the chair just like it was, then left. After getting the phone number, I drove back to the woods and waited. Just before sunset, he came back and the black Nova that was Al Carson's. They got out and went into the house at dark. I would take the receiver and put it close to the microphone. It was dark enough. I had the night vision helmet on, and I made my way to the crawl space. The door was unlocked. I crawled in, then pulled the door shut. I could see good, and I moved anything that was in my way. I knew about where the den should be, and I could hear voices. A concrete support was just what I needed. The concrete footing would help keep the receiver from the dirt. I could hear Al Carson. They were talking about paying someone off and that week was doing good; still had Sunday to go. Bill was talking about a deal in South Carolina. "How are we going to get supplied. Dan say he can get more when a boss leaves in a month or so. Well, seeing is believing. Want a burger?" he asked Al.

"You fixing yourself one?"

"Yeah, two."

"Fix me two also." The TV came on. I crawled back out, put the little lock on, not locked, and then I went through the woods to my car. I turned my unit on, and it was like listening to someone in the next room, so I was recording while listening.

"Want everything on it?" Bill asked.

"No onions," Al said.

"Pickles?"

"Yeah," and he had two plates loaded, with two Bud Lights. "The fight will be on shortly," Al said. I got as comfortable as I could. I would stay till they went home or slept.

The ultimate fighting came on, and I could hear the fight good. I fell asleep about twelve. The fight was still on, and Al and Bill talked about a new contact in South Carolina and how they could supply them. "We need someone else," Bill said. "Got any idea?"

"No. It was hard to get Dan." The fight ended, and Al said, "Time for me to go." He got up and said, "See you tomorrow." Al just waved by. I heard a little noise; then things went quiet.

I drove home. There was a new black Dodge truck parked in the driveway, four-wheel drive, automatic, with black leather seats and interior. It was beautiful. I went in, and everyone was sleeping. I knew Tom had got it. I showered and went to bed; it was two thirty. I lay in bed late. It was seven before I got up. Dad asked about the truck. "First time I saw," I said. "It was ordered. I guess they delivered it." Two sets of keys were on the table. Dad and I went out to look it over. I unlocked the doors and sat inside. It had that new smell. "Let's go for a ride," I told Dad. He shut his door, and we left. It had great power and drove great. The seats were good. "Want to drive it?" I asked.

"Not really. I'm enjoying being chauffeured." We got on I-20, and I opened it up. I got to eighty-five, and it had plenty of power left; then I got off at Highway 138 and turned around back home. It had great pickup. The bedcover was black and would lock. I got home, and Dad asked how much did it cost.

"I don't know, Dad. The company got it for me."

"It's nice," he said.

Mom had breakfast for us—pancakes, eggs, bacon, and grits. Brendon and Andres were up, and that was the first time in over a week we were all together. "What are you going to do with the Honda?" Brendon asked.

"We all can use it," I said. "If you keep the yards cut and cleaned." They both grinned. They were through eating, and they headed for the yard. I sat talking to Mom and Dad for over an hour. They were trying to pick out of me what I really did at work. I danced around the answer, but I let them know they were close when they asked if I worked for the government.

Dad said, "We know enough," to Mom.

I started to leave, when Dr. Hampton called. "Chris?"

"Yes, sir."

"This is Dr. Hampton. Have you learned anything?"

"I know the truck driver that delivers your medicine—Dan, you call him—is taking the medicine to some men I am after now."

"When do you want to arrest Dan?" he asked.

"Let's catch Al Carson and Bill Scott before we let them know we are after them."

"Keep me in touch," he said.

"Dr. Hampton, before you go, would you like to work with me a day or so."

"Yes," he said. "When?"

"Now. Is that OK?"

"Where can I meet you?" he asked.

"Wendy's."

"OK, in one hour I'll be there," he said. Tom had asked me to keep the doctor informed. I'll show him, I thought. I knew I would be sitting and watching a long time. After showering, I dressed in slacks and a brown shirt. I went to the Honda and got my tools and gun and things and put them in the truck. I had noticed the truck was full of gas. I drove to Wendy's and got the doctor.

"Want anything?" I asked. "I'll take a large Coke, fries, and chicken nuggets. It may be a long day," I told him. He ordered water and chicken nuggets. We did small talk. I told him about the listening to the microphone and watching the house.

"It sounds good to me." He was wanting a little excitement, I thought.

We drove out his road, and when we got in front of the house and passed it, there were three cars parked. We went to the road, then out the wooded road till we came to a small clearing, and parked. I turned my receiver on and listened to the men talk. Bill was taking in the money and getting more supplies for Al Carson and Terry Woods. "Here is a hundred Valiums and a hundred Vicodin."

"I need another fifty Vicodin," Al said. Bill got him another fifty. Bill went to get another beer.

"Want another?" he asked Terry.

"Yeah," he said. We sat and listened for over an hour.

Dr. Hampton talked very low. "We can hear them, but they can't hear us," I said. Then he spoke a little louder.

"This is what you do most of the time?" Dr. Hampton asked.

"When I get the information I want, I'll act on it, but now we need to know their setup and all the people we can. Right now we know three plus Dan, the truck driver. They must have other men selling for them."

Al told Bill, "I've got to go. Larry and Scott need these supplies." Then he called someone and said, "I'm on my way. Meet me at Scott's house." I guess he was talking to Harry. I cranked up and went to the main road and waited up till I saw the black Nova pull out. When he got a good ways from me, I pulled out and stayed back as far as I could. When we got to Covington, I got closer. We went through town, then on the old Atlanta Highway for three miles. He pulled down Tully Road. It said Dead End, so I passed it and went down a little ways, then came back and turned down Tully Road. The Nova was parked at 1142, and I kept going. At the end of the road, there was a turnaround. I parked and took out my map. No one was watching, so I sat pretending to read the map. About five minutes, a black Ford F-150 pulled up, and one man went to the door, then went in. I waited ten minutes, then drove by the truck, getting his license number, LRX 273. When I got on the old Atlanta Highway, I went toward Covington. I pulled in a driveway of a house for sale and waited a couple of minutes. Later the Ford truck passed. I pulled out and followed Larry. He went to town and parked at the shopping center in front of

Kroger food store, then went in. I parked and watched. Ten minutes later, he was back, and he just sat in the truck. A little later, a young man walked up and got in with Larry. Five minutes later, he got out and went to his car. I waited. I wanted to know more about Larry. I expected him to leave, but he just sat there. About fifteen minutes later, a man dressed with a suit came up and got in Larry's truck, then a little later got out and went to his nice Buick, and Larry cranked his truck and pulled out. I followed him a little ways and decided to get his address from his tag number. I told the doctor we had a good day; we know of two more contacts. Then I asked where I could take him.

"Thanks, Chris, for letting me go with you."

"You're welcome. Where can I take you?"

"Back to Wendy's," he said, and I did. "Keep in touch." Then he gave me his cell phone number. It was a Saturday evening, and I was going to the dojo tomorrow and have a good workout. I called Tom and gave him all the new information.

"Good," he said. "I'll get what I can, see you," and hung up. There was Scott Thomas on Tully Road and Larry in a Ford truck, LRX 273 tag number. I got to the house in my new truck; it was perfect. I always wanted one just like this; then I remembered I hadn't thanked Tom, so I called him. "Yes," he answered.

"I love the truck, thanks."

"You're welcome," and we hung up.

I talked to Mom and Dad for over an hour, then showered and went to bed. I woke early and had a good run. Mom had breakfast ready, and I ate hardly. Mom got ready for church. Dad and I sat around and talked about Iraq. "Think you will have to go there?" he asked.

"I don't know," I said, "but I wouldn't mind." Uncle Cho called. He was coming down later. He had some business tomorrow in Atlanta. Good, I thought. Dad always enjoyed his company, and I did also. I knew he would bring some vegetables. His squash and tomatoes were great; everything was. He grew organic only, no bought insecticides. I called Mike. He said he would meet me at noon. Andrew got up, and after he ate, he had a new game he wanted to play, so we played his new war game. I left at five till twelve, and Mike was just getting there. We had to clean up.

"I'm glad you came," he said.

"Yeah, I see why." It only took an hour. We mopped the floor, put everything in its place, then put the mats down to have a workout. It went good. We sparred until we both had a good sweat. After resting and drinking some water, we started back. Mike had a good jab. His hands were fast, and he hit hard. My feet were my best weapons, and he did lots of kicks, but I was ready. "You have the fastest feet I know of. You could make lots of money fighting."

"It's not for me," I said.

"You don't like money?" he asked. "By the way, your truck looks great. What kind of gas mileage do you get?"

"I don't know. I just got the truck." Then he took me to the floor. "Stay focused," he said. He had a good arm bar on me. I tapped; he let me up. "That's enough for me," he said.

"Me too, thanks," I told him.

"You're always welcome," and he grinned.

I went home to a good dinner. Uncle Cho had smoked some ribs, and we had fresh squash, tomatoes, lettuce, string beans, and okra. "Wow, that was good," I told Mom and UC.

"Glad you liked it," Mom said. Uncle Cho asked about my new truck. I told him the company had it for me.

"Good place to work for." We sat around the table talking. UC was telling us about Dorothy and the kids; then I remembered the stilts Dad made.

I got them and told UC, "Come outside. I have something to show you." He and Dad followed me outside. I let the lever down to stand on them. I got on them and lifted my foot while I mashed the buttons, one side, then the other, and I stepped up until I was eight feet high. He was impressed. Dad went to his car and got four Velcro straps and gave them to me. They had a sewed loop to fit over the stilts. The top was smaller than the bottom. After sliding them on, I tried them out. They locked my feet good and my legs good. I started taking steps; they were fine. I walked around with them on.

UC said, "Let me try them." I lowered myself and showed him how to work them. After he got high, he took steps. "Only your dad could think of something that smart." He was right. Dad had also made a case to carry them on my back, one on each side. I was impressed. "They make good weapons," UC said. The weight was around three pounds each. "Yes," he said. "They make good weapons. What would happen if you pointed them at someone and mashed the button?" he asked Dad.

"That last section would shoot out like an arrow," Dad said. "I made it so it wouldn't destroy the stilts if you ever used it to shoot out."

"That's great. It sure didn't look like a weapon you could shoot." After looking it over good, I put it in the truck.

Monday morning, I got up at five thirty and had a good six—or seven-mile run, then went in for breakfast. We had fresh blueberry pancakes with cheese and eggs, with blueberry muffins. That's when I like milk. I drank a large glass. I ate grits with my eggs and then muffins and milk. Andrew and Brendon were still in bed. I left for Bill Scott's place. I got there around nine and listened to some soft music while I waited for someone to talk. I fell asleep at ten fifteen. I woke to someone talking. Al Carson had come, and he and Bill were talking about one of the girls that worked for them, Page. She had disappeared, and she had eleven hundred dollars. She owed Bill. Her sister works at Wal-Mart, and she got off at seven. "I'll pay her a visit tonight," he said. Bill told Al not to hurt her bad yet but to let her know she must get Page back with the money.

"I have fourteen hundred now. Where is the other six?" Bill asked.

"I'll have it tomorrow," Al said, "and I need a hundred Vicodins." Bill got the medicine and gave it to Al.

"That makes eleven hundred, Al."

"Yeah," and wrote it down in his little book. "I'll see you later," he told Bill and left. I cranked up and got ready to follow him. I saw him leave, and I got to the main road before he was out of sight, but I stayed back. We got to Covington and went to Highway 278 and out it toward the hub. He passed the hub and turned down another road; then he stopped at a trailer. I passed and turned around and looked for a place I could stop but couldn't find one. Al had stopped at Highway 11. The house number was 2240. I got back to the hub and parked. I went in the little store and got some lemon drops candy to eat and a bottle of water. I went back to the truck. I was parked, so I could look down Highway 11 for Al. Twenty minutes later, Al came by. I followed him into town. He went to a shopping center and parked. I did the same. About ten minutes later, a nice-looking girl drove up in a blue Ford, got out, and went to Al and got in the Nova. They talked for a few minutes; then she got out and went to her car. I followed her. After writing down her tag number, we went to Bell's grocery store. She went in and stayed a little. Then she got two sacks of groceries, then went to Oak Hill Street 4291 and went in. I watched for a few minutes, then left. I went home. Tonight I was going to Bill's place and watch.

It was early, so I went to the dojo. Mike had a class going. I went to the barbells and started lifting. An hour later, the class was dismissed. Mike asked if I wanted to work out.

"Sure," I said. I put on my headgear, and we started jabbing. I did a roundhouse kick that caught him off guard; he went to the floor. We waited until he had his senses back.

"Let's call it a day," he said. "Them feet of yours are deadly. I haven't ever been kicked that hard."

"Sorry," I said. "I wasn't thinking."

"Don't be," he said. "I want a good workout and got it." I started cleaning up the dojo. After a few minutes, he started mopping. I had the mats put up, and I went for a mop. We were through in a few minutes, and then we talked about his next fight in a week with Moto the Assassin, an Oriental with a good record of sixteen and three.

"How long you going to fight?" I asked.

"Until the dojo is paid for at least two more years."

"Well, I'll see you later. I've got work to do." He knew not to ask what.

I left and went back home and got some things. I changed pants and left. No one was there, I got to Harper Landing Road and drove out it to the landing. Several trucks with trailers were there, and a few people were on the docks. I turned around and went back to my hiding spot and turned on some music. I could hear the TV playing at Bill's place. After an hour, I saw the Nova pull up; then a good-looking blond got out and went in. I heard her tell Bill she needed a fix. "I need a fix too," he said. "You're beautiful with your clothes off," he said. Then things went quiet for a little while.

Then she asked, "That hold you a little while?"

"Yep," he said. I heard him go somewhere. His voice got lower; then he was back. I had changed to my camo clothes, and I got my stilts and went toward the house. I had to go around the back to stay in the dark. When I got to the side window, I had good cover. I put the stilts on and went up at the window. I could see good inside. Bill was in his shorts, and the girl was dressed in slacks and blouse. She had something she was snorting through a straw. When she finished, she lay back in her chair. Bill asked if she wanted to go to South Carolina with him.

"When you coming back?" she asked.

"Tomorrow afternoon," he said.

"When you leaving?"

"An hour or so," he said.

"Let me see if I can get a sitter." She called someone and asked the person if they could spend the night with Mary. "I'll pay you," she said. "OK, I'll bring her over in a few minutes. OK, Bill, I'm going home and I'll be right back."

"Hurry," Bill said. She left; then Bill came into the den carrying a briefcase and sat down, opened the briefcase, and took out lots of money and was counting it. Then Al Carson came up. He went to the door and knocked. Bill said, "I'm coming," and went to the door. Then he went back to his counting.

Al asked, "Want a beer?"

"Yeah," Bill said.

Al got two and was sitting, watching Bill finish, and Bill said, "Not enough," and went to his bedroom and came back with more money and counted more.

A car pulled up, and Al asked, "Who was that?"

Bill looked out the window and said, "It's Jane."

"What she want?" Al asked.

Bill said, "She is going with us."

"To hell," Al said. "She is nothing but trouble."

"She will be OK," Bill said.

"Not with me," Al said.

"She is going," Bill said, "and I don't want any shit either. Go out and keep her out till I finish with this money."

Al went out. "I don't like it," Al said. I lowered myself and went to the corner of the house. Al was fussing with Jane.

"You bastard," she called Al. "You never worked and you never helped with Mary."

"You bitch, all you ever wanted was a fix. Now look at you your body. It's used for your drugs." It got worse. They got louder, and Al hit her with his fist. She went down. Bill came out.

"What's going on? I could hear you all the way to the back of the house." Jane still hadn't got up.

"You hit her, you ass?" and came over to her. "You OK?" Bill asked. She didn't answer. He bent down over her. She didn't move. He went into the house and got a flashlight and came back. Blood was coming out the back of her head. "My god," Bill said. "You killed her." They were both bent down over her. "She is dead," Bill said. He stood up.

I couldn't see them clearly, but I could hear Al say, "I only hit her light."

"Shut up," Bill said. "What you going to do? You got to get her away from here."

"I don't know," Al said.

"You got to take her and bury her somewhere."

"This wouldn't have happened if you hadn't asked her to go. You know since the divorce, we only fuss and fight."

"Don't get me in on this," Bill said. "You killed her, not me."

Al got wild. "You caused it," and Al hit Bill, knocking him down, then kicked him. Bill went for his gun in his pocket. Al kicked him in the face. Bill got the gun out and was trying to get a bullet into the chamber. Al kept kicking him, and Bill went limp. Al leaned against a tree and was crying out of control. I watched. Bill got control and went for his car and backed up to the body, opened the truck, and picked up the body and got it in the trunk. I was so nervous. I went behind Al and hit him hard in the ear. He went down. I had to call Tom.

"Tom?"

"Yeah," he said.

"I got problems."

"What's wrong?" I told him. "What's the address?" I gave it to him. "Get the recorder from the house and I'll take care of it."

"Yes, sir," and I hung up. I went to the crawl space under the house, got the recorder, and came out. I saw the briefcase and got it and left. At my truck, I called Tom.

"It's taken care of. If you are in a safe place, watch until the police come."

"Yes, sir."

"You did a good job," Tom said. I was almost shaking. "Just relax," Tom said, and I told him everything I knew. I could hear a siren; it was the sheriff department. It was two. I had my binoculars, watching the police turn the outside lights on. I watched, and after an hour, I pulled out and drove home. It was almost three. I took a shower and lay down.

The next morning, I had a good run, then went to the office. Tom was there and asked about the tapes. I gave them to him. He told me to sit down; then he called the Newton City Sheriff Department. Talking to the sheriff, he told him everything again; it was on loudspeaker. Tom told him he was to be kept out of this totally. "Yes, sir," the sheriff said. "We have Al Carson and Bill Scott. Bill told us everything and we are after seven more people now, including Dan Thompson with Allied Chemicals."

Tom said, "I want an exclusive write-up, do you understand?"

"Yes," the sheriff said, "but let me approve it first."

"OK, yes," Tom said and hung up. "Write me a story on this, Mr. Reporter."

"Yes, sir," I said, and I went to my office and started writing the drug ring and its capture and killing.

Tom made a copy of the story and faxed it to the Covington paper and sent another copy to the *Washington Post*. I had the briefcase with me, and I gave it to Tom. He opened it and was very surprised. "How much money is there?" he asked.

"I don't know, sir." He started counting; it took over an hour.

"Seven hundred and fifty thousand, three-quarters of a million," he said. "Good. We will put it in our war chest."

Tom called Dr. Hampton and told him about the ring being arrested now and about the death of Jane Oldham. "I don't think you will have any more drug problems."

Dr. Hampton thanked Tom and said, "Call me if I can ever help you," and hung up.

"That is a fine doctor. His father was a friend of mine in the army. Chris, I need a follow-up story for the papers." That evening, Tom called the sheriff department and was told seven more people had been arrested and Bill Scott had told everything, not wanting to be in on the murder with Al Carson. I wrote up a follow-up story and gave it to Tom. "Now go home. Take this week off and next and now let your beard and mustache grow." I was surprised. I got the Covington paper and read about the ring being busted and all the names of the members charged. It was signed, "By the Reporter." So that was my new name, the Reporter.

CHAPTER XI

That week I went to the mountains. It was nice to relax and fish, but best was the working out with Uncle Cho. We raced on stilts, we meditate, and we had good workouts. Most of the time I saw Dorothy and the children. How they were growing. I took them to Toccoa one day and got them a new set of clothing. We ate at the pizza house, then went to a movie; afterward, to the ice cream store. It was a good day. I was hoping UC and Dorothy would have some time alone. It was nine before we got home. I called UC twice while we were out, letting him know it would be late when we would be back. The next morning, I had a good run, then breakfast. We worked a while in the garden, hoeing out the grass; then we watered it good. I went home on Wednesday. I wanted to work on Mom's flowers. I enjoyed it. Then I went to the dojo for a good workout. Mike was glad; that Saturday he had a match with Moto the Assassin, and he wanted that win bad. "I'll come tomorrow if you want me to."

"Oh Yes, I do." He thanked me again, and I left. Ashley came over most evenings, and we would go out to a movie or dinner. School had started, and in a way I missed it. That Sunday Mom had all of us go to church. She cooked a great meal—squash, okra, salad, baked potatoes, corn bread, and turkey.

Monday morning, I had a good run, then went to work. Tom asked if I would like a mission. "Great," I said. "Where?"

"Iraq."

"Sounds great," I said.

"But first you will go to Dubai for two months for some special computer training, then to Baghdad. You will work in a computer store and learn what you can."

"When will I leave?"

"Wednesday, a flight out of Dobbins in uniform with this beard and mustache." He laughed. "You will get lots of attention. You're off till Wed," he said, "but be here by eight. Your flight is at ten."

"Yes, sir," I said. Then I went around to see everyone.

Johnny said, "You lucky dog. I'd love to go with you."

Sarah gave me a hug. "Be careful. You know it's dangerous."

"I will," I promised.

Ann hugged me. "You're a handsome dude," she said.

I grinned. "That's nice coming from such a lovely person."

I went home and played around with the computer. Tom e-mailed me. "Chris, you have a new Web site. It's listed as the Newsman Covington News and the *Washington Post* deposited your money for the stories, good going," and signed off with a smiling face.

On Tuesday I spent the day with the yard. When Mom and Dad came home, I hung around the kitchen, talking, and that evening I played games on the TV with Andrew and Dad. "Can you tell us where you are going?" Dad asked.

"Oh yes, I'll be in school in Dubai for a while."

"School in Dubai? Their schools better than ours?"

"Only certain schools. Their computer school is as good as the best in the world."

"I hear only people of the palace could get in," he said.

"My company has pull," I said. I went to bed at ten and got up early for a good run. I was back by six thirty. I showered and told everyone good-bye.

"Wow, you are handsome in uniform," Mom said. I kissed her and left. Dad would drive me to town. He wondered why I wanted out in front of an insurance company.

"Pretend you didn't bring me here," I said.

"All right." I gave him a hug, and he left.

I took my duffel bag through the office spaces, to the back; then I took the elevator to the basement. No one was there, so I took my key and unlocked the door and went down the hall to another door. I looked through the eyepiece, and I heard the door unlock, and I went through it. Tom was in his office. He went to the professor's door and knocked. "Come in." Tom opened the door. "Chris is here," he said.

The professor came into my office. "Take your clothes off except your shorts."

"Why?" I asked.

"Your new tan," he said.

"Really?" and I stripped down to my shorts, and they both put a paste on me and started rubbing it all over me. After fifteen minutes, they were through. I was as dark as someone with a dark tan. They both looked me over.

"Good," Tom said. "Chris, we are going to put a microchip behind your ear." He was showing me. It wasn't as big as a dime. "You will only feel a sting, the shot, and it will be over."

"What does it do?" I asked.

"It's a listening device and we can tell your location anywhere in the world."

"You said listening device. How much more can I hear?" I asked.

"Many times," he said. "It's adjustable."

"OK, I'm willing." The professor opened a doctor's bag, took out a bottle of something, a razor, a needle and thread, and a needle of a shot. He wiped a spot on my ear with something; then I felt a little shot. He put the needle in the garbage after breaking the needle off. He was looking at my ear; then he did something I couldn't see. He and Tom were doing something for about five minutes.

Then he said, "What do you think?" Tom gave a good inspection.

"You're good, professor."

"Thank you."

Tom said, "Well, you're ready to finish your tan. We will go out." He opened a closet door. It had a large mirror on it. They left the room, and I put the paste all over my butt and all over my front. I wiped it all clean, then put my shorts on. I opened the door, and they came back in and looked all over me again. "Looks fine to me," Tom said. "Now you can dress, Chris. To activate your listening device, you can put your finger on it and mash gently. One time, it will come on. If you mash it twice, your hearing will double. If you mash it three times, it will be mighty loud. To cut it off, mash it again. Now if we want to send you a signal, we can turn our unit on and talk to you, but we can't hear you except if you touch it. While we have our unit on, it will sound off, so one touch means yes, two touches means no. Do you follow me?"

"Yes," I said. "One touch is yes, two touches means no."

"Good. Now we can follow you on your missions. If you ever need help, we can always get to you." The Tom added, "We need to leave in fifteen minutes."

"Yes, sir," so I finished dressing. The professor called to me, and I went to the cafeteria. Everyone was there, and they all let me know they were there to help me anytime.

"Good luck." I shook hands with and kissed Sarah and Ann, then shook hands with John, Alex, and the professor.

Tom and I left. A car was in front in a no parking zone. We got in and left. At Dobbins Air Base, we had someone waiting for us and who drove us to a C-5A, and the plane was ready. I shook Tom's hand and got aboard. Ten minutes later, we were taxiing off. Tower told us we had a runway, and we were off. Three marines were in the plane, and we talked. One asked me what unit I was with. I avoided the question. Later I was asked about what I did. I again avoided the question. All the men had at least one tour in Iraq. One was on his third tour. One older sergeant said, "He can't answer our questions. Look at him, third army patch, a beard. That means intelligence, ain't that right, Lieutenant?" I smiled and asked where they would be stationed. Two at Baghdad, one was unknown. Then the men asked me how I got in intelligence. Was it hard? I couldn't tell anything. I talked about Covington. One man was from Decatur, one from Macon, the other from Atlanta. James, from Macon, asked if I was a lifer.

"I don't know yet," I said. How many years had I been in? I wouldn't answer. We talked about fishing, hunting, and sports. Everyone liked baseball. I liked football best, but I like baseball too. The trip was long and tiring. The marines talked about missions they had been on, friends that didn't make it, and how lousy the Taliban were—they had no regard for life unless you were a believer of the Koran. It is awful to have such, believing so many different ways.

It took most of two days to get to Saudi Arabia; then I went on to Dubai for more schooling. On arrival I went to the computer science technology of the computer system. I went with a box of candy to Professor Mohammad Al-Hidi. The secretary told him I was there. "Send him in," he said. He was smiling with a look of friends. "And you are Nerij Bhardwaj."

"Yes, sir," I said.

"Thank you," he said as I handed him the box of candy Tom had sent from France.

"Mr. Quick sent his regards and hope you enjoy the chocolates."

He smiled. "He spoils me. Is he doing good?"

"Yes, sir, he is well." I handed him a letter from Tom.

"Nerij, you will be staying at the school dorm, room 362." He handed me a Manila folder with a layout of the school grounds and every bathroom, restaurants, gym, classroom, library, major computer room always open. "Your clothing will be in your closet. You have your choice of underwear." He called for a school host. His name is Zoka. We talked of the weather, a big camel race in two weeks, about the school for only the finest Arabs. "I am your sponsor."

"Oh," I said. "Thank you, sir."

"I know you will make me proud of you."

"Yes, sir." Then a knock came to our door.

"Come in." The young man stopped at the entrance. "Zoka, this is Nerij Bhardwaj. Please show him around." I shook his hand and followed this young man, who said nothing. I asked him about a restroom. We stopped at a door with a picture of a man.

"I will wait," he said. It was a well-kept restroom. I used it, and we went through the building to another building and took an elevator to the third floor, room 362. It was in roman numerals. He opened the door, and I went in. There was another bed, empty, and two closets and a chest of drawers, a small kitchen, a coffeepot, sink, microwave, a refrigerator well stocked with all types of sandwich meat, and shelves that had a good stock of food. "I will be back," he said and left. I had a bath; then I looked through the uniforms and selected a white robe and blue trim.

I lay on my cot, and thirty minutes later, Zoka was back. He knocked. "Come in," I said.

"Nerij, would you like to see around the school?"

"Yes," and I got up. I fixed my cot. I followed Zoka. He would take me through the school.

"This is your classroom," he said, and we opened the door and went in. It was full of Apple computers and nice chairs; then we went to the cafeteria, to the gym, and then outside. A large section was full of bicycles, all blue with white trim. After going to a nice pond, there were tables and good sitting places all around the pond. Ducks were swimming around, and birds were everywhere, with bird feeders all around. It was a beautiful place. There were a few people around sitting at the tables, with their laptops computers, some just talking. Zoka asked if I was hungry.

"Yes, I am."

"Good," he said. "Dinner is being served." We went to the cafeteria. "Is there anything else I can show you?"

"No, Zoka, I am fine."

"Then I will see you later."

"You're not eating?"

"Oh no, I just work here. I am not allowed. Thank you," and he left. All the students were dressed the same; the workers had plane white on. I went through the line and got what I wanted, then sat down. As I sat there, a young man came in, got his food, and looked around. When he saw me, he came to my table and politely asked if I wanted some company.

"Yes," I said. "I'm Nerij Bhardwaj."

"I'm Mohammad Hamin Odin. Where are you from?" he asked.

"Sabun, Syria."

"How did you get this school to come to?"

"I won a computer contest and got to come here."

He then said, "My father insisted on me to come here."

"Then you don't like it here?"

"No, I don't. I am tired of school."

"Yes, I know what you mean. I like to travel and see new places."

"Where have you been?" he asked.

"Not far, but I want to see more."

"What does your father do?" he asked.

"He is a mechanic. He works on all types of machinery."

"Does he have a car?" Odin asked.

"Yes, we do."

"Do you drive it?"

"Yes, I have driven it."

"My father has a Toyota but we have a driver."

"You never drive?" I asked.

"Oh no, my father won't allow it until I am through with my schooling. That's why I'm here. I want to go to America. I hear even women drive."

"That's what they say," I commented.

"Don't you want to go there?"

"Yes, it would be great." We finished eating and I told Odin I would see him later.

"Wait," he said. "Do you know much about the computers?"

"I guess I enjoy it."

"Would you help me?" he asked.

"If I can."

"What room are you in?" he asked.

"Room 362."

"I'm in room 312."

"I'll see you later," I said and left.

I lay on my bed thinking about home; then I remembered Tom wants me to e-mail him. I put my laptop on the desk and sent him a message about my being there and about Professor Mohammad Al-Hidi. I sent Mom and Ashley a few lines and said I was fine. I lay on my bed thinking about how this mission could help me to go to school here. I knew Tom would know how to handle things. After I did my e-mail, I lay back down and was thinking, when Tom sent me a message. He told me he was turning my listening device on; then I heard and felt my ear pop. I was surprised. Then Tom called me on my cell phone. "How are you?" he asked.

"Fine," I said.

"I want you to try your hearing device first on low, then medium." I gave it a little bump. It was so loud. I told Tom it was great. "Now try it on medium." I thumped it again. I could hear people talking in the next room.

"It's loud," I told Tom.

"Good," he said. "Your GPS shows us you are in the school building."

"I am," I said.

"I'll talk to you tomorrow." I lay on my bed and listened to two people talk. It was about school; it would start in two days.

The next morning, I had a good run. Then a good shower and breakfast. Odin sat with me, and we talked about what we would do when school was out, and we also talked about our girlfriends. "Would you like to go for a bicycle ride?" Odin asked.

"Sure."

After we ate, we went to the bottom room and got two ten-speed bicycles. I let Odin lead the way. Dubai was a clean city, very busy, with buildings and things being built. All the buildings were modern. We rode through the dock area and looked at many nice yacht, and Odin said, "We have a boat like that one." He pointed to it. We went out a boat dock and stopped at the boat. "Yes, it is just like ours." The interior was blue and white.

"It's very nice," I told him. We rode all morning. Odin had much stronger legs than I thought. It was a good workout for me.

"It's time for lunch," he said. "Ready to go back?"

"Sure," and we rode the three or four miles back to the school. In the cafeteria, more students were there. "There must be fifty or more students," I told Odin.

"Oh yes, there will be close to two hundred enrolled. They will be coming in all day."

"How many classes are there?" I asked.

"Ten," he said. "This is a two-year school to get a diploma. We are in the finish class. It's very hard," he said, "but we will be experts. You haven't had any finish classes yet?"

"I thought I had."

"Where? This school is the best there are." That caught me by surprise.

"I had special tutoring," I told him. "He owned a computer store, and I worked for him and went to school at his shop. He is good," I told Odin.

"Would you show me a few things I am having trouble with?"

"If I can, I would be glad to." We went to my room and used my computer.

"My problem is programming in the Amazon."

"Make me a program chart," I told him, and he did. "Now adapt the words to the chart." He started but couldn't get far, so we started there.

After an hour, he said, "You are very good, you have helped me a lot. I'm going to my room. Can I come back in a little while?"

"Sure," I said. When he left, I started doing push-ups. After a series of fifty-four times, I did sit-ups. I was at two hundred and twenty when Odin returned.

"After all that riding, you do exercise?" he asked.

"I believe in exercise," I said.

"My father is like that. He gets on me for not doing more. I ride my bicycle everywhere. That keeps me in good shape." I was through with my sit-ups, and Odin had his computer. It was a nice Apple, adapted with the latest equipment. My computer was much better but looked like an old Arab-made unit. "Can you show me how to set up an intrum file," and we started. Then after a couple of hours, Odin was doing good.

"You are quite good," he said.

"You have helped me a great deal, thank you. It's time for dinner," he told me. "Are you hungry?"

"I will get fat if I keep eating like this."

Odin said, "We will work it off," and laughed. "I will see you downstairs," and he left.

I ate a small steak and some fruit. Some of the students still had their regular clothes on. This group of young Arabs looked like the upper class.

My Arabic was doing pretty good, but I was still missing some words, but Odin said he could understand my Syrian Arabic very good. After we ate, we went to the school ground and walked around. Odin spoke to several students and introduced me as Raj, the Syrian. "His sponsor is Professor Al-Hidi." That was a big sponsor, it seemed.

"Oh yes," was the reply. We sat watching a small pond with a water fountain in the middle. Ducks were swimming around, and there were nice places to sit and study around the pond.

"This is my favorite place," Odin said. "I like the water."

"I do too," I commented.

"I do most of my studying right here," he told me.

"Do you have many friends?" I asked.

"My best friends have graduated and gone home. I have to get my advanced schooling. My father is very good with the computer and wants me to work in his office with him."

"What does he do?" I asked.

"Father is in charge of the advancement of research and development of water and air department."

"Wow, that is quite a job, and you will join him?"

"Yes," Odin said with a smile. "Father is well paid for his position. We talked for over an hour, then walked back to our building and to our room. "See you in the morning," he told me as he walked away. I nodded and went in for a shower and lay around.

The next morning, I was up before daylight. I had a good run; then I showered and went for breakfast. Odin was there. "You're late," he said. "We only have thirty minutes before class." I hurried. I had oatmeal with peaches in it. We were in class with five minutes to spare. The professor was not there until exactly nine o'clock.

"I am Professor Al-Nundee and you will address me that way. You will speak when you are recognized and not before. This is a six-week course and I expect each of you to do your best or get out now." He looked around the class. He pointed to each student he didn't know and asked their names.

When he pointed to me, I stood and said, "I am Nerij Bhardwaj from Syria," and sat back down. The class began. There was a computer at each desk. The seats were padded and comfortable. The desk had a drawer with a notebook and paper, ink pins, and dictionary. There were twenty of us, and each of us had a nameplate. We put our name on it and placed it in front of our desk. The professor could address us from it. We were given a book written by Professor Al-Nundee. It had a leather binding, very nicely made. The first day, we were told to read chapters 1, 2, and 3. Each chapter had instructions for us to use our computer, and we were directed to do those lessons and read about our programs. I found them pretty easy, so I kept reading until chapters 4 and 5. At the end of the day, Professor Al Nundee was walking around and looking at our progress. He stopped behind me, and I kept reading.

"Raj?"

"Yes, sir."

"Why are you reading chapter 5?"

"Sir, I have read this book before and I was reviewing it now."

"Oh? Where did you get this book from?"

"My tutor was from India. It was our best book. I guess he had a copy. It did not look like this one, but it was written by the fine expert Professor Al-Nundee."

"You flatter me, Raj. I spoke to Professor Al-Hidi. He gives you high recommendation."

"Thank you, sir. I will try to live up to his good words." He moved on around the class, looking and talking to different students. At three, we were through and were dismissed. I brought my book and went to my room. After a short time, we had dinner. I did not see Odin, so I went walking. This was boring, and I had six weeks to tolerate. I stopped at the pond and sat. I noticed two students looking my way and talking. I turned my hearing up one time. I could barely hear them, so I made it louder. I could hear them easily; they were talking about me and Odin, probably the worst students in school, and how Odin could not possibly get through this course without help. I just kept reading. I was at chapter 9, with four chapters to go. When I looked toward the two students, they would laugh at me, then turn their heads. On the third time, one student made a gesture I didn't like. I got angry and stared at him; then Odin came up from behind me and surprised me with a "got you" motion. I almost jumped out of my seat. The noise was loud, and he had a good laugh. I turned my hearing down two bumps, then one bump. The young man across the pond was still watching me. "Who is that?" I asked Odin.

"Don't mess with him," Odin said. "He is the bully of the school. That is Dannude. He is very strong and he likes to fight. We cannot fight except once every two weeks. We have boxing. Then we can get in a match." We started walking away, and Dannude also started walking in our direction. Odin said, "Walk faster or Dannude will catch up with us. He likes trouble.

He will pick a fight." I didn't hurry. By the time we got to the building, Dannude caught up with us.

"Who is this donkey of a man?" he asked Odin. I turned toward him.

"If I am the donkey, you must be the donkey's ass." He grabbed my front clothing and twisted it. I reached up and got two fingers and bent them backward until he went down on his knees. "Don't ever do that again," I told him and let him go.

"I will meet you in the fighting circle," he said and left.

Odin said, "Oh, you shouldn't have done that. He cannot be beat."

"Anyone can be beat," I said.

"How did you know how to do the finger thing?" he asked

"Just training," I said.

"Are you a fighter?" he asked.

"I have had some training."

"You are not afraid? He is so big and he is very strong."

"But he is slow," I said.

"He fights very well. He has never been beaten in two years, I have seen him fight many times."

"Don't worry," I told Odin. "He is no problem." In my room I studied for another hour; then I did push-ups and sit-ups. This was getting too boring for me, this place.

The next day, class went slow. We were put in four-man groups. Odin had talked with two of his old classmates, Silini and Ochum. They were slow learners and had low grades. During the day, our team had four hours to work out the problems. We were programming and setting up new programs of our choice. We chose galaxy formation. That evening after class, we went to the library. It was everything a library should be. We got two books on astronomy, and the library had a computer connected to a large blackboard we could use. That evening we started with names of different star formations. We selected one hundred, and after listing them, we numbered each formation. Silini was the hardest to teach, with everyone trying to show him. It was doing all of us good. We worked till nine. Odin said, "You are very good and make learning a pleasure." Silini and Ochum agreed.

In class the next day, Professor Al-Nundee wrote each subject, with the group learning it. There were five groups. The professor said it was the first time astronomy was used as a group study. That week went slow, and on Friday we were instructed to be ready to show our progress the coming Monday. That Saturday we went to the gym. It was a small area with weights and a punching bag and a couple of exercise benches. Dannude came in and stared at me. "It's you and me next weekend," he said. I ignored him, and that made him mad. "I'll show you what a donkey's ass really is," and he left. We worked that afternoon in the library. We had all our star clusters sectioned off.

On Monday the professor came to each group. We were the stargazers. "Good," he said. "I like what you are doing, but you have a lot of research to complete. That much you have chosen." We worked on sectioning and error corrections that day, and that evening our group went back to the library. Each of us took twenty-five star clusters and researched them before we worked together. It took us until ten, and everyone was getting tired. Tomorrow we will take a telescope and do some stargazing. That pleased everyone. Each member of our group had a favorite planet and solar system to program. The next day, I had completed seven of my solar systems and helped each person. Ochum was the hardest person to help, but we got five sections completed. At that time he was getting to know how to log each of his clusters. That evening we checked out a telescope from the library; it had a star finder. We took ten minutes each turn, and Odin found it fascinating. Silini had never used a telescope as good as this one, and Ochum said this was a good subject and was glad we chose stargazing, Silini had our solar system with our planets. He was enjoying the craters on the moon and couldn't get away from how big they were. We all took turns looking at the moon. Silini used our solar system to make his first program. It was a clear night to observe the stars.

On Wednesday at the cafeteria, Dannude made a point telling me Saturday was my ass-kicking time. I told him, "You're cute." He got red in the face and wanted to grab me but walked away.

Odin said, "This isn't good, Raj. You don't know how bad he is."

"Don't worry, Odin. It's nothing to worry about." At the end of our second week, Professor Al-Nundee asked me if I wanted to have our match called off. I didn't realize it was known so much. "No, sir, I will be OK."

"It's not a disagreement," he said. "Dannude has been a smart aleck since he came here. I'll be glad when he is gone." The match will be in the gym at noon. A billboard had the match listed at eleven, along with two other matches. Saturday morning, I had a good run; then I showered and had breakfast. As I got my food, I noticed people looking at me. I nodded at a young man and sat down. Odin was not in there. I took my time eating, and Odin came in.

"The big day?" he said.

"I guess." After eating and sitting, I noticed Dannude looking at me. I nodded my head at him, and he grinned. It was eight thirty. Silini and Ochum had sat down with us, and we talked about riding our bicycles to the pier later.

Ochum said, "We might need to plan it another day."

"Why?" I asked.

His reply was, "You might not feel like the ride later."

It began to bother me, and I said, "Look, all he could do is give me a whippin', if he could."

"Last year he beat one boy up so bad, he had to go to the clinic and get stitches and he couldn't come to class for two days. He is a bad ass."

"Even bad asses can lose. Do people bet on this fight?"

"Oh yes, they give two to one odds on Dannude."

I got all the money I had and gave it to Odin. "Put this on me," I told him.

"You are serious," he said.

"You bet your butt I am." We walked around the pond and sat and talked.

At ten thirty, I told Odin it was time to go to the gym. I had to get my gym trunks first. We got to my room, and I put them on under my clothes, and we went to the gym. There were lots of students there, and Professor Al-Hidi and Professor Al-Nundee. Someone in the gym called out, "Ilinda and Solon, come forward." Two men went to the middle of the gym on some pads. They were asked, "Do you want to have this match?" Both agreed that they did, and boxing gloves were put on each of them; then a head protector was put on each one. "Now fight," he said. The two young men hit each other several times. Finally one got the best of the other one, and the loser said he had enough. Then, "Raj from Syria and Dannude, come up." I went to the middle, and gloves were put on me and Dannude. When they started to put the head protector on me, I said no; then Dannude said no to his. I had refused to wear shoes, but Dannude had his on. We were asked if we wanted to have this match.

"I do," I replied.

And Dannude also said, "You bet your ass I do."

"Then fight!"

I let Dannude swing at me twice; then I hit him in the mouth. He was mad and tried to grab me. I hit him two more jabs. At that time, he did a kick. I turned as it caught my side, and he tried to punch me. I dodged and hit him in the nose, making it bleed. He grabbed me in a bear hug. Both of my arms were pinned down. I rammed his nose with my head, and he let me go, swinging madly. I backed away. He ran at me, swinging, and I kicked his leg out from under him. He went to the floor hard; then he got up, cursing me and swinging. I hit him again in the nose, and blood was coming out heavy now. He started kicking at me but was missing. I had enough of this clown, and I hit him in the nose again; and as he swung at me, I did a head kick, and he hit the floor. I put my knee on his stomach, cutting his breathing off, and I asked him if we could stop; I had enough. "Yes," he said, barely able to speak. I got up, and the crowd was laughing and talking loud.

Odin came to me and was laughing. "You are a fighter and you didn't tell me."

"I'm no fighter," I said.

"But you are." I went to my room for a shower and changed clothes. Odin, Silini, and Ochum were there. I dressed and asked if they were ready to go biking. We went down to the basement where the bicycles were, and everyone we saw spoke to us and said hello. We rode down to the water and followed the road to the dock. Silini couldn't go fast, and we had to take our time for him to catch up with us. Bicycles were not allowed on the docks, so we walked out and talked about things we were going to do. Ochum's family was rich. They had about two horses his father played polo on and a big home in Saudi Arabia. His father was an advisor to the prince Alahani Al-Hedomine. Silini's family wasn't rich but still was wealthy. They lived in northern Saudi Arabia with the wealthy people, a large home with over one hundred workers. His family did maintenance, building, and construction for the rich families. His father was an architect and was well-known throughout the country.

"What does your family do?" Ochum asked.

"Consulting work," I told them.

"What do the advise on?" Silini asked.

"Computer, and research."

"Oh," he said. "That is why you are so smart."

"Thank you," I replied.

"Are you rich?" Odin asked.

"We live well," I told them.

"Where in Syria do you live?" Odin asked.

"Hamah, in the northwest." I started back. They had made me the leader and followed me when I went. On our bicycles, I went on farther down the coast and would stop to look at the big ships and nice yachts.

Silini said if we don't start back, we will miss dinner. We had stopped to watch a group of men unload a large truck. They made several comments about the rich students. We started back. Silini was a slowpoke. We got back in time, but lunch was almost over. Several people spoke to us. We ate, and I asked if they wanted to do some stargazing.

"Yes," Ochum said. "That is better than TV."

We checked out a telescope and learned they had another one also, so we got the two and went out to a sitting area and set them up. We had several people wanting to look, so we let them, and they would say, "That was a good fight." I would nod in recognition. Odin had got his laptop computer and was working on his star formation. This week we want to work hard and get most of our work completed; everyone agreed. On Sunday we all brought our computer to the pond, and we had a good place in the shade to work. I had twelve of my solar systems completed by the end of the day; I had two more. Everyone worked good. We stayed after dark, till nine, with the telescopes. Professor Al-Nundee joined us that evening and looked at the moon.

"It always fascinates me to think of the Americans walking on the moon," he had said earlier. Our extra studying would pay off later. He was glad to see our group working hard. He had his doubts about Odin and Silini passing before but now was more confident. "That was a good fight," he told me when he started to leave. "It did Dannude good to see he wasn't so great."

On Monday we were allowed to work all day on our projects. Some students had almost finished their project, but they would not get the best grades. They took shortcuts, the professor said. The week went fast. I had seen Dannude twice, and each time he spoke to me, and it looked like we were going to be friends. That Saturday I finished my project and started helping Odin more. Silini was doing OK, but Ochum was lagging behind. He only had half his work finished. I told him he had to work harder. That didn't please him, but when we started a good bike ride, he agreed he needed to study and didn't join us. We rode all morning and got back in time for lunch. We agreed to study that afternoon. I worked the rest of the day with Ochum, and all day Sunday we had made good progress. We would be finished by the weekend, and those that were through could submit their test early. I turned my work in the middle of that week. We had less than two weeks before completion. On Saturday we helped Ochum and Silini. By Sunday evening we were all finished. Our group was the first group to be through. We had all week to come and go to class as we pleased. On Friday the winning group would have the honor party.

It was Friday afternoon when Professor Al-Nundee addressed the class. "I am proud to present the honor of the highest group score and best grade for the achievement of our special class. The highest award goes to our astronomy programmers, group 3, Mohammad Ochum Al-Issak, Mohamad Hamin Odin, Al-Hidi Silini, and group leader with a ninety-seven average, Nerij Raj Bhardwaj, sponsored by Professor Al-Hidi, our most completed student. Please give them a good round of applause." Everyone stood up and clapped for us. "It is an honor. Please address us, Nerij." This was not what I wanted.

I stood and said, "Thank you, Professor, for those kind words but the person that prepared us for such an achievement was you. Will everyone please applaud Professor Al-Nundee." Everyone stood, and we clapped. That got me off the hook. We had cake and drinks brought in, and we had snacks. Everyone was happy to have finished the course, except three students that didn't make it. They would take the course over. Tom had let me know to catch a plane to Baghdad, and I would be met by a Sergeant Gill. A plane would leave Dubai Sunday at two in the afternoon. Two more days and this would be over. Our group made promises to stay in touch. We all had a good time. Around dark, a messenger brought a note to Ochum. He had a package waiting for him.

"I wonder who this is from," he said, and we went to the main entrance. No one was there, but a van marked Delivery was in front. Ochum walked to it; then two men grabbed him and started pulling him in it. I ran to help. He was almost in as I got there. I hit one man, and then I was struck in the head with something. I fell as the van pulled away. Things were blurry. I tried to get up but couldn't. People were gathering around me, when I realized I was being helped inside. They took me to Professor Al-Hidi's office. I passed out, but I awoke to the professor wiping my face with a cloth, and he asked me to drink some water; then things started coming to me. I asked about Ochum.

"Someone has taken him," the professor said.

"Who? Why?" I asked. The police came and started asking questions. Another student saw what happened and was telling the police. After all the questions had been answered, I went to my room. I was asked to stay around in case I was needed, or maybe I could identify someone. I called Tom and told him what happened.

"That isn't good," he said. "You don't need to be involved. Just do what they say and keep your telephone with you."

"Yes, sir," I said. I felt bad I couldn't help Ochum. I lay on my bed thinking about what had happened. My mind kept going back to the man I hit. Had I seen him before? There was something about him that I couldn't get off my mind, but where? When? I couldn't get the two together. I didn't rest much that night. I decided to go for a bicycle ride, but first I changed clothes and put my worst clothes on and rode down to the boat dock. The bicycle would give me away. If anyone saw it, they would know I was a student. I left it and walked down the pier, looking. I put my turban on and sunglasses. After looking all day, I went back to the school. There I saw Professor Al-Hidi. He said Ochum's father had come and was wanting to talk to me. He would be here in the morning. After eating I went to my room and lay down. A knock came to my door. "Come in." It was Professor Al-Hidi and Ochum's father. He was very worried, and we talked about when our group went riding and what we did. I told him everything I could think of, but nothing helped. After an hour, they left. Mohammad Al-Issak thanked me and went away very sad. That night I was restless but finally went to sleep. The next morning I learned a ransom letter had been delivered. They wanted one hundred thousand dollars equivalent in rupees by Wednesday. If the money or police interfered, Ochum would be buried in a box alive. I felt sick knowing how this might happen. I had to do something, but what? I called Tom and told him the news. He said the Saudi Police were the best in that part of the world. That night I kept thinking, maybe the man I hit would have a bruise, or I might recognize him. I went to sleep thinking about the next day. That night I took my clothes and poured coffee all over them, and the next day I would go early to the pier.

The next morning, before daylight, I left for the pier. I got there as the sun came up. I walked all up the line of ships and back down almost at the last ship. Only two left. I stopped and sat on the seawall. A truck pulled up, and a man started unloading; then I saw him. It was the same group of men we watched unload a truck before, and there was the man I had hit. His eye was bruised; that was the face I remembered before. I turned my hearing up and sat like I wasn't concerned about them. They were watching out for anything unusual while they worked. The ship was the donalley. I left the area, looking all around the ship. I had to get on it. No ropes or anything hanging down I could climb up. At the front of the ship was a chain anchor, which would be hard to climb up, but there wasn't anything else. I walked on out of sight. I knew nothing was suspicious about what I had done, but once I was a good distance away, I stopped and looked at the ship. How could I get onboard undetected? I need help, someone to drive me back tonight, but who? I ran back to the school, and I wanted to tell someone whom I could trust. I called Tom; he was excited I had located the man but was very concerned about me trying to go to it alone. "I will call Professor Al-Hidi. Don't do anything until I talk to you again."

"Yes, sir." I ate lunch, and Tom called me back.

"OK, Chris, you handle this but see the professor now. He is getting you help." I went to the professor.

"Come in, come in," he said. "This is great. You have helped so much. Tom assures me you are as good taking care of this matter as anyone. What can I do?"

"I need someone who is strong and not afraid to fight. We need guns with silencers and two inner tubes from cars."

"I know someone. It is my nephew. He is smart and strong." The professor called his nephew and asked him, "Want to do something good but dangerous?" He grinned. "Come to the school now. I will be waiting." He hung up with a smile. We sat and talked; then he used the phone again. "Detective Von-Addis please." He waited, then said, "Von, this is Nundee. I need a big favor. Can you come to the school now? I'd rather not talk on the phone. Yes, an hour would be fine."

"Sir?" I asked. "Is it wise to let the police in on this now?" He looked at me.

"I am quite aware of the situation but we have to have guns and I think Von will be of big help." I was beginning to wonder if we might be overdoing things. We talked for a few minutes; then the professor's nephew came. "Naonie, this is Raj. He is one of my friends. This is our problem." I let the professor talk. Naonie's face went serious when he was told about the kidnapping. He looked at me.

"Raj, what is the plan?"

"We have to get onboard the ship without being seen. Then we can see if Ochum is there, but if he isn't and we alert the kidnappers, they will kill Ochum and we will never find him alive."

"The man you hit, are you sure it's this man on the dock?"

"Yes, I am sure. We must keep him from getting away and alive." We talked for a while; then Detective Von-Addis came. We told him what was going on.

Then he said, "I heard about the kidnapping and the department is very concerned, but if anything goes wrong we will be in big trouble." The detective was a big man, and I did not think he could get onboard climbing the anchor chain. I wasn't sure I could easily, and I looked at Otto. Could he make it? I was getting concerned.

The professor told Von-Addis, "This could be big for you if things go well."

"Yes, but I am working with two men that are not trained and this could go bad for me."

"Just get me two pistols with silencers and we will forget you know anything."

"Oh no," he said. "I must help and do what I can." I asked Von-Addis if he could get us some night vision. "I think so," he said. "Have you ever done anything like this before?" he asked. I did not know what to tell him. I had to keep my true identity unknown.

"I am capable of doing this," I told him. "I was going to do it by myself." He looked at me, then the professor, and wondered what he was getting into; but if things went bad, he would not be involved.

"You understand?" he told the professor.

"Yes, that is understood," and I nodded my head. I asked Otto if he could get us a rope big enough to climb, maybe thirty feet long. Also two inner tubes we can float on.

"Yes," he said.

"We will go at midnight," I told them.

"It's supposed to rain," Von-Addis said.

"Good," I replied. "Better cover. We need a wet bag, something to keep the guns and equipment in from getting wet. We can do this," I said.

Otto said, "Yes, we can." Von-Addis said, "I have things I must do and I'll get the guns and night vision and I will meet you back here at ten tonight. Here is my card. If anything came up, call me that is my private number."

The professor said, "Thank you, Von," and he left.

Otto said, "I need to get the tubes and rope. Anything else?"

"Your phone number?" I asked.

"Sure," and he wrote it down. "Thanks, Uncle Hidi."

"I'm counting on you, Otto."

"Yes, sir," and he left.

"I'm going to my room and rest. Will you be here later?" I asked.

"I'll be here." As I started to leave, Ochum's father came.

"I heard from my son," he told us. "This morning a delivery boy brought this phone and the kidnapper called about the money. I'll have it tomorrow when the money is here. I am to have the flag out front brought down halfway. Will you do that for me?" he asked Professor Nundee.

"Yes," he said.

"Then a courier will come and pick up the briefcase. Then I will get a call where Ochum will be, but if the police or anyone interferes, they will bury Ochum and I will never see him alive." Tears were in his eyes, and he was shaking. The professor got up to console him.

"We will do all we can, Mr. Al-Issak."

"Thank you, Professor. I'm sure you will." I excused myself and went to my room. I found the clothes I would wear, some shorts and a dark T-shirt. I noticed my stilts. The harness they were in would not interfere with anything, and maybe they would be of some help. I laid down. It was Saturday, almost five, and I was tired.

I woke; I had a bad dream, and I looked at my watch. It was almost eight. I called Otto. "This is Raj. Is everything OK?"

"Yes, Raj. I got a good rope and some cord, two tire inner tubes, and two cans of Fix A Flat to blow the tubes up."

"Good," I replied.

"I am on my way there," he said.

"Thanks," and I hung up and called Detective Von-Addis. "Is everything OK?" I asked.

"Yes, Raj. I'll see you before ten."

"Thanks," and I got my shorts on and my stilts and went to the professor's office. He was in a lounge chair resting.

"It will be a long night but please call me the minute anything happens."

"Yes, sir. I will keep you informed." I programed his phone number, Otto's, and the detective's so I could call them easily. "I need two zip lock bags to keep my phone dry." He called the cafeteria and asked for two small zip lock bags. Otto came, and we talked.

"Want to take a drive down the pier?" he asked. It was getting dark.

"Yes," I said. "We can make a drive-by." I had my turban and street clothes on over my shorts.

The professor asked, "Can I tag along?"

"Sure," Otto said, and we got in his car. The rain had started. We went down the highway, then turned on the pier road and drove down the road. As soon as I saw the ship, I told the professor as we went by the truck that they were unloading. We noticed two men sitting inside. We didn't look at them and just drove on by.

"Those were lookouts," I said. As we got to the end of the ship, I turned and looked at the anchor. The chain was tight. There must be a strong current, I thought. One thing I hadn't noticed, the anchor chain went in a hole three or four feet down from the top of the ship rail. That would be a problem. I would have to get over the rail and get a rope down for Otto. A small boat was tied to the ship, and a set of steps was lowered. We went back to the school, and Von-Addis was pulling up as we did. We went inside and made our decision on boarding. Von-Addis had a wet bag with two pairs of night vision and two Walther P38 pistols with silencers.

He said, "I have a .30-06 rifle with a nightscope in the car."

"Looks like we are all set."

Von-Addis said, "You know if you shoot anyone and they are not involved, you will be in big trouble, and me too. Raj, I am counting on you to be very careful."

"I will I promise."

"Let's go," he said. "It will take some time for you to slip aboard." We got the tubes and rope from Otto's car; the rain had got harder.

"That, I like," I told them.

"Yes," Von-Addis said. I asked him about his name.

"It isn't Arabic?" I asked.

"No," he replied. "My father is German and my mother is Arabic." He drove to the pier road and down past the ship. The two men were still sitting in the truck.

"Lookouts," Otto said.

"Yes," we agreed. There was a driveway between two buildings near the end of the ship.

Von-Addis said, "I will come from the back to a spot I can see." We drove another mile, then the driveway back of the buildings. "This is it," Von said, and he pulled in, and we drove to the front, stopping before we were out. We barely could see the truck through the rain.

"I will call you when we get onboard," I told Von. Then we saw a light blink twice coming from the ship.

"A signal," Von said. "Two blinks must mean all clear," he said. That lookout is outside in the rain. The light was in the middle of the ship, near the ladder and boat tied up. I had taken off my clothes except the shorts, and I put the stilts' harness on. There were some boxes covered near the pier's edge. We got to them, and the rain made it perfect. No one could see us. We blew up the inner tubes, and I told Otto to lower our things to me after I was in the water. It was a wall at least fifteen feet high. I threw my tube in and jumped in after it; it moved away fast. I had to swim for it, then paddle back. Otto lowered our things to me, then dropped his tube in. I grabbed it; then he jumped in and swam too. We tied a cord around the tube and pulled them. When we got to the anchor chain, I tied my inner tube to it, then began climbing. The chain links were large, and it was harder than I thought. There wasn't much room to get my fingers through, and that made it hard to grip. I got near the top, and it must be three feet from the chain to the edge of the boat. I was having trouble getting on top of the chain. Finally I got my legs around the chain, and I was not doing good getting on top; then I thought maybe my stilts would help. With my legs locked and one hand holding on, I removed a stilt, and it was able to go through the chain; then I was able to climb using the stilt to help. I took the other stilt and put it through the last link and worked my way on top of the stilt. It was shaky, but with my feet against the chain and on top of the stilts, it worked. I eased my way, looking over the edge. I couldn't see anyone, and I climbed over the edge. I lowered the string down to Otto. He tied the rope to it, and I pulled it up and tied it off. He tied the string with our things, and I pulled them up. I put the night vision on and the pistol in my pants. I could see a watchman almost out of sight. Otto was having trouble. He stopped near the top and pulled my stilts out of the chain. I was glad he made it to the top.

"I don't know how you made it up that chain." He put his night vision, on and the pistol, he held. I got the phone out and called Von.

"We are onboard. We see one lookout and I will stay in touch." There were plenty of things to get behind from the front of the ship. We were sure no one was behind us and moved casually. There was a captain's room. It was lit up and was maybe twenty feet high. It was empty. There was one man standing under the captain's tower, looking toward the truck. When we got a few feet away from the lookout, I motioned Otto to stay still. I moved toward him. His back was to me, and I locked my arm around his neck and chocked him. He passed out, but he kicked and fought. He was trying to hit me with a rifle. I took it before he fell to the floor.

"What if he comes to?" Otto said.

"Let's use the cord to tie him up," and we did. Also Otto gagged him. We pulled him over to another place and moved toward a stairway, going down.

Otto said, "The truck just blinked his light." I blinked twice, not sure I was doing right. I had my phone on vibrate, and it vibrated.

"Yes," I said low.

Von said, "I saw the light. Is everything OK?"

"Yes, that was me."

"Good," he said. "The two men are still sitting in the truck." I thumped my ear implant. My earphone came on. I could barely hear the men talking, so I bumped it again. It was loud. I could hear Otto's heart beating fast. The men were playing cards. I couldn't hear how many, but I thought four. They were talking about the share of the money they would get tomorrow. I knew these were the kidnappers. One man was asked to go check on Schoney.

"If he falls asleep, Lonard will be mad."

"Who could go to sleep in this rain?"

"Go see," the voice said. I motioned to Otto. We moved back on the deck behind the stair door.

Shortly a man came up and hollered, "Schoney!" He was looking around. He shut the stair door and at that time saw me. I kicked him hard beside the head. He hit the floor hard. He tried to get up, and I kicked him in the head again. He was out. Otto started tying him.

"No more cord," he said, "but these two were tied good."

"They will be concerned about this man. I think there are three more."

"How do you know?" Otto asked.

"I could hear them," I said.

"How?" he replied. "I didn't hear anything."

"Good ears," I said. "We better take the other three or they will alert the others."

"Are you sure there isn't more?"

"No, but I don't think so." We got our guns ready and went down the steps. "Are you ready?" I asked Otto. He was shaking. I opened the door and rushed in, my gun pointing. There at a table sat three men. They were very surprised. One went for a gun, and Otto shot him. It hit his leg; he fell to the floor. He was still trying to shoot at us, and Otto shot him again; this time in the stomach. He lay still. I was pointing my gun at the other two.

"Put your guns on the table," Otto said. Only one had a gun. He put it on the table. "Where is the student you took?" Otto asked. They looked at each other.

"What student?" one asked.

"The one you kidnapped," he said.
"We don't know anything about a student. We are just ship hands."
"You lie," Otto said. "Want me to shoot you so the other one will tell?"
"We don't know anything." Otto pointed his gun at the man doing the talking.
"I'll ask you one more time. Then I am going to shoot your knee off."
"I don't know anything," and Otto shot and hit his knee, and he screamed. "I'll ask one more time and hit the other knee."
"I don't know anything," he begged.
"Here goes your other leg."
"No, please, I'll tell you," the other man said. "Shut up." Otto shot him in the leg, and he passed out. "Where is the boy?" Otto asked.
"In the storage area."
"Are there anyone else onboard?"
"Yes, one man with the student."
"Where is the storage?" Otto asked.
"In the front of the ship."
"Show us."
"I can't walk," the man said, begging. "I didn't have anything to do with this," he said.
"Get up."
"I can't." We helped him to his feet, holding him up; he was bleeding. "I didn't do anything. I just was here."
"Help us and it will go better for you," Otto said. We had him at the door. Otto said, "If anything goes wrong, I will shoot you first." He moaned every step we took. We went to the front of the ship, and a door was closed.
"In there," he said low.
"Call out the man," Otto told him.
"Raymoul, Raymoul, do you want someone to relieve you?"
"I was sleeping," the voice said.
"Get him to come out," Otto whispered.
"Raymoul, want this tea?"
"Yeah," the voice said, and I could hear him coming. I stood at the door. As the door opened, I was on him. He fell back and grabbed his gun. I was close enough to hit him with my stilt. I hit him again, and he didn't get up.
Ochum was lying on a cot, tied up and gagged. I untied him, and he said, "Raj, it's you."

"Yes, Ochum, you are OK now." Tears were in his eyes.

"Oh, Raj."

I called Von. "We have six men shot and tied. Ochum is OK."

"Stay where you are and protect him. I am calling backup for these men in the truck," Von said.

"OK, we will wait here." Otto found some rope and tied up both men, and I told him to call the professor.

"Al-Hidi," Otto said, "we have taken the ship and rescued your student."

"Praise Allah, praise Allah," the voice said. "Is he OK?"

"Yes," Otto said. "He will be OK." Then Otto said, "We have Inspector Von getting backup now. There are still two men in the truck. Uncle, we had to climb up this chain to get in the ship. We whipped three men and tied them up and we had to shoot two men. I may have killed one and Raj was wonderful. He would hit and kick the men so fast, they didn't have a chance and he can hear like a cat. He is great and helped so much." I almost laughed at the way he told things, but it wasn't over yet.

"Stay here. I'm going on top and see what is happening."

"OK," Otto said. I went topside, and everything was quiet; then I heard gunshots. It was Von shooting the .30-06, and the men in the truck were driving off. Police from both directions were closing in on the truck. I watched but couldn't see much. The rain had slowed down but was still coming down. Now at least ten cars were there, and men were all over the dock. Otto called me. "We got trouble up there?"

"No," I said. "They just took the truck and police are everywhere." We are fine, everyone is tied up, a couple men shot, one may be dead. I called for an ambulance.

Von said, "We will be out there as soon as we can get a boat." He added, "You did a great job." I asked to be left out of it. "Hide the guns," he said, "and the night vision, until we are alone. Is Raj your real name?" he asked.

I hesitated. "Yes for now."

"Then it will be OK. I don't care. You did everything and planned it well."

I said, "Thanks I owe you one," and he hung up.

I went down with Otto and Ochum. The man shot in the leg was moaning. "I need help," he said.

I went to Ochum. "How you doing?" I asked.

"I'm well. Have you called my father?"

"I will now," and Ochum gave me his phone number, and I called him. "Mr. Al-Issak? Yes, here is your son." I handed the phone to Ochum. He started shaking, with tears in his eyes. He told his father how they took him and how they treated him.

"They were going to kill me when they get the money, I heard them say." I sat by Ochum, my arm over his shoulder. He couldn't stop weeping. Tears kept coming down, and he finally stopped shaking. He hung up. "My father is on his way." He held my hand. "You have saved my life. You have helped me so much," and he hugged me.

Otto said, "I'm going topside, OK?"

"Yes, go get some fresh air. Ochum, do you want to go topside?"

"Yes, please." The men were tied good, so I left them. I went to check on the man in the other room. Everything was good, and I went topside.

Two hours later, I was with Professor Al-Hidi, Ochum, Mohammad Al-Issak, and Otto. The police had a boat, and Detective Von and Professor Al-Hidi had brought Ochum's father, and we went into the captain's quarters, talking. An ambulance took one man to the hospital; one man was dead, and five men were arrested. The police got all the information from Detective Von and were asking Ochum questions. I gave a statement, and Otto was the hero of the day. I only answered the questions when I was asked.

I had called Tom. He said, "You did a great thing," and was very happy. "Now don't get too much publicity. Your plane leaves for Baghdad tomorrow. Be on it if you can," and I told him I would call him later tonight when this was over.

The professor said, "Raj, none of this was possible without you. You found the man you had hit. You watched the boat. You are my friend for life like Tom."

Ochum said, "They would have killed me, Raj, if you hadn't been so good. I would die after Dad paid them. They said I could identify them, so they couldn't let me live. Thank you so much."

Ochum's father said, "I want you to have some money, and Otto also."

Otto said, "I could use a car."

"Help Otto," I said. "I don't want your money, sir, but thank you. Please know without Professor Al-Hidi and his choice of people and help, this would not have been possible."

"I know," Mr. Issak said. "Al-Hidi is a good and professional man and I thank him so much."

"I'm leaving tomorrow and I have some things to take care of. Detective Von-Addis, you put all this together and we could not have been successful without you. I thank you so much," and I shook his hand. "Can you get me back to the school."

"I will start working on it," he replied.

Mr. Al-Issak went to Von-Addis. "I will be talking to your superiors and they must know what a valuable person you are and I thank you also for all you did."

Von-Addis went outside to talk to his captain. "Yes," the captain said. "We will get this finished so they all can go. We can finish what we need tomorrow." It was already three fifteen in the morning.

Von-Addis drove the boat with all us to the other side. "We will have to confirm all our statements before you leave, Raj."

"Yes, sir. Can we do it after breakfast? My plane leaves at two."

"I think so," Von-Addis said. "It's been a pleasure working with you, Raj."

"My pleasure also," I said.

The professor asked Mohammad Al-Issak which hotel he was staying at. "The Hilton." He thanked all of us again and said, "If ever I can do anything for any of you, please let me know. I mean it." We left Ochum and his dad, thanking us. "We will be over in the morning," Mr. Al-Issak said, "and get all this finished."

Ochum held my hand a moment. "Get some rest, Raj, and thank you so much, Otto," and we drove back to the school. I went to my room and showered and went to bed.

I slept late; it was eight fifteen when I woke and went down to the cafeteria. The professor and Otto were sitting at a table. I joined them. "Morning."

"Good morning," the professor replied. "Slept well, I hope?"

"Very well, thank you."

"Tom called. I gave him a good rundown on things. He is quite happy about you and how things went."

"Great," I said.

"Raj, Mohammad Al-Issak wants to do something for you and Otto. He is very wealthy. Let him do something. It will make him feel better."

"Maybe a small gift, but not money."

"Good," the professor said. "You know, he is in charge of all transportation, transit airlines, shipping, railroads."

"That's great," I said, "but if I take something, I would feel what I did was for a reward."

"But it wasn't. We know that and I understand you spent lots of time helping Ochum to pass his class and that was a lot."

The professor looked at me and said, "Von-Addis will be here with his captain at ten and Mohammad Al-Issak and Ochum will be here also and we can finish this."

"Good," I said.

"Raj, where will you go from here?"

"To Baghdad, sir."

"What will you do there?" he asked. I am a news reporter, sir. Now that I have my master's in computer science."

"Are you going to make a story about this kidnapping?"

"No, sir."

"Why not? It should be a good story."

"It wouldn't do much in American paper."

"I will always be here and a friend to you and Tom."

"Thank you, sir. I don't think it would be good for the police to know anything about me except I went to school here and Ochum is my friend, and I got lucky spotting one of the kidnappers."

"Yes, Raj, his name is Hiliano, from Somalia. The captain, Ulrich, he is the one that planned this, and the others were to get money for helping. He confessed to everything."

"That's good," I said.

The professor said, "The police are very good at obtaining information and Ulrich was planning to kill Ochum, so he couldn't identify anyone. Praise Allah this has ended this way. That is why Mohammad Al-Issak wants to do something for you."

At ten, Captain Torroso and Von-Addis came; then Ochum and his father came. "Raj, the captain said I am recording your statement, do you understand?"

"Yes, sir."

"Now tell me how this started."

I started with the kidnapping, then how I walked to the waterfront because I thought I had seen Hiliano there, and I spotted him and how I got Otto to help me watch the ship and how we contacted the detective Von-Addis, not knowing for sure. We wanted to watch and be sure these were the people. We couldn't bring all the police until we had more proof, with Von-Addis making sure we were careful. "And with all his great help, we were able to achieve this, and the police are the real people who is to be accredited for this success. Of course with all you have done, Captain Torroso, with Detective Von-Addis." The captain was very pleased to hear he was involved with his leading detective.

The captain said, "Raj, you and Otto have been of great help in capturing this gang and we will always be grateful for this. Now our investigation is complete. We have statements and confessions that will complete our file. Thank you." We all shook hands. The captain and Von-Addis left. Ochum and his father stood.

"Raj and Otto, we can never thank you enough for what you have done." He handed me and Otto a business card. "Please call this man and let him know what kind of car and what color. I will be very hurt if you refuse this little gift." Ochum gave me a hug. I shook his father's hand, and they left, with me promising Ochum I would stay in touch.

Otto said, "This is wonderful. I have to go." We shook hands. "Uncle, thank you for the trust you have in me," and he left. I sat.

The professor said, "Raj or whoever you are, thank you for being here at the right time and so much help. Allah has guided you here. I have spoken to Tom and we will stay in touch. I will go now and I hope I will see you. Please order yourself a car or truck or you will offend Mohammad Al-Issak."

I shook his hand and went to pack the rest of my things.

CHAPTER XII

I got off the plane, and I was looking for a marine sergeant, Derrik Gill. Tom had told me this was the only person that knew my true identity. He alone would get me what I needed. His contact was a Colonel Talbert, Tom's friend. I spotted a marine at the inspection gate. As I got near, I noticed him looking my way. He was looking over everyone. He caught my eye and locked on it. I gave him a wink. A little smile came on his face. As I got through the gate, Derrik didn't make contact with me, but I noticed him following me. I went to a spot at a private area, and he came to me. "Chris?"

"Yes."

"Derrik." We shook hands. He had a strong handshake, and I can see he was very fit. "Sir, you have a hotel room at the Carlton. All your things are there. I suggest you change to civilian clothes here. Do you have any with you?"

"No," I said.

"I have a change for you in this locker," and he handed me a key. "I don't know how I am to help you, but whatever you need, let me know. I understand you are a newsman and I think you are also a serviceman. These things I don't have to know, but I assure you, I and only I will ever know. I was told you have a vehicle coming. Now you have a truck waiting in the parking area of the hotel. He handed me a key. "It's a white Toyota pickup." He handed me an envelope. "There is American cash and also euro money. Let me know if you need more." He gave me a business card. It said Derrik, with a phone number on it. I looked at the number and handed it back to him. He smiled.

"One of those with a great memory."

"Good," he said. "My memory is pretty good also." I smiled. I knew I could trust this man; already I liked him. "I understand you are Nerij Bhardwaj from Syria. I will always address you by that."

"Thank you," I said.

"Is there anything else I can do for you?" he asked.

"No, that's everything."

"Then I will go," he said. "The lockers are at the other end of this building." We shook hands, and I went to locker number 111 and got a small bag out with clothes in it—slacks and a white shirt and white shoes with soft soles—and went to the restroom and changed. At the front I took a cab to the Carlton.

At the desk, I said, "I'm Nerij Bhardwaj. I should have a room?"

"Yes, Mr. Bhardwaj." He handed me a key, room 421, and I went to it. It was a nice two-room and bath. I looked over it good for anything suspicious; it looked clean. I called Tom from my cell phone.

"Yes," he said.

"I'm here and things are fine."

"Good," he said. "This evening at eight, call me."

"Yes," I said. "Until eight," and hung up. I lay on the bed thinking. After a few minutes, I did my exercise. Two hundred push-ups, four hundred sit-ups, knee bends, and some loosening-up movements; then I showered and got ready to go out. I was getting hungry. The Carlton had a good restaurant. I had a salad and steak, taking my time looking around at the people and mentally adjusting. I was at a nice place to sit. At eight I called Tom.

"How are things?" he asked.

"Well," I said, "and there?" I asked.

"Very well. Everyone said hello. Tomorrow you must register as a newsman and then go to a secure area and inform our people you are there. You will be given a list of the dos and don'ts. You should have all equipment delivered. Four types of cameras and recorders. A newsperson, a Hal Bailey, from the *Washington Post* will show you the ropes. Anything you need?"

"No, I'm fine."

"Good," he said. "Stay in touch."

"Yes, sir," and we hung up. I went back to my room. A knock come at my door. I opened it; it was a deliveryman with a large package. I tipped him and laid the package down. It was three 35mm cameras, two movie cameras, and two digital cameras. There was a nice carrying case, a magnifying glass, a good map of Baghdad, plenty of film, directions to hidden places for money, and other things. The carrying case was special—my name with Washington News in big letters out front. My closet had all the clothes I needed. I was set; now for a good story.

The next morning at the dining room, I was paged. "Raj Bhardwaj." I raised my hand at the waiter.

"I'm Raj."

"Thank you, sir," he said and left for the front desk; then he came back with a very nice-looking blonde carrying a newsperson's backpack.

"Raj?" she said.

"Yes."

"I'm Hal." I stood and shook hands with her.

"Pleased to meet you. Please have a seat." She took off the backpack and hung it on a chair.

"You're new?" she asked.

"Is it obvious?"

"Yes, you don't have your equipment with you," and she smiled.

"Yes, I'm new."

"First thing," she said, "always have your equipment. You never know when you will need it. Also everyone will know to give you what ground they want you to know, and have."

"I see." My oatmeal and cereal came, and Hal ordered her breakfast.

She asked, "So you are from Syria?"

"Well, Dubai last, but my family came from Syria." I had trimmed my beard and mustache, but it was still long.

"You speak good English. You must have went to school in America."

"Yes," and I kept eating. Her food came, and we didn't speak until we both finished.

"I'm going to speak to Captain Mask. He is in charge of us newspeople. Want to tag along?"

"Yes," I said. "Let me get my gear."

"I'll wait for you here," she said.

"Be right back," and I went to get my carrying case, which also could be carried like a backpack. Hal drove an old Toyota car. When we got to the safe zone at the blockade, two marines stopped us.

"Hi, Hal," one said. "Who is the new guy?"

"Raj. You have him as Nerij Bhardwaj."

"You're clear," he said, "but get a new ID. This one isn't current."

"Yes, sir, I will."

"Thanks, Bill." Then we went through the fire zone. We stopped at a big tent marked Number One, and we went in. "Captain Mask?" she asked a private.

"Hi, Hal, you doing OK?"

"Yes, and you, Tommy?"

"Yep, ninety-six more," he said.

She smiled. "Your family?"

"They're fine," he said. Captain Mask had someone in now, so we sat and waited. A few minutes later, a newsman came out.

"Hal."

"Hi, Louis," and we waited while Tommy announced us here.

"Go in now," he said, and we did.

"Hal."

"Yes, sir."

"Who is this?"

"Nerij Bhardwaj," she said, "with the *Washington Post*."

"Sit down," he said. "Hal, you have been warned about going to the hospital without a guard?"

"Yes, sir," she said.

"What am I going to do with you?"

"Not worry so much," she said.

"Too hell," he answered. "You want to be like that Alabama gal, with your head cut off? Or any of the other nine dead newsmen? You don't think I don't catch hell when it happens. Where is your interpreter?"

"He is sick," she said.

"And where this time?" he asked.

"At the edge of town, one of the victim's family."

"And you need an interpreter?"

"No," she said. "Nerij Bhardwaj is fluent. He is from Syria."

The captain asked me in Arabic, "Do you speak good Arabic?"

I answered, "Yes, I do."

"OK," he said, "but it will be at noon tomorrow before I have someone available."

"OK," she said. "Noon tomorrow."

"Yeah, like I believe you."

She smiled. "Well, you told me."

"Yeah, be careful, we have rumors."

"Thanks, Larry," and we left; then we went to a tent that said ID and Passes. I got my picture taken, and thirty minutes later, I had my ID and pass. At her car, she said, "You know, this is my story and you will not have your own while I show you around for two weeks."

"Understood, understood," I said, and we drove through Baghdad to the poverty area. I used the map while she drove. We found the house and went to the door. She knocked. An old woman cracked the door.

"I'm Hal from the *Washington Post*." I translated. The old woman held out her hand, and Hal put some money in it, and she let us in. Hal opened her case and took out two coloring books and a box of crayons. A little boy and girl were standing in the door of the next room. She tried to give them to the children.

"No," I told Hal. "First ask the parent." Then I asked the old lady her name.

"Rhonda Halbin," she said. I told her my name was Nerij Bhardwaj.

"Could the children have the coloring book?" She told the children to come take the present. They grinned and went to the corner of the room where a window was and looked at the coloring books, then started coloring.

"Where are you from, Nerij?" she asked.

"Syria," I told her.

"Where in Syria?"

"Hamah," I said.

"My son is married and living in Tallesh."

"I have been there many times," I said.

Hal asked, "What's she saying?"

"I told her where I am from. Her son lives there now in a town called Tallesh, not far from Hamah, my home."

"What are you doing with this lady?" she asked. "What is your name?" she asked Hal.

"This is Hal. What is your last name?" I asked.

"Brooks," she told me.

"Hal Brooks," I told Rhonda.

"This is my first time with Hal Brooks. I just started," I said.

The old lady studied my face, looking for lies. "Where is the man she was with at the hospital?"

"Her interpreter is sick and Hal is showing me how to get started as a newsman. Since I speak Arabic, we came anyhow."

Hal could speak some Arabic but not much. "Ask Rhonda about her daughter in the hospital."

"How is she?" I asked.

"I don't know," Rhonda said. "I haven't had a way to see her."

"It's been four days since I was there," Hal said.

"Want to go see her?" I asked.

"Who will watch the children?" she said. "But if you would take some things to her . . ."

I asked Hal, "Can we take some things to her daughter?"

"Lotus? Isn't that her name?" Hal asked.

The old lady said, "Yes, it's Lotus Halbin."

"Yes, Nerij, we can go by and see her on our way and maybe get a statement." Hal asked me to see if we could film our meeting. I asked. Rhonda wasn't sure about that.

I told Hal, "We're rushing things. Let's win her confidence first." Hal pointed to the money she had given Rhonda. Then Rhonda put the money away. "Not now," I told Hal. "Let's win the old lady over. She is very suspicious about anyone she doesn't know." I talked to Rhonda for a few more minutes, then asked about the things to carry to Lotus. The old lady went and got some clothes and put them in a sack and handed them to me.

Hal said, "It doesn't look like we can do much here," so we told Rhonda we would be back tomorrow if that was OK.

"Will you pay me?" she asked.

"Yes," I said, "we would."

When we got in the car, Hal asked if I could drive. "Yes," I said. On our way, Hal turned the tape recorder on and asked me questions. As we listened to the recordings, I told her everything. I didn't know she was recording. We got to the hospital and parked. We went to the second floor. There, a long row of cots were full of men and women; no children. We walked down and stopped by a cot with a young lady, I thought. She had her veil on, but her eyes were green and watery; she had been crying. Hal asked her how she was.

Lotus replied, "Not good."

"I have things for you," handing the bag of clothes to her.

"Where is Mother?" she asked.

I translated, "She had to stay with the children."

"How long will you be here?" Hal asked.

"How would I know?" she answered.

"Do you need anything?" Hal asked.

"I want to go home," Lotus said.

"What happened when you got hurt?" Hal asked.

After a little pause, Lotus said, "I was looking for some vegetables, when a man came from a car. He was hollering, 'Praise Allah, Allah is great,' then the explosion. That's all I remember, until I woke up here."

A nurse came up and said, "Lotus, do you feel like walking around some?"

"I'll try," she said.

"Good." She asked, "Can your family help you?"

I said, "Yes, we can help."

"Good." Then the nurse said, "Let me help you get up." Lotus sat up, and Hal took one arm, and the nurse took the other, and she slowly stood up. The nurse asked me to hold her arm, and I took her with Hal, and Lotus tried to walk. She took a few steps. The nurse had left, and we took several steps before Lotus wanted to go back to bed. The nurse came back. "That was good, Lotus."

"When can I go home?" Lotus asked.

"You have a concussion and your leg, we removed a piece of metal. It's been four days. I would say if you are doing good, day after tomorrow." I asked Lotus if I could take some pictures for Hal.

"Tell her I will pay her," Hal said. Lotus said she could. Hal took out some money and handed it to her, then started taking pictures. After the interview, we went back to the hotel. "Your first day and what do you think?"

"I like it," I said.

"Good," Hal replied. "I'll see you in the morning, good day," and left.

At my room, Tom called. "How are things going?" he asked.

"My first day, good I guess."

"Chris, Professor Al-Hidi called. He said you had not selected a car from Mohammad Al-Issak and asked me to tell you he will be very disappointed if you do not except this gift."

"What can I tell him, sir? He wants to buy me a car for helping with Ochum."

"Let him," Tom said. "You can use one, where you are."

"All right," I said. "How about a white Toyota truck? I'll tell him where he can send it."

Tom said, "OK, I'll stay in touch." Tom hung up, and it was good to hear from him. I started exercising—first push-ups, then sit ups, running in place, bending, and kicking. After a good workout, I got ready to go eat.

In the restaurant, Hal was sitting with two men. She asked me to join them. "Nerij, this is Ralph and that's Albert." They both had their carrying case. I had forgotten my equipment, and they noticed it.

"New I guess," Albert said.

"Yes, you noticed."

"You will learn it's the time you don't have it you need it. It always happens." Their food came, and I ordered a salad and steak.

Albert talked the most, mainly about the human bomb that killed seven and wounded thirty-six. "The young man that blew up the people was only eighteen and his family didn't know he was going to do it."

"Yeah," Ralph said. "Usually they brag to their family and let them know it."

"It won't ever stop," Hal said. "In the old days, they would go into a crowd of people, stabbing as many as they could. Now they have bombs and can take out many more."

"Where are you from?" Albert asked.

"Hamah, Syria," I said.

"That northern Syria?"

"Yes, northwest."

"You speak great English," he said. "You schooled in America?"

"Young Harris, Georgia."

"I've heard of it," Albert said. "Are you Moslem?"

"Yes," I said.

"Tell me why you think you should kill people that don't believe like you."

"I don't, but some people do."

Hal spoke up. "No religion, remember?" Nothing else was said. "I'm going on an interview," Hal said. "Want to go?" looking at me.

"When?" I asked.

"After we eat."

"Sure," I said.

Albert replied, I've been trying to take you somewhere for three months and you won't go. Now this new guy comes along and you go with him. I'm jealous."

Hal said, "This young man is safer," and laughed.

I finished eating and said, "I'll get my things, be right back." I hurried and got them; then I drove Hal to an out-of-town address. This time I wore my turban. I felt more Moslem that way and thought it would help with the interview. We found the right place. I knocked at the door, and an old man came.

"Yes?" he said, with the door barely open.

"I would like to speak to Undrea," I told him.

"Who wants him?" he asked.

"Nerij Bhardwaj," I told him.

"Why?" he asked.

"An interview about working for us." Hal had told me she had said she would try to find him some work, but she wanted to know more about the young man that did the bombing. Undrea knew the young man. I could see someone in the back of the old fellow.

"I will see them," Undrea said and opened the door. "Come in please," and we did. Undrea was tall and skinny.

"I am Nerij Bhardwaj," I told him.

"Have I seen you before?" Undrea asked.

"No, I'm new in Baghdad. I am Syrian."

Hal spoke to Undrea. "He works with me," she said.

"Did you find me some work?" he asked Hal.

"Not yet but I am looking."

"I might have some work for you, Undrea. Do you speak English?"

"No," he said, "but I learn fast."

"In a couple of weeks I will need someone to show me around, if you are interested."

"O yes, I am."

Hal had some money. "Can I film you?" Undrea looked at the money.

"Yes," he said, reaching for the money. Hal handed it to him and turned her camera on.

"The man that blew himself up at the market, who was he?"

"His name was Al La Honel."

"Where do you know him from?" Hal asked.

"From school. A friend saw Al La Honel get out of a car, then walk up to those people, shouting, 'Allah is great!' Then he did something and blew up everyone."

"Why do you think he did this?" she asked.

"For the money and for Allah."

"Who pays him to do this?"

"The Taliban will help your family."

"Was Al La Honel Taliban?" she asked.

"If he would do this, I think so."

"How long was he Taliban?"

"That's all I know," he said.

"Have the Taliban tried to get you to join them?"

Undrea would not answer her. "That is all I know."

Hal, seeing he would not answer, said, "Thank you. Do you know where Al La Honel lives?"

"I might. I could find it," he said.

Hal said, "It would be worth some money."

"I will try to," he said.

"May I came back another day?"

Undrea looked at me. "When do you think you might have some work for me?"

I looked him in the eye. "In a few days. I will stay in touch."

"Where do you stay?" he asked.

"The Carlton hotel."

"I know where it is," he said. "Can I believe you?" he asked.

"You can."

Hal said, "We will be back in two days, if that is OK." I translated. He nodded his head; yes it was, and we left.

"Nerij, will you drive?" Hal asked.

"Sure," and I started back.

"I want to go by the hospital," she said. "Take a right at that next street." There were plenty of places to park, but Hal directed me to a special place. "Less chances of anyone stealing here. You can see the car better."

"Do you have any trouble?" I asked.

"No, but most Americans do. I watch close," she said. We went to Lotus; she was sitting up. Hal nodded to Lotus, and I caught her eye and winked at her. She looked away, then back at me for a moment.

"How are you doing?" I asked.

"Not good. I want to go home," she said.

"You will soon. You look like you are doing good."

Hal asked, "Do you want me to give you a ride when you go?"

"Please," Lotus said. A nurse was working with a child beside Lotus. When she finished, Hal asked when Lotus could go home.

"In the morning," she said.

My translation made Hal look from me to the nurse, then asked, "How is the concussion?"

"I guess OK. We can only tell by the headaches."

"Does she still have one?" I asked.

"Yes, but not real bad." Hal's face went to a little smile. Hal pulled out a small package and handed it to Lotus. I figured it was girly things, so I turned my head while Lotus looked.

"Thank you," Lotus said.

"We will go now. We will be back in the morning." Lotus smiled and knew Hal was a good person to care.

Hal looked around the hospital for any news or anything of interest; then we left. "The people trust you," she said. "That is good, for you to have a better relationship than us Americans." I was glad she could not tell. We drove to the safe zone, and the guards asked Hal if she was being careful.

"Lots of rumors now," one said. "We are on extra alert," he said.

"I'll watch out."

One guard asked if I was helpful with the natives. "Nerij is not from here. He is from Syria. Be careful. Stay out of zone 10, 11, and 12."

"OK," she said, and I drove on to the tent area. We went in, and the captain saw us.

"Hal, there are rumors. It isn't a good time to wander around."

"I'm careful," she said.

He looked at me. "With a new newsman from Syria and you don't speak Arabic, you're looking for trouble. At least your interpreter could see some danger, but this man is useless."

"How about dinner, Larry. Are you hungry?"

"Sure," he said. "How could I pass up a chance to talk to a lovely gal." He got up, and we went to the mess hall. The captain told us about the rumors from one of our good informers. "Something big, he thinks. Maybe a car bombing on the base," he said.

"That isn't good," Hal said.

"We have a new safety device. We have a quick way to blow up any attempt. It's set up between the first guards and the second guards. Hal, why don't you use one of the company security? At least when we cannot give you any people."

"Too costly," she said. "I can't afford it and the company wants payment for it."

"You will get hurt or killed," the captain said. "If you stay long enough, bureaucracy the way. When are you going home?" he asked.

"No time soon," she said.

"I can't make you be safe or I would."

"I'll be OK," she said.

"I have to go," the captain said. "As much as I like looking at that pretty face."

"Thanks, Larry," Hal said as he left. We drank coffee, then left. At the gate, Hal told the guards, "Be careful."

"Thanks," they said as we drove away. At the hotel, I went to my room and called Sergeant Gill.

"Glad you called, Raj. I have a notice to pick up a truck and work on it for you. It comes in this morning."

"What are you going to do to it?" I asked.

"I'm making a place for an AK rifle and also an easy-to-get-to pistol, a homing device, night vision, an electric burglar alarm, what else can you use?" and he laughed.

"Sounds like the works," I said.

"How is it going?" he asked.

"Good, I guess."

"Raj, there are lots of rumors about an attack, so usually it means something. Be extra careful."

"Thanks, Sergeant, I will."

And he said, "I'll call you when the truck is ready, good-bye," and I hung up. I started exercising—push-ups, sit-ups, knee bends. I needed a kicking bag, and I looked around the room for a place to hang one. My room had two deep windows, and I found a good place to hang a bag if I had something to hook to. I called room service, and thirty minutes later, a young man came u.

"What is your name?" I asked.

"Petwan," he said. I told him what I needed and asked if the hotel would get mad if I hung something from there. "Not if they don't know," Petwan said. I handed him a five-dollar bill. "I will find you something," he said, and I showered and lay on my bed and fell asleep. I woke to someone knocking on my door; it was Petwan. He had a hammer and a couple of concrete nails. "Where do you want this?" he asked. I showed him the place. He stood on a table I had and drove the nail into the ceiling.

"Great," I told him and gave him another tip. I had a knapsack, and I filled it with an old jubba, an old local robe, and hung it up. It was six feet to the jubba, so my kicks were high. It felt good, and as it bounced around, it didn't make noise or damage anything. I did kicks for over an hour, then got ready to go eat.

Hal wasn't there, but Ralph and Albert were. They invited me to sit with them. Ralph asked, "How is your interview coming along with the bomber friend? What is his name?" I saw they were trying to get a lead on a person.

"Onda, I think."

Ralph said, "You're not sure?"

"No, I'm not sure." He didn't know if I was lying to him or was not very bright; either way, he didn't ask anything else.

Albert said, "I hope you are not going in that unsafe zone, are you?"

"I listen to Hal," I said. "I don't know." My food came, and I started eating.

"What did you do before you were a journalist?" Albert asked.

"School, studying and working to be a newsman."

"How did you get this assignment?" Ralph asked.

"Lucky, I guess."

"Unlucky," he said. Hal came in and sat with us.

"What was the friend of that bomber's name?" I asked Hal.

"They pumping you for my leads?" she asked.

"Yes, Ralph wants to know."

"Watch those two," she said. "They will try to steal a story from you."

"Oh," I said and looked at Ralph.

"In the morning I am taking Lotus home."

"I will be ready," I told her and excused myself and went outside.

Four rocking chairs were in front; two were being used by locals, but I sat anyways. One man dressed nice asked my name and said, "I am Rynea. This is Zebaid."

"Raj Alture," and I shook hands with them.

"You from Iraq?" Zebaid asked.

"No, I am from Syria. Hamah, in the north."

"I've been there," Rynea said. "Good area."

"Yes, I enjoy it," I said.

"I stayed at the Bilton Hotel."

"I don't remember the Bilton," I said.

"No," he said, "the Bilton was in Hatacha." I wondered why Rynea was trying to test me; I would keep my eye on him.

"What do you do?" I asked Rynea.

"Enjoy life," he said.

"Must be nice," I told him. He had looked at my newsman identification, noticing my newspaper name. "Nice meeting you," I said and went to my room. I woke early and started exercising. I liked my kicking bag and favored my exercise on it, then sit-ups, push-ups, leg bends—anything; it was boredom now. I wanted something more. At breakfast Hal joined me, and then we went to the hospital for Lotus. Hal had a sack with things for her, and she was glad we were there. She went to a room to dress. She had her burka and hijab on. I could only see her eyes, but I noticed her looking at me. On one occasion I winked at her. I couldn't tell, but I thought she smiled. I drove to her house. Hal said, "You came here without me telling you where to turn. You are good with directions."

"Thank you," and I smiled at her.

"Ask Lotus if I can film her." She took out some money so Lotus could see it. I asked.

"Yes," Lotus said. Hal gave her the money and started filming as we went to the door. Rhonda had opened the door and went to Lotus and started hugging her.

"Come in, come in," Rhonda told us, and we did. Hal was recording everything. I translated what they were saying, mostly about being in the hospital and so many people hurt there, some with limbs gone, and now how could they make a living. I asked many questions about the bombing, but Lotus didn't know much. She had taken her hijab off now; she was so lovely. Her skin was so perfect, green eyes, lovely eyebrows, and cute mouth—my kind of gal. The children were wanting attention. I asked if they were hers. "No," the mother said. "They're my son's. He has not come back now for eleven months. I'm afraid something has happened to him. My Lotus is not married or promised yet."

I smile. "I am not married or promised yet either," I said.

"Good," her mother said. "Do you like my Lotus?"

"Yes, she is so lovely."

Rhonda took my hand. "You must come back to see us. Will you?"

"I will," I told her. Lotus left and went out of the room. Hal asked what we were talking about. I told her, and she smiled.

"You would be a good catch." I pretended to blush. Hal gave Rhonda some money, and we thanked them and left. "You should go back to see them. Lotus likes you."

"Maybe," I said. We went to the army base to see what we could learn.

Two young soldiers from the one or first were at the first guard post. "Hi, Hal, you doing OK?"

"Yes, William, I am. How is your dad doing?"

"Not good," he said. "It was a bad heart attack. Dad just stays around the house doing nothing and Mom is really worried."

"I'm sorry," Hal said. "I hope he gets better," and we drove to the second guard post.

"Hi, good-looking," a sergeant said.

"Hi, handsome," Hal came back with.

"When we getting married?" he asked.

"After the honeymoon," Hal said.

"I'm ready," Sergeant Denny said. "Let's go." Hal laughed.

"Long engagement," she said. "Ten, maybe twenty years."

He said, "Can't wait that long. I'll be an old man." We drove to the officers' tent and went in.

The clerk said, "Hal, the captain is in a meeting. He will be tied up for a while."

"What's going on?" she asked the private.

"With the attack?" he asked.

"Yeah," she said. "We lost any men?"

"Yes, one and three wounded."

"Anyone I know?" she asked.

"No, they were in the Sixth Cavalry."

"We get any prisoners?"

"Yeah, five. One big shot. Got him at interrogation. They say he is spilling the beans on things."

"Good. I'll see you later."

"Hey, I didn't tell you anything."

"No, you didn't," Hal said, and we left.

"Mind if we go to the PX?" I asked.

"Sure," and we went to the store on post. I got several things—some perfume (two bottles), chopstick, chewing gum (ten packs), five different kinds candy. Hal laughed and said, "You're going to make a big impression."

"I hope," and grinned. We went back to the hotel.

"I'm hungry," Hal said. "And you?"

"Yes. I'm going to freshen up and come back to eat."

Hal said, "Me too," and I went to my room. I called Sergeant Gill, and he told me about the attack on Samaria.

"We lost one man. One more seriously wounded. We got Omar-Hundi. They got him up at Sixth Cavalry, going over him. Your truck will be ready tomorrow, and how are you doing?"

"Slow," I said. "Maybe things will get better. I'm getting in with the locals, a family that was in the last bombing. Maybe I can learn something."

Sergeant Gill said, "I'll bring the truck to the hotel tomorrow morning and leave the keys at the desk. Be careful." And we hung up. I had mail from Tom and family. I answered, cleaned up, and went down. As we ate, I asked Hal if there was another place she eats at.

"On post," she said and grinned. "Not very safe most places and Captain Mask doesn't like you not following the rules and can make it hard on you."

"I see. Well, it's not bad here. It just gets old. You got family back home?" I asked.

"I'm divorced, no children. I like the adventure but I would like to speak Arabic better."

"Take a course. You're smart, it won't take long."

"On-the-job training helps but my interpreter, I sometimes wonder about him. By the way he will be here tomorrow. One good thing, he helps to keep me out of trouble. He knows the trouble places to avoid." I told her about my truck coming tomorrow. "How did you rate that?" she asked.

"A good friend took care of it for me."

"You buy one?"

"No," I said. "I ordered a new Toyota truck."

"How did you get it shipped here?"

"I don't know. He e-mailed me and said it would be delivered here in the morning."

"He has pull," she said. "Look, Raj, you can hang around with me a little longer if you like. I don't think you're ready to do it alone."

"I am going to hire Undrea."

"OK," Hal said, "but I get the story from him first."

"Sure, you got it," I promised.

"We will start there in the morning," she said. "He will tell more knowing he is going to work for you."

"How much should I pay him?" I asked.

"I pay Tushon ten dollars, American."

"Cheap enough," I said.

"It comes out of your pocket," she said. "You don't have an expense account, do you?"

"Yes," I said.

"I'll be damned. I've been here total seventeen months and I don't get one."

I quickly said, "They will take it out of my stories, if I ever get one."

"You will. It just takes a little time to get started. I think you will do good," and she smiled at me.

The next day started us going to see Undrea. Hal asked if he got the bomber's address. "No," Undrea said, "but we can go by his house. I'll show you."

"Ready to start to work?" I asked him.

"Yes, oh yes, I'm ready now."

"Good."

I told Hal we could drive to the house. Undrea would show us the way. After Undrea told his family he was going to work, we drove to the outskirts of Baghdad, making several turns, then came to a unit of living places; and Undrea said, "Tullen Lallar lives in the left side in back ha—."

"What's his name again?"

"Tullen Lallar," Undrea said.

"Does he have family?" I asked.

"Yes, two sisters and mother. His father is old and cripple." I asked if the Taliban would take care of the family now. "Yes," Undrea said. "They will give the family a little money each month, enough to eat on." We drove around the area. Hal asked me to find out if he knew other bombers. I did, and Undrea said he now knew four different bombers from school in the last three years.

"How do the students get to be Taliban?"

Undrea saw he was answering too many questions. "I don't know," he said. We drove back to Undrea's house, and Hal gave him some money. "Will you come get me tomorrow?" he asked.

"Yes," I said. "I will see you this time tomorrow."

"I will be ready," and he walked away. We drove back to the hotel. Hal had enough information. This was the first time the bomber's name was known. She could write a follow-up story now. As I went in, the desk clerk said he had some keys for me; there were two sets of keys. I went outside and spotted a new white Toyota truck, and I went to look. It smells new inside, and I cranked it. I looked to find the rifle and pistol; they were hidden good. I called Derrik, and he said to meet him, and I went to the army post. Derrik was at the second stop, waiting. He got in and had me drive to an area where no one was. The rifle was hidden behind the backseat, in a compartment that had a special way to get in it. The pistol was in a swing-down place under the dash.

"You pull a lever here," he said, and the pistol swung down. The rifle had a pair of binoculars and night vision equipment hidden with it. Derrik showed me how to set the alarm system; everything was hidden and looked normal. I thanked him and left. "Stay in touch," he said as I drove off.

At my room, I did exercises for a couple of hours. I worked up a good sweat. I showered, then went to eat. Hal was there talking to Ralph. "Seen Albert?" she asked.

"No," he said. "He had a lead he was following up." I joined them talking and then went outside to sit. Hal joined me, and we talked about home and what we would do when we got back.

"I want to come to America," I told her. "I would like to see the Grand Canyon, New York, and Hollywood."

She smiled. "Quit the bullshit," she said. "I know you're not who you say you are. First place, the truck you got came from the army. I saw a sergeant bring it up. Second, you don't come on as a newsman. I don't know who you are, but I would guess not a newsperson."

I smiled. "Thank you," I said, "for such a nice thought. The army said they wanted to examine the truck before I got it, and did, I guess."

Hal looked at me. "You're hard to figure out. I will." I told her about my home in Syria, about going fishing and visiting my uncle in Libya. Hal said, "I'll see you later," and left.

It was early yet, and I decided to go see Rhonda and Lotus. I drove to the house and knocked. Rhonda came to the door. "Come in, Nerij." I had a sack of things and candy and gum for the children. I gave Rhonda the two bottles perfume, one is for Lotus, and shared the candy with the children. Lotus had her hijab on, and I looked into her eyes, green, very pretty, and I told her so.

"I came to see if you would like a ride to the market."

"Yes," Rhonda said, "but Lotus will have to stay with the children."

"Let's take them with us," I said.

Rhonda said, "That would be nice."

"Good," and we went for a ride. Rhonda sat up front with me; Lotus, in back with the children. Rhonda said this is the first time she ever rode in a new truck.

"You must be wealthy," she said.

"No, but I am not a peasant." She directed me to the market, where we got lots of vegetables, some fish, and I got a gift for each of them. The children wanted a kite. Lotus got a new burka. Rhonda also got a burka; it was a full-length robe, black with a blue waistband. They were so excited.

I enjoyed listening to them. Darren, the boy, ate candy the entire time. Sofia, the girl, didn't talk much but chewed gum. Everyone laughed when I would tell about the ocean and the sailboats; it was a good afternoon. When we got back, Rhonda insisted on me staying for dinner.

"Lotus is a good cook. You will see," and I stayed. We had fish, cabbage, and two other vegetables—I didn't know what, but it was good. I talked about school in Saudi Arabia, about the ocean and big ships, and people on ski boats. That was what they liked best, the ocean. I told them about gardens my family always had. Their life was simple; they lived from day to day. They had electricity but no radio or television.

"I have to go back," I told them. It was already eight, and I was never supposed to be out this late, too risky. "I will see you in a couple of days," and I left.

At the hotel, Hal and Ralph were sitting on the porch. I parked and sat with them. "Have you seen Albert?" Ralph asked.

"No, not in a couple days."

"Us too," he said. "Something is wrong or he would have been back."

"Do you know his interpreter?" I asked.

"We know him but don't know his address."

"Have you reported this?" I asked Hal.

"If he isn't back by morning, I will," she said.

Ralph said, "He may have gone to see a lady friend he knew."

"Oh," I said.

"You go see yours?" Hal asked.

"I went to see Lotus and Rhonda. I took them to the market and had dinner."

"It's less likely you would have trouble like Americans, but you still are at risk."

"We have Taliban at home," I said. "I know how to avoid them, I hope." I went to my room, concerned over Albert; maybe he is at his girlfriend's house. I went to bed.

Next day after breakfast, I drove to the army post. The front guards now knew me and my truck and would not search me. I went to the PX and bought a TV and a portable radio with extra batteries; then I went to see Rhonda and Lotus. I got there, and Lotus come to let me in. I parked close, and I got the TV first, then the radio. Rhonda was overwhelmed. "You are so wonderful to us," she said. "May Allah bless you a thousand times."

"Thank you," I told her. "God looks after good people and you are good people." Lotus had taken her hijab off and wanted to know if I would have lunch with them. "No," I said. "I have to go," but first I got the TV working. The little antenna helped some, but I would have to get an outside antenna to get good reception. I drove to Undrea's house and got him. We went riding around, talking. We both asked each other lots of questions. He was twenty-two and has one brother (eleven) and two sisters (eight and nine); no mother. His father works for the government. He maintains a building in town.

"How much money will I make?" he asked.

"Fifteen dollars for five days; work."

"That is wonderful," he said. "This is a very nice truck," he told me. "I feel like someone important riding around with you."

I said, "You are important."

"Thank you, Nerij." We went to the market. Our windows were down, and Undrea would holler to people he knew. We stopped and got some fruits, and I wanted to be seen around. We went to the hospital; nothing was happening to write about. Later that evening, I took Undrea home. "Come in please," he asked me. "Meet my father." So I did. "Father, this is Nerij. My father, Al-La-erale." We gave each other a little hug. I also met his brother, Teron, and sisters, Myan and Opale.

"Very nice to meet you." After talking a few, I excused myself and left. When I got to the hotel, I learned Albert could not be found. Captain Mask was mad. Albert had not been reported missing for three days. This wasn't good, I thought. If the Taliban had him, we would find out soon. I had dinner with Hal, and she was very worried. Albert had a wife and two children. He was from Arizona, and now his family would have been told.

Hal said, "You see why Captain Mask tries to keep us journalists out of certain places unless we have a guard with us."

The next morning, the army had a news conference with all journalists about the raid last week, when they captured Omar-Hundi. We lost one soldier, and one had a bad injury. He also told of a journalist missing. He would not release the man's name until his family had been informed. We had lunch at the mess hall, and Captain Mask sat with the newsmen. He told us if we wanted to die, then just keep on going where we don't have protection. While eating, a courier brought news that the Taliban had reported capturing a newsperson and gave his name, Albert Dean. Tears went to Hal's eyes, and she got up and left. After eating, I drove out to get Undrea. His father came out with him. We talked for a few minutes. Al-La-erale told me to be careful; bad things were going on. I asked him if he knew about Albert being taken hostage. "Yes," he said; he had heard. I wondered how he knew since we just found out, but I didn't ask.

We drove around town; then we followed the Tigris River a few miles. "How far is it to the next town?" I asked.

"Four—or five-hour drive," he said. "The town of Al Kut, bad place," he said. "Lots of trouble there."

"Any idea where they take prisoners?"

"Who?" Undrea asked.

"The Taliban."

"The Taliban is all over the place. They hide in every city. I sure would hate to be taken by them. They are bad. They will kill your family if they don't like you."

"Have you ever had trouble with them?" I asked.

"Praise Allah no," he said.

"My friend Albert Dean, a journalist that was just taken by them, they may kill him."

"They will ask for something first," Undrea said.

"I need some news," I told Undrea.

"What kind of news?" he asked.

"About the war, about the politicians, corruption in the government, anything like that. Each story, I will give you a bonus," I told him. I was near Lotus and Rhonda's house, so I decided to stop by. I told Undrea; they were friends. "You know them?"

He said, "Yes, I like them."

"Why?" I asked. "Do they have a father?"

"No, their father was Taliban and killed for not doing something," he replied.

"I didn't know."

"Be careful with them. They must know some of the bastards," he said sourly.

"Why, do you not like them?" I asked.

"Only a fool would like them," he said. "They are mean and cruel if you don't do what they want you to do." We stopped, and I went to the door. Undrea said he would wait in the truck. Lotus came to the door. She had her hijab on, but her eyes told me she was glad I was there.

"Come in, Nerij," and I did. Inside she took off her hijab, and I told her how pretty she was. We talked a few minutes, and I told her and Rhonda about Albert Dean; and I told them if they wanted to go to the market,

I would come back tomorrow and take them. Darren came to me and started talking. I reached down and picked him up; he was all smiles. Lotus said, "The children really like you."

"I like them too," I said. "I like all of you. How is the TV doing?" I asked.

"Wonderful," Lotus said.

"I'll pick up an outside antenna," I told them.

"You are too good," Rhonda said.

"I'll see you in the morning," and I left. Lotus looked outside and saw Undrea.

"Your new guide?" she asked.

"Yes, he works for me now." I drove to the army post, and Undrea had to be searched, and I had to put him on the list. I took him to be photographed and to be registered; then I went to the PX. They had an antenna. I got it and several things—six cans of spam, peaches, pears, chewing gum, candy, and Undrea wanted an advance on his salary. He got spam and candy. I had to buy it; the locals could not buy from the PX. That was all right; he was very thankful. I went in to see Captain Mask. I have to wait a few minutes, but I didn't mind.

"Come in," he said. "What can I do for you?" I told him I was just checking in to see if everything was all right. I told him I had a young man Undrea that I had just registered and photographed. "You realize they will sell you out for a few dollars, don't you?"

"Yes, sir, I am watching out."

Captain Mask wasn't very nice to me. He said, "That's all," and started back with his paperwork.

I left and drove back to Rhonda's house. I got the outside antenna put on the roof. Derrik had put a toolbox in the truck, and all I needed was a hammer and screwdriver. Undrea helped me attach the line to the antenna, and it only took a few minutes. The antenna was great. I could get six TV stations now. Rhonda was very happy. I told them I would see them in the morning. Undrea spoke to Rhonda, and they had seen each other over the years. As I took Undrea home that evening, he asked if he could sit in the back tomorrow and go to the market with us. "Yes that would be OK," I said.

Undrea was very polite, and I thought he would be a good person to work with. "I'll see you tomorrow," I told him as I left and drove back to the hotel. Hal was eating when I got to the cafeteria, and I sat with her. "Do you realize they are torturing Albert at this moment?" she said, and she pushed her food away. "What are we doing here?" she asked. "These people don't want us and they want to harm us. I don't know," she said. "It could be any one of us, and who will be next?" Tears were in her eyes.

"Yes, it's a bad time," I said, "but we can hope and pray for Albert." I got an idea; maybe the Taliban would sell Albert back to us. Anything was worth a try. If I could get a Taliban leader to call, maybe we could trace his phone back to him. Undrea said the town Al Kut was full of Taliban; maybe I could drive down there and leave a phone number for someone to call for a reward.

In my room, I called Tom. "Good to hear from you," he said. When I gave him my plan, he said maybe it would work, so he gave me a cell phone number, and he could trace it. I made a message with the number on it, and then I had several copies made. After I took Undrea and Rhonda to the market tomorrow, I would drive down to Al Kut and try it. At my room I did exercises for almost two hours, then got ready for bed.

I woke early and did some kicking to limber up, then went to eat. At nine I went to get Undrea. I told him my plans to go to Al Kut. I had dressed totally Moslem, with my jubba and turban on; then we went to see Rhonda and her family. They had eaten and in minutes were ready to go shopping. The children were happy to go and wanted to ride in the back. Rhonda said it was OK with her, so they rode with Undrea. He played with them, and they had a good time. Rhonda told me, "You look very handsome. What do you think of my Lotus?"

"I like her," I said, "and I like you and the children."

"We all like you, Nerij. You can see my Lotus out sometimes if you like."

"Thank you," I said. "I would like that, but I can't get serious about anyone. My work as a journalist carries me all over the country and it is dangerous, so I cannot have much of a personal life. You do understand, don't you?"

Rhonda answered, but I had told her I wasn't going to get involved with anyone, and that didn't make her happy; she was hoping for a son-in-law. I asked Lotus if she would like to go for a ride in the future. "Yes," Rhonda said, "she would like to go." Her mom did all the talking for Lotus, and I figured it was best to get the idea in their mind that I would be leaving sometime.

We made several stops at different vegetable stands and got lots of food. At one place I got everyone a present, even Undrea. Before noon we drove back to Rhonda's house. I had told Rhonda about taking the circular to

Al Kut. "Give me one," she said, and I did. I did not tell her I knew her husband was Taliban before he died, but I knew she must know some of his associates. "Thank you for being so good to us," Rhonda said and gave me a hug.

We drove to the river and followed it for fifty or so miles. Undrea told me our best bet was to go to the market to pass out the circulars, and when we got there, he would go to talk to the people. I sat in the truck eating fruit. After an hour, we were out of circulars. We had passed out over fifty; maybe we would have some luck.

Tom and the professor had set a computer up for any call they might get. The professor spoke good Arabic and would do the talking. Our drive back, we took our time stopping and looking at the occasional boat. We would talk about what we would do someday. Undrea wanted to be in politics. He was studying books he had and wanted to improve his education.

CHAPTER XIII

After taking Undrea home, I went to the hotel. Hal was there on the porch talking to the two men I had met a few days before. I sat down and listened. "Maybe something will come out better than you think," one man said.

Hal looked over at me. "Did you go to Al Kut?" she asked.

"Yes and passed out circulars. Maybe we will hear from it." I watched the two men leave.

Hal said, "They are police that hang around, trying to learn something about us."

"I talked to them one day. That was why they asked so many questions," I commented.

I went to my room and did exercises for over an hour, then got ready to eat. I called Tom, and he said they hadn't heard anything, but it was early. "Everything OK?" the professor asked.

"Yes, a little dull but OK."

"Good, keep in touch," and I hung up and went to have a salad.

The next morning, Tom called early and said they had been contacted. "They asked for fifty thousand dollars, American. I asked to speak to Albert Dean before we would pay for him. Their location was in Al Kut. We know about where but don't have an exact location. They said they would call back, and we are waiting and ready."

"Good," I said. "Maybe we can get an exact fix on them."

After eating I went to get Undrea, then drove to the outskirts of town. I enjoyed looking at the different places. We got to the Tigris River and parked, watching the few boats on it. After a few minutes, Tom called. "I have a fix on Albert. Are you alone?"

"No," I said. "I'll call you back."

"I'll wait," he said. I drove Undrea home and called Sergeant Gill.

"Can you get away tonight?" I asked.

"Can do," he said. "Where do we meet?" he asked.

"I pick you up at six thirty," I told him, "at the front guard post."

"I'll be there. Armed?" he asked.

"Yes," I said. "Sidearm." I called Tom. "Can you give me the coordinates? I'm ready," and he did. I put it in my GPS and told Tom my plan. "I would go there tonight and look over things."

"Good," he said. "Call me when you have something."

"Yes, sir," and hung up. It was only two; I had time to eat and rest. It might be a long night.

At six I started to the army post. I was early, but Derrik was there waiting. "You're early," I said.

"You too," and smiled. I told him what was happening. He was in a suit. I asked him to put a turban on. He laughed but knew we didn't want to draw suspicion on ourselves. He had large sunglasses on, and we fit in the locals.

It was an overcast day and looked like it would rain soon, and by the time we got to Al Kut, there was a slow, cold rain. I was glad; better cover. The GPS took us to the other side of town, where there were not many houses. We went to the location on the GPS and drove past it; then we drove around, looking at other places, then went back. Lights were on; it had an eight feet wall around it and was a two-story house. We parked down from the house and got the binoculars and night vision out, looking over things. After an hour, we saw a car come out of a big gate. The driver closed the gate and locked it. "Let's follow him," I told Derrik. We stayed back a long way with our lights off. For a few minutes, the car went a couple miles, then stopped at a house with no lights on. Two men got out and went in, then turned the lights on. I felt no one was there except these two men. If there was some way we could get them to talk, we would take them. We watched the house for two hours before deciding to leave and go back to the first house. The lights were on, and we sat and watched for a few minutes; then I wanted to do a look around. Derrik had a pair of walkie-talkies, and he would look out for me. I had my stilts, and I wore the harness, and I got my pistol out. Derrik got the rifle, and I went to the side of the house and put the stilts on, and I raised myself up to look over the wall. I watched for a few minutes to be sure, but I saw nothing. I raised myself up and went on the wall. I lowered myself down to the ground, and then I put my hearing to a higher level; only rain, nothing else. I went to a window to look in but didn't see anything. I eased around the house, but no one was watching outside. From the back I raised myself up to look in a window, but it was dark inside. I tried the night vision and couldn't see anything. On the opposite side of the house, a window was lit up. I got to it and looked inside. One man was lying down watching TV. He was middle-aged and wore a pistol. That was what I hoped for. For some reason he was armed. At the front corner of the house, a small window was lit up. I looked inside and saw a man sitting down with a rifle leaned against the wall. I could hear something, but it sounded like a radio trying to pick up a channel. It was very low. I turned my hearing up again. The rain sounded like rocks hitting a metal roof. It was so loud, but the noise turned into a loud moan. That could be Albert. My heart raced. I kept listening; then I heard a cry of pain. It was definitely someone. I moved away from the window and called Derrik. I told him what was going on.

"Someone is on the roof," he said. "They are in the front. Be careful." My side of the house was darkest, and I told Derrik to watch and let me know if they moved. I was coming over the wall. "You're clear," he said. I can still see him looking around at the wall. I raised myself and went over; then I followed the wall to the back of the house, then moved away. At the truck I turned my hearing off and got in. We were far enough away that we could not be seen.

"I think Albert is there. I could hear someone in pain, making noise."

"What do you think we should do?" he asked.

"Nothing now," I said. "Their people at the house are more. We need to take out that guard on top before we can do anything. Let's go back to the base and I will call in first." We drove around the area for a good look at things; then we drove back to Baghdad. It was almost four in the morning. I told Derrik to get some rest. We would probably go back tomorrow night.

"Will do," he said and left. I didn't want to wake Tom, so I would call in the morning.

At eleven, Tom called me. "We just heard from Albert," he said, "and we promised to make the payment tomorrow." I told him what I found. "Good," he said. "The call came from the same house. It was from the day before. It must be him. What are your plans?"

"I'll take Derrik and two more men tonight and get him," I said.

"Is four of you enough?" he asked.

"I think so. Any more and it might be too big a mission."

"OK," he said. "I'll call and have Derrik get more sharpshooters. Call me when this is over," he said, "and good luck."

I called Derrik and told him what was going on. "We need two men," I told him, "with rifle scopes and silencers."

"Sir?" he asked. "If more men are on top, we would need to cover all sides."

I thought about it. "You're right. Let's get three men for inside and four men covering us. We need to be certain."

"Yes, sir," he said. "We have a unit with five men. That would be perfect."

"Good," I said. "We will leave here at dusk." I called Tom back. "We are going to use a team of five men to watch our flanks."

"Good," Tom said. "Sounds better." I began to work out. I exercised for an hour, then went to eat. Hal was there and asked if I heard anything. I wanted to tell her, but I couldn't, not yet. I said, "But I have a good feeling about him."

"I hope you're right," she said.

"Any new stories?" I asked.

"No, nothing of importance. You're gone a lot," she said. "Anything with you?"

"No, nothing good."

Hal said, "I told my editor to start looking for a replacement for me. I'm going home for a while."

"Good," I told her. "What will you do at home?"

"A vacation, maybe Miami or the Bahamas. Just relax in the sun and drink martini."

"Sounds fun and I hope you do."

I drove to see Undrea, and we went to see Lotus and her family. "Want to go to the market?" I asked.

"Yes," Rhonda said. "Thank you so much." They were ready in minutes, and we went to the market. We got fish, several vegetables, rolls of bread, and Undrea got food for himself. We drove to the river. Undrea and the children at the back were having fun. We threw rocks into the water. I talked to Lotus about farming.

"It must be nice in Syria. We can't grow anything much, and a garden all the time would be great." I told her about watermelons and cantaloupes in America. "America would be wonderful to live in. If it's true, you can go where you want, gardens, even fishing." She had heard all kinds of lakes and ponds.

"It's true," I said. "They have all that and lots more."

"What more could they have?" she asked.

"Great parks to see, big mountains, lots of rivers, many animals to hunt at the right time." She was amazed at my story.

"It's true?" she asked. "You have seen this?"

"Yes," I told her. "I have seen all these."

"Are you going back there, someday?" she asked.

"Yes, some of my family live there and I will go there again."

"You are so lucky," she said. "Is it dangerous to live there?"

"Oh no, not at all," I replied. "Many highways going everywhere. America is a big country. In the north it's cold in winter. In the south, it's warm all the time."

"The Americans are so lucky. If only we had some of those things," she said. I drove Undrea home first and gave him that week's pay; then I took Rhonda and her family home.

"Please come anytime, Nerij. You are so kind to us. May Allah always bless and watch over you."

"Thank you," I said. "I'll be back soon."

Lotus spoke up. "Yes, please, and thank you for the drive." I gave her a wink. She turned away smiling.

It was only five, and I had over an hour to do something. I drove back to the hotel and started with my computer and laid out my plan—where each should be and how I would enter the house, the outside people we would see and take out, but the three people were our problem.

Derrik called. He had another car, an old Chevrolet we would use also. He said, "I have a good surprise for you."

"Oh? What?" I asked.

"You'll see," he said.

"OK, me on my way to the post. I'll be there in fifteen minutes."

"Can do," he said and hung up.

I got to the first outpost and was stopped and searched. "You can go," they said.

Then at the second post, one corporal said, "Yes, Nerij, you're clear." I wondered how he knew my name; then I saw the old blue Chevrolet with five men in it. I stopped, and two men got in with me, one carrying a cooler.

"Celebration beer for our success."

"Not quite," Derrik said. He sat up. "This is Corporal Hainey," he said.

"My pleasure," he said as I looked in the mirror at him.

"Nice to meet you," I replied. About five miles out of town was a nice place by the river, all quiet, and we could see for a long way. We stopped for our briefing. "OK," I said. "I'm Lieutenant Doan."

Sergeant Gill said, "This is PFC Moore. That's Rodriguez, Harper, and Shane." All had assault rifles with night vision; two had long-range rifles with scopes and silencers. I looked each one over. They were as young as me or younger, except Derrik; he was the oldest.

"Me, Derrik, and Hainey are going inside. The rest of you make certain no one comes in or out on top when we start. Take out anyone outside. We can see there is an eight-foot wall around the compound. I will go over first and open the gate. You pick a place to cover us from. There will be at least one man on top. You have to get him before I go in. We wait until dark before we move in. Any questions?" No one spoke up. "Good. Let's move." We loaded up and went on toward Al Kut.

On the way, Corporal Hainey asked, "Lieutenant, are you army or marine?"

Sergeant Gill spoke up proud, "We're marines." Hainey shut up from that. Everyone was camouflaged, except me in my jubba and turban. It was just getting dark when we got there, so we parked out a ways at a good place. The men had walkie-talkie and were using them; then we drove to the house. The other car moved around to a good place and parked after two stops to let men out. We sat for an hour; then we saw the gate open. The men that left yesterday were leaving.

"Let's take them," I told Derrik, so we followed. When they stopped, we pulled up to them and jumped out, pointing our guns at them. They froze. We made them go inside the house; one was young, and the older one told him to shut up. I asked them questions, but neither would answer. I told Hainey to take the older one to another room. We had them tied good, their hands in back and their feet tied together, and Hainey helped the older one jump to the other room. I pointed my pistol at the young man and said, "When I count to three, I will kill you if you don't answer me. How many men at the other house?" He didn't answer, so I said, "One, two, three—"

Derrik said, "Wait, I can make him talk." He went to the truck and brought the cooler in. He was in back of our prisoner. *What was he doing?* I thought. When he opened the cooler, a cobra snake rose up, and it scared me. He got the snake behind the head and came up to the prisoner from behind, holding the cobra close to his head. He moved enough for the man to see the cobra at his face. He screamed and moved away all he could. The man started jerking, shaking all over.

"Please don't," he said. "I'll tell you, I'll tell you, please don't."

I asked again, "How many men in the house?"

"Three men inside, one outside on the roof." I felt sure he told us the truth. Derrik put the cobra back in the cooler. There were ice in it so that the snake could barely move. I grinned at Derrik.

"Great idea," I told him. We tied the two prisoners good, gagged them, and blindfolded them and laid them in the back of the truck, hog-tied. We covered them with a tarpaulin and went back to the first house.

"Anything happening?" Derrik asked the group watching the house.

Shane answered. "One man on top," he said. "What happened to the two men you followed?"

Derrik answered, "We have them in the truck."

"Dead or alive?" he asked.

"Watch," Derrik said, and for an hour we did, and nothing happened; it was time.

"Going in," I said. I could see the man on the roof barely.

Shane said, "I'm clear for top target."

"Go," Sergeant Gill said, and I couldn't hear, but I saw the man fall backward. I moved to the wall and put my stilts on. As I raised myself to the top, I took a long look around the front and side of the compound; it looked clear.

I called in, "Going in," and then I went over the wall with my legs; then I lowered myself to the ground and took my stilts off. I moved to the side of the house and looked in each window. As I passed at the back of the house, a window was lit, and I raised myself to the second floor. No one was there, so I waited a little. Nothing happened, so I lowered myself and went to the back. It looked clear, and I went around to the side. The grounds looked OK, and I went to the front. On the ground level, a window was lit, and two men were inside. I had increased my hearing once. I could barely hear them talking, so I increased my hearing again. The men were loud now. They were talking about the money coming tomorrow. Everything looked clear, so I moved to the gate. "All clear," I said. "I'm opening the gate." I checked good for any alarm, and I couldn't see anything; and I opened the gate a little, and Derrik and Hainey came in. We shut the gate but didn't lock it, going back to the lit window. I listened but could only see the two men talking.

One man said, "I hope Hisane be ready to eat soon."

"Me too," the other one said. I told Derrik we have to go inside now, and we moved to the front door. I had my door openers with me, but it was a look-alike I had never seen, but I tried what I had. Nothing worked. One back door was strong looking, and I didn't think we could get in without making a lot of noise. Maybe we could go in through a window. One window was above us. I raised myself to it, but it was locked. Derrik and Hainey watched the two men inside, and I went to the back of the house and raised myself to the window. It was locked, but it had one pane that was cracked. I told Derrik to take out the two men if I alerted them. Then I broke out a pane to get in. I had duct tape in my supplies, and I taped the window before I broke it.

I told Derrik, "I'm going in now," so he and Hainey were ready to shoot the two men. The window made a noise when I hit it with my elbow, but it didn't fall to the floor. I pushed it some and lowered the glass to the floor. I reached the lock and unlocked the window. It was a little noisy as I raised it. "Everything OK?" I asked Derrik.

"Looks good here," he said.

"I'm going in," I told the group, and then I went through the window. I was holding my backpack and gun with one hand.

As I got through the window, I heard someone at the hall saying, "Bring me some tea." I moved beside the door. I could hear him going to a room.

"Anything happening down there?" I said very low to Derrik.

"No, these two are still here." I waited and listened. When another man came up, he had tea, I guess for the leader. That meant four men at least instead of the three we were told. *How many more?* I thought. When the man went back downstairs, I lowered a rope to Derrik to come up. I tied it to my two stilts, and it worked good. After Derrik was up, I told him there were at least four men. We would take out the one on the top floor. If the two men at the room were alerted, Hainey would take care of them. Two of the outside guards had come to join us now. Derrik had Hainey to come up with us, and now we were going to enter the hall. I eased the door open and looked. Good. Nothing. Now I went out and moved to where I heard the leader go. His door was almost shut but open enough to go in quickly. Derrik was to follow me, and Hainey was to guard us. I opened the door fast, and on the bed was a very surprised man. I had my gun pointed at him; so did Derrik. The man looked at a pistol lying beside him. I nodded no. Derrik went to him and held his rifle to his head, and

I gagged him and tied him up; then I heard noise. Gunshots. It was ours, because we used silencers, and the shots were muffled. I started to the hall when shots were fired from inside. They were AKs. I knew the fight was on. I heard someone scream. It was a death cry. Hainey was shooting at someone across from us. Shots were hitting around me. I moved quickly out into the hall. Someone ran across the bottom. I heard someone hit the floor Hainey was shooting at. Derrik went past me and down the steps. I followed. Where was Albert Dean? Derrik opened the front door, and two rangers came in. The back had two doors closed. I could see one dead man on the floor. That meant two more at least. I saw blood at a door. Derrik lay down, pointing his rifle, then motioned someone to quickly open the door. Hainey got ready from the side, opened the door fast, and moved sideways. Derrik shot; the man went down, but only one man. That meant the last room still had others.

I was concerned they would kill Albert, so I hollered, "Come out and you will be OK. If you don't, you will die."

He answered, "I am unarmed."

"Come out with your hands up," I said. I heard noise, and the door opened. A young man came out with his hands up. I went in; it was empty. Where was Albert Dean? Had we come to the wrong place? "Where is your prisoner?" I asked. He looked puzzled, as if he didn't know what I was talking about.

Derrik said, "I'll be back," and left. Five minutes later, he was back with the cooler. We still had two men covering the outside, but now all the rooms had been checked; no one. Derrik opened the cooler, and the cobra stuck his head up. Derrik moved the cooler over near the young prisoner. I asked him again, "Tell me where he is or I will let the cobra have you." He didn't answer. Derrik picked the cobra up and started toward his face. The young man pointed down under us; there were no steps. "How do you get down there?" Derrik moved again near the man. He was shaking.

"A door in the front room," and he pointed. I went in there and couldn't see anything except a rug. I pulled it back and saw the door.

I went back to the prisoner. "Is anybody down there with the newsman?" He shook his head yes. Derrik and Shane came with me. I hollered down, "Put your weapon down. If you fire at us, we will fire back and you won't come out alive." No answer. I got the young prisoner and told him to tell whoever was there to come out. We have everyone now and will shoot everyone if he fires at us.

"Hisane, come out or they will kill all of us."

Hisane hollered back, "I will kill this man if anyone comes down."

Derrik said, "Tell him all our bullets have been dipped in pig blood." I looked at him, wondering. Derrik said, "Pig blood contaminates, making them unholy, and they can't go to the hereafter.

I hollered down, "Our bullets have been dipped in pig blood. None of you will be mortals and you'll die like cowards."

Derrik was leaning down, trying to see the man. As he looked lower, he pointed to a spot. He rose up and then moved over and pointed down, then said low, "If we all shoot at once, we can probably get him." Shane and the other ranger got ready.

"No," I said. Then I asked the prisoner, "What is your name?"

"Al-lon," he said.

"Al-lon, who is your leader?"

"He isn't here," Al-lon said. He left earlier.

"Bring in the two prisoners in the truck," I told Derrik. He left, and outside he got the two men untied, except their hands, and brought them in. "Who is your leader?" I asked Al-lon. He pointed at one of the men. "Take his gag off," I told Shane; he did. "What is your name?" He spit at me. I started to hit him; then I told Derrik to get the cobra; he did. "Now put the cobra near his face." The man started. "Tell me or die," I said.

"Olonda," he said.

"Olonda, we have dipped all our bullets in pig blood. Tell the man down there to come up. If he kills the newsman, we will kill all of you like the cowards you are. Put the cobra near his face," I told Derrik, and he did. The cobra moved slow but turned toward Olonda and started spreading.

Olonda said, "Move him, move him."

"Tell the man down there not to hurt the newsman and come up."

"Come up, Atar. We are all going to die if you don't."

"Is that you, Jarraz?"

"Yes," he said, "it's me, come up."

The man in the basement said, "I'm coming up unarmed," and then he started up.

He was young, and when he got up, I hollered down, "Anyone down there?" and there was no answer. "Are there anyone else down?" I asked Jarraz Olonda.

"No," he said. I told Shane to check it out. He took a mirror from his backpack and reached down where he could see.

"It looks clear," he said, "except a bleeding man hanging. It's probably the newsman." Then he went down, followed by Derrik. "Come down, Lieutenant."

They had tied the prisoners and had them lying on the floor, and I went down. Derrik and Shane had lifted the newsman off the two meat hooks in his hands. Blood was all over his arms. His shirt and shoes were off. His two nails had been ripped off, and his feet cut in lots of places. His chest and stomach had little cuts all over it. I got sick and almost threw up. Derrik had tears in his eyes. "The bucher," he said. "We should kill them all." Shane had called for our medic, and he came down. He gave Albert Dean a shot of morphine. It was two in the morning. Now we got all the prisoners together. There were five alive and one dead, plus Albert Dean.

"Hog-tie these men up and put them in the back of my truck and cover them." I went outside and called Tom. "Sir, I hate to call at this hour but we have Albert Dean. He is alive but cut up bad. We have no casualties, but enemy one dead and five prisoners."

Tom said, "This is wonderful. Where are you?"

"We're at the home in Al Kut, about to leave. We have two computers and the leader, Jarraz Olonda. The house is cleared out and is there anything you can think of for us to do before we leave?"

"You're clear. I'll call Colonel Talbert and he will meet you. Go to the army post. Good luck and great job. By the way, you'll be coming home real soon."

"Thank you, sir," and hung up. We started back to the post. Our medic was with Albert Dean in our truck; the rangers were following.

At the base was a group of officers, including Colonel Talbert, Captain Mask, and a general. They took Albert to the hospital. Sergeant Gill reported to Colonel Talbert with me. He shook my hand. "Lieutenant Doan, it's a pleasure. You're to get a medal along with Sergeant Gill. You have done a great job. Your Colonel Tom, my friend, has informed me of your good deeds. Thank you." I saluted him and shook Sergeant Gill's hand and drove away. At my hotel, I showered and went to bed.

Next morning, I was concerned about Albert Dean, and I hoped I would be able to write a story and turn it in. It was eleven by the time I went to eat. Hal was there and said, "Do you know anything about Albert?"

"Rumors," I said.

"What rumors?" she asked.

"I heard he was at the hospital."

"On base or in town?" she asked.

"I'll make a call," I said. I went outside, and Hal followed. I called Sergeant Gill. "Derrik, have you heard anything about Albert Dean."

"Physically he will be OK, but he is in a coma, drug induced. He may lose his left hand, but they don't know yet." I have thanked the team last night, but I told Derrik to thank each one again for me. "I will, sir. Are you going home now?"

"Yes," I said, "in a few days. I'll see you before I go."

"Great," he said. "Good luck. I don't know anything yet but I will tell you if I hear."

That afternoon, I went and got Undrea and then Rhonda and Lotus. The children and Undrea sat in the back as we went to the market. I bought Lotus and Rhonda new head scarfs and the children more coloring books and more crayons. Undrea got a headpiece, a kufi. Rhonda got fish and vegetables and said, "You must have dinner with us tonight."

"OK," I told her, but I had things to do before then. I left, and Undrea and I went to the hospital. Lots of people were there, but no death by the Taliban; then we went to the army base, and there I had Undrea to stay in the truck while I went to check on Albert. No one would tell me anything, so I went to see Colonel Talbert. He wasn't available. I called Derrik.

"Yes, Lieutenant, where are you?"

"I'm at the infirmary," I said.

"I'll be right over." So I waited. When Derrik came, we went to a special place, and a nurse said no one can be allowed in. Derrik said, "This is the man who saved him. Is he awake?"

"No," she said. "He hasn't been awake yet, but I can tell you they are operating on his hand shortly."

"Thank you," I told her, and we left. "Thanks, Derrik," and I went to the PX. I got spam, peaches, pears, potted meat, a loaf of bread, mayonnaise, and a gallon of ice cream. I had a cooler and put the ice cream in it. I took Undrea home and said, "I'll see you tomorrow," and he left.

I called Tom. "How are things going?"

"Good," he said. "Colonel Talbert is sending the computers to me and says the newsman will be OK, he thinks. Our group said tell you hello and I want you to come home this weekend. Colonel Talbert will arrange your flight to the States. It's Wednesday, so you have a couple of days to close things out there. Is that OK with you?"

"Yes, sir, that's good with me."

"Keep in touch and good-bye."

"Good-bye, sir," and I felt good about going home. It had only been four and a half months, but it seems longer, I thought.

I knocked at Rhonda's door. Lotus opened it with a nice smile. She was not wearing her burka or hijab but a simple white dress used around the family at home. She was so lovely. I had a large box of things, the food, and I set it on the table and went for the cooler. "Something special," I told her. When I got back, they were going through the box of food.

"For us?" Lotus said.

"Yes, for all of you." I described the spam and how to fix it, then the potted meat, and how to use the mayonnaise. They knew about peaches and pears, the rich folks' food, they called it. I had six cans of each one.

"You are so good to us, Nerij. How can we ever repay you?"

"You're my good friends. That's enough."

"Lotus, you keep Nerij company while I finish the fish."

Lotus said, "Let me show you around."

"OK, sure, I would like that." We went to the kitchen. Her mom smiled.

"I'm almost through," she said. Then we went through the bedrooms and back to the den. Darren and Sofia were playing with their pictures in the coloring book, talking about the animals. Lotus bent over to pick up something. She wore no bra, and her breasta almost fell out. They were beautiful. As she rose up, she saw me looking and smiled. Oh, how my heart pounded.

"Would you take me riding some evening, Nerij?" That made me wonder what she was thinking.

"Yes," I said.

"Good. I love to see the sky and river at night."

"Me too. I'll be leaving soon," I told her, and she looked so sad.

"When?"

I said, "Just a couple of days."

"We will miss you so much. Will you come back?"

"Sometime, but I don't know when."

Then her mom came in with the fish and said, "Let's eat." She told Darren and Sofia to wash their hands and come eat.

As we ate, Rhonda was saying how nice it was for me to take them to the market. "Nerij is leaving soon," Lotus said.

"Oh, we will miss you so much. Is it your work?" she asked.

"Yes. I will go to America for a few weeks."

Lotus asked, "Will you come back to Baghdad?"

"I don't know when they will send me."

"More fish is on the stove." She ask, "Are you ready for some?" She was getting up.

"Yes, one more piece." This time she brought the pan and passed all the fish out. "It's so good. You are a fine cook."

"My Lotus is too. She did most of it." Lotus was quiet. I touched her hand.

"You're a fine cook." She made a small smile. "Now I have a treat for us. We need small bowls for the ice cream."

"What is that?" Rhonda asked.

I took out the ice cream and said, "Try it."

Lotus opened the container and dipped her spoon in it, then tasted. "That is great," she said. Then she dipped everyone some.

The children were wanting more. "I've had enough," I said. "You eat all you want and when I come back next time, I will bring more." So everyone had another big bowl. It was so nice to see the smiles on their faces. What a hard life these people have, I thought.

"Mother, can I go for a ride with Nerij?"

"Where would you go?" she asked.

"Maybe to the river and watch the stars."

Her mother said, "Yes, it would be OK. Nerij would protect you. But remember, you're not engaged."

"I know, Mother. Will you take me now?" she asked.

"Yes, sure, I will." Lotus got up and put her burka and hijab, then started for the door. I followed, and we went toward the river, only a couple of miles away. Lotus told me how to go. She said there is a fine place outside of town, not many people around there.

As we drove, Lotus took my hand in hers and said, "I have never felt the way I do for anyone else but you." I knew things were going too far, but my feeling for her was more pity than anything.

"I feel you are a very special person, Lotus, but I have to go away and I don't know for sure if I will ever be back for sure."

"That is why I wanted you alone," she said. "I may never have a chance to know anyone as good and nice, so I can't lose this chance with you." We got to the river. The road ran along beside it. Here there were trees and a good place to pull over beside the road. The river was wide here, and a boat was going up it. We stood beside the truck, watching the sky, and Lotus got my arm and put it over her shoulders and put her arm around my waist, hugging me and looking up, with her lips wanting me to kiss her. I did, and she put both arms around my neck, pulling me closer. My heart was racing. I tried to control my emotions but couldn't. I wanted her as much as she wanted me. I turned her against the truck and kissed her more. Now we were both breathing hard and losing control of our emotions. She touched my hand and placed it on her breast. There was no stopping now, and we got in the backseat of the truck and stayed for over an hour.

On our way back home, Lotus leaned over and had her head as close to mine as she could. "Will you try to come back sometimes?"

"Yes. If I can come back to Baghdad, I will, and I will always think of you wherever I am."

"I'll miss you so much and thank you for all these great memories," and she squeezed my hand. We had got to her house, and she pulled me over to kiss me again before we went in. Rhonda was watching TV with Darren. Sofia had gone to bed.

"Were the stars bright?" she asked.

"Yes, Mother, they were beautiful."

"I will be back before I leave." I told Lotus and Rhonda good-bye. Lotus walked me to the door and put her hand on my shoulder.

"I will see you again?"

I said, "Yes," and left. At the hotel, I called Tom and asked, "Have you heard anything about Albert?"

"No," he said. "Colonel Talbert said he has a flight coming to America on Sunday morning. Can you be ready?"

"Yes. This is Friday. I will be ready."

"Good," he said. "It will be nice to see you. Good-bye."

"Good-bye," and I hung up. I showered and went to bed.

On Saturday morning, I ate at the hotel; Hal was there. "Have you heard? They have Albert in the hospital. No visitors yet and he will be OK. One of the army men is a special friend that told me. Did you know?"

"Yes, I mean no. That is wonderful." She looked at me, puzzled.

"You did know, didn't you?" I smiled. "I have friends too."

"Do you have the story about him?" she asked. I told her I'm leaving Sunday. "Where are you going?"

"Home, after I get this story published."

She said, "Good. You earned it," and I left for the army post. I went to Colonel Talbert's office. He was there.

"Come in, Lieutenant Doan." His secretary went out and shut the door. "What can I do for you?"

"I was concerned about Albert."

"Good news. He woke up last night and ate soup. He is going to be OK. He knows about his hands. He is so happy to be here. He told the nurse about the torture and they both cried. It was quite an ordeal. He wanted to know how we found him. I told him we had an inside man. He pleaded to us to let him meet the person that saved his life and got him out of that hell place. I asked Sergeant Gill to speak to him and I think he is there now."

"Good. I know Gill will take care of things. He is a good man."

"Yes," the Colonel said. "He will get a medal for this mission and you too, Lieutenant."

"I understand you have a plane leaving for the States Sunday?"

"Yes," he said. "Around ten in the morning."

"Sir, in case I don't see you again, good luck."

"Good luck to youm Chris," and I saluted him and left.

I drove to pick up Undrea; then I went to see Rhonda and her family. I stopped by the PX and got a box of food for them, including ice cream. When I knocked, Lotus came to the door with her house dress on. It was thin, and she wore no hijab. I went in, and when she saw Undrea, her smile left. She went to put her hijab and burka on. The children were excited. "Are we going to the market?" Darren asked.

"Yes." I smiled and said, "Also a ride to the river for lunch." He went off running.

"We're going to a picnic," he said.

Rhonda came in and gave me a hug. "It's so good to see you again, Raj. I'll sure miss you. So will everyone."

"I'll miss all of you also." Lotus came back. "Let's go to the market, then a picnic?" I asked.

Rhonda saw the box of food. "The spam," she said, "it's great fried, like fish, but more tasty." I had ten more cans. "A picnic sounds great," and they started getting ready.

Undrea asked, "When are you leaving?"

"Tomorrow," I said.

"I will miss you too," he said.

"I may be back. We will see."

"Maybe," he said. We drove to the market. We had plenty of vegetables, but we got some other things. I had bread, mayonnaise, a can of ham, spam, and ice cream, also two large Coca-Colas. We were set. When we got to the river, we ate, then talked, while Undrea and the children threw rocks at the river. We talked about our childhood. Rhonda had things bad. Her family was poor, not much food and never doing anything. She was raised in a small town two hundred miles in the country; then Bi-Ali came along, and she married him, and they left and came to Baghdad. He was bad off when the Taliban offered him money to come with them; then three years ago, she got word Higiabi, her only son, was killed in a truck accident. He was the children's father; then six months later, Bi-Ali was shot. Now it was only her and Lotus with the children.

"I knew he should not have joined the Taliban, but he needed the money bad." She had tears. I felt so sorry for them.

"Let's enjoy the picnic," Lotus said, and we walked around. "It was nice to get away," she said.

"When are you leaving?" Rhonda asked.

"Tomorrow," I said. "In the morning. You know, Lotus is very fond of you."

"Yes, and I like her and all of you very much."

"I hope and pray to Allah you will come back to see us."

"I will. I believe I will come back to see you. I believe I will be coming back to Baghdad sometimes."

Lotus came over and leaned against me. I put my arm around her shoulders and held her close to me while we talked. I knew only engaged people did this, but everyone knew I was leaving, and this was our last time together. My phone rang; it was Tom. "Chris, I have some good news."

"Oh," I said. "What?"

"There is a reward on Jarraz Olonda, one hundred thousand dollars."

"That's great," I said, thinking about the financial problems Lotus's family have. "Can I give it to the people that helped me most?"

"Who is that?" Tom asked.

"Rhonda Halbin and daughter Lotus."

"Is that who you are with now?" he asked.

"Yes, they are my real associates here."

Tom said, "That can be arranged. You need an address and full name and I think it will clear."

"Great," I said. I had my back to Lotus and Rhonda, but I was speaking English, and they realized it.

Undrea had joined us, and I asked him if he had this truck, would he come twice a week to take the family to the market and other places they needed to go? "I would, I promise. Allah has blessed me," he said. "Praise Allah."

Lotus said, "Walk with me, Nerij." So we started down the river. "This is the last time we will be together. I will wait for you if you ask me."

"No, Lotus, you will find a good person. Just keep looking, but I will always be a good friend and I will try to come back." We got back, and everyone was eating ice cream, and we got some. We ate the whole gallon. I drove Undrea home first and told him I would pick him up at eight in the morning.

"Thank you so much, Nerij. I will look after Rhonda and Lotus and the family."

I gave him two months' pay and said, "Good luck."

Then I drove to Lotus's home. Rhonda and the children went inside. It was already dark. Lotus started kissing me. "Let's go inside," she said, and she led me to her bedroom. Rhonda was in the den watching TV. I didn't like what I thought was happening, but the kissing started again, and Lotus took off her clothes. It was dark, but she pulled me closer to her. My heart was pounding out of my chest, but I was almost helpless as we lay on the bed together.

As I was leaving, Lotus said good-bye and stayed in the bedroom. I gave Rhonda a hug and then told the children good-bye and drove back to the hotel. Hal was sitting on the porch, and as I came up, she asked, "What have you heard about Albert?"

"My people say he is going to be OK. He ate soup this morning and talked to his nurse, then went back to sleep."

"Nerij or whatever your name is, I wonder if you know more about getting him back than you can say. When are you leaving?"

"In the morning," I told her. "It has been good knowing you," I said, "and we will meet again, I'm sure." I took her hand and squeezed it. I went to my room and packed. It was ten, so it would be four at home. I called Tom and asked how they were doing with the new computers.

"Good," he said. "We got more leads we are working on."

"Can I write a story now on Albert's capture and our getting him back?"

"Yes," Tom said, "but let me have your final write-up."

"OK, sure," I said, "and good night."

"Good night," and we hung up.

I woke early with the anticipation of going home. I did a good workout, then showered and went down to eat. Ralph was there with Hal. We did small talk; then I said good-bye and went to get my things. I went to Undrea and told him he might have to wait outside until I sent the truck out to him. "Good-bye, Nerij. I will always remember you," and I drove. Inside I had called Derrik and asked him to clean the truck out and told him I was giving it to Undrea. We met at his barrack. I went to the latrine and shaved that awful beard and mustache off and put on my service uniform. It felt good getting out of my jubba and kufi. Derrik had cleaned the truck out and gave it to Undrea. He was back now. "You look good," he said. It was time to go to the plane. As I got outside and was loading my things into Derrik's Hummer, Hal pulled up. As I turned in her direction, a big grin came over her face, and she waved good-bye. I could only smile.

"Good-bye, Hal." We got to the C-130, and several people were there—Colonel Talbert, Captain Mask, and the men that was on our team from Albert's recovery. I shook hands with everyone and then got onboard. The plane taxied to the takeoff, and we were on our way home.

CHAPTER XIV

I got to Dobbins Air Base the next afternoon. The plane's captain had let me sit in front some before we got there. I got a message to meet Tom at the service desk. A jeep took me to the main terminal, and when I got to the service desk, no one was there. I stood there for five minutes, and the professor came. "Chris." We shook hands. "It's good to see you." Tom had something come up and sent me to get you. We got to the parking lot and found his car and went to town to the office.

It was a nice homecoming. The office had food, cake, and wine for our party. The cake said, "Welcome home Chris." Then Tom came in, and that made it great. He is such a good person, and he always shows appreciation for anything you do extra.

That afternoon, he took me home. Dad and Mom knew I was coming, but I wasn't sure when, so it was somewhat of a surprise. After a long talk, I wanted to get to my story about the rescue of the newsman Albert Dean. The story started on the night our reserve team went to a home, knowing the captive was there through good reconnaissance. The men had to scale an eight-foot wall and with a Taliban on the housetop and five more inside. The team had to enter the house from the second floor, capturing one of the leaders, and then went down to the main floor, taking three more prisoners, then learning their captive newsman was hanging like a piece of meat by hooks through his hands and was in the cellar with another guard. After, they secured the guard and released Albert Dean. The mission by our rangers was one of the first to lose no men and capture six prisoners. It sent a message. Our men do not give up or give in. They should be congratulated for a fine mission and the life saved of Albert Dean, reported by the Reporter.

I sent the script to Tom for approval and went to bed. The next morning, Tom had sent the approval back with minor changes, facts the enemy shouldn't know. I faxed it to Mr. Albert with the *Washington Post* that morning. He had sent me a "good going, Mr. Reporter, watch the paper tomorrow." Everyone was working except Grandpa, and I went with him for a ride and a little shopping. He told me some jokes, and we talked about the war in Iraq. After we got a haircut, we went home. Ashley would be over around three. I was looking forward to seeing her. Mom got home around four. Brendon and Andrew got there also at the time, and Dad got there late. He was working overtime and wouldn't be home until seven. It was so good to see Ashley and to hold her. We went for a ride and to be alone. "I hope I'm the only girl in your life," she said.

"I have only you," I told her.

"Do you have girlfriends when you are gone?" she asked.

"Girlfriends, no. Friends, yes."

"I'll wait for you until you're ready," she said.

"I know, honey, but it's important for you to finish school, while I am establishing myself. I have a story that should be in the *Washington Post* tomorrow."

"That's great," she said, and we hugged and kissed. Then I told her Mom is fixing a pot roast, fried squash, and biscuits.

"Let's go home."

The dinner was great. Only Mom could cook that good, I told her while we all ate and talked. After dinner, Dad, Brendon, Andrew, and I played games on the game machine. They were good. They played so much. Dad and I barely had a chance. When they beat us, it was a big thrill. Dad played like it was only luck, but they knew they were that good. Ashley left at ten and said she would see us tomorrow. I went to her car and kissed her bye.

That week went by slow. No one was home during the day except Grandpa. We spent lots of time together. He is very smart, and we had great conversations. The following week, Tom called. "Chris, I know you have only been home a short time, but I have a good friend that has a problem. Maybe we can help him. It's Dr. Hampton. Can you meet me at the drugstore in an hour?"

"Yes, sir, I'll be there."

"Good. I'll see you then," and we hung up. It was two fifteen, so I would be there at three. I got there at ten after and sat drinking water. I knew he would drink a Coke float with me, and when he came, I ordered two large Coke floats, and we went to sit at a booth. "Chris, Dr. Hampton's father was in the air force with me and we were best friends. We promised to always stay in touch but he is gone now. I try to stay close to his son, Dr. Hampton. Someone broke into his office and stole his computer, along with many files. Heath has a patient list of the most important people in town, one of which is being blackmailed now, and two others have been contacted. The blackmailer says he will expose private information if the money isn't paid. I want to help him if we can. Would you look into this for me?"

"Sure. I like Heath Hampton. Does he know I will be calling him?"

"Yes," Tom said.

"Good."

"He is in his office now."

"I'll go by and see him," I said.

"Thanks, Chris, stay in touch."

"Yes, sir, I will."

"Good luck," he said and left.

I drove the few blocks to his office. He was still working. "I'm here to see Dr. Hampton," I told the nurse, and I waited a few minutes.

"Dr. Hampton will see you now, Mr. Doan," and she led me to his office. "He will be in shortly," she said, and I sat in a large overstuffed chair. Dr. Hampton came in.

"Hi, Chris, how are you?"

"Fine, sir, and you?"

"Healthwise, good. Chris, I have a problem. Someone broke into my office and stole a computer and lots of files. This looks bad for me and one patient is being blackmailed now and two others are being also. I know how good you were capturing those men stealing the medicine from the hospital and thought you might help."

"I'll be glad to do what I can, sir."

"Thank you so much, Chris. This is a file on Larry Butler. He was asked ten thousand dollars or the file would end up in the newspaper. He paid the money. Now they want ten more thousands."

"Can I talk to Larry Butler?" I asked.

"Let me call him first and make sure it's OK. I know everything I tell you will stay between us."

"Of course," I said.

He picked up the phone and called. "Larry, this is Dr. Hampton. I have a special friend that is trying to help with our problem. He is a local person with the highest security and he has helped me with the gang that was stealing medicine from the hospital. He caught them. Do you remember about this last year?"

"Yes," the answer came. "I would be glad to get some help with this matter," he said.

"Good. His name is Chris Doan. I'll have him to contact you. Thank you, Larry. I'll stay in touch," and he hung up. Dr. Hampton gave me two other names and numbers. "I'll call them first," he said, "but you have something to work with now. Thank you, Chris."

I said, "I'll call you tomorrow." He gave me his private number and asked me to call him after seven if I could.

That evening after dinner, I went to my room and called Larry Butler. "This is Chris."

"Yes, Chris, thank you for calling."

"May I come out and talk to you?" I asked.

"Yes, you can," he said. "When?"

"At your convenience," I told him.

"Now or anytime," he said.

"Good. I'll come now then," and he gave me his address. I knew exactly where he lived, a big house out Highway 115. It only took thirty minutes to get there. He met me at the door.

"I know you," he said. "You played football for Newton High School not long ago."

"Yes," I said. "Larry, I'm asking you to be very discreet about who I am. My work is a secret also."

"I like that."

"What is happening?" I asked.

"Well, you know someone broke into Dr. Hampton's office, that somebody is blackmailing me. It's my wife. We have friends that if they knew her health problems, they would ostracize us and that would hurt her very much. I paid them ten thousand dollars. Now they are asking for more."

"I'm afraid they will always be wanting more. How did you pay them?"

"Two weeks ago I got this call telling me they had the file and would turn it over to the *Covington News* if I didn't pay them. I got very mad and said I wouldn't. They said they would give me a couple of days to think about it. Nancy, my wife, was so upset knowing people would know she had AIDS. Was wanting to move from here. I couldn't do that. I have seven hundred acres. I raise cattle. My wife does lots of work in the community and is in charge of several projects. It means so much to her. She is a wonderful person that made a mistake. She was engaged to her college sweetheart that got it and she is paying for his mistake. Now we all are. This man called me again and said he would give me my file and all the information if I would pay him the ten thousand dollars. I had to believe him, so I met a man one night behind Wendy's and gave him the money. He left. I did not get a look at him. He wore glasses, large yellowish kind, with a cap and he stayed behind me while I sat in the car and he left from behind. We were walking, then going through the back in the trees. I don't know much other than he was white, large, from maybe six feet one, and he looked stout from his hairy arm. He wore a ring on his wedding finger, that looked like a school ring. That's all I know."

"When did he call you back?"

"This past Saturday, four days ago," he said. "His partner wouldn't give me the original file. I only got a copy when I paid him but he promises me this will be the last time he will ever ask for money. I don't believe him." Larry was looking sad now.

"Does your phone show you who is calling?" I asked.

"Yes and I have the number."

"Great. Now here is my number. You can reach me anytime." I gave it to him. "Have you got a tape recorder you can keep on you all the time?"

"No, I don't."

"I want you to get one and be ready all the time to record."

"OK." He looked at me. "Do you think we can get him?"

"If we do things right, I believe we can." I said I got his cell phone number and the number the crook called from. "When he calls the next time, tell him you don't have all the money yet but you will have it tomorrow."

"Thank you, Chris. I hope you can help."

I told him, "Be ready when he calls. Then call me right then."

"I will," he said. I went home.

Ashley had come, and we went for a ride. It was a pretty fall day, and I was enjoying being home. Dad grilled steaks for dinner, and we sat around and talked. My cell phone rang, and it was Larry. "Chris, I just got a call and I am to meet him in two hours. I told him I won't have the money until tomorrow. 'OK,' he said but I better have it. Then he will call me to set up a meeting place."

"Good, Larry. I will see you in the morning."

"Thanks, Chris. Good-bye."

I called Tom and told him what was happening and gave him the number Larry had given me. Tom said he would try to back trace it and set up a traveling line to it. "I'll call you back," he told me. The next morning, Tom called and said he had a trace on the phone number. It came from Highway 136, but he didn't talk long enough to get an exact fix on it.

"How far out is 136?" I asked.

Tom said, "About five miles. I'll call when I have something else," then hung up. Around ten Dr. Hampton called.

"Chris, I just got a call from Dr. Amberham. He had his files and computer stolen a couple of days ago and the people are wanting money or they will release his file information to the public. I told him to stall the blackmailer as long as he could. My nurse mother works for Dr. Amberham and she told her about my computer and files being stolen. It hasn't been reported to the police because this can't get out to the public. Too much information in the wrong hands."

I told him about the blackmailer wanting more money from Larry. "We have something working, Dr. Hampton. Maybe it will work out."

"Thanks, Chris. I appreciate the help."

"Yes, sir," I said and hung up.

I called Larry and told him I would set up to follow the person tonight when he meets the blackmailer and to call me as quick as he could when he finds out where to meet. "I will. Take care," and hung up. I went to my room and took out a map of Newton County, and I knew what I needed, one more person.

I had a sandwich for lunch, but now I'm hungry. I thought about a good salad. I had the TV room to myself. After fixing a nice club sandwich with a glass of milk, then watching world news, I must have fallen off to sleep, and the phone rang. It was Dr. Hampton. "Another doctor had his files stolen, Chris. These are the best doctors in Covington. It's got to be a ring operating here, Chris. Are there anything I can do? Watch for you or following you to help. This is happening to me and I am well capable of helping."

Yes, I needed him. "What time do you get off?" I asked.

"My last patient today is four forty-five so I'm through by five, unless you need me sooner."

"No, five would be fine," I said.

"Let's meet at Wendy's."

"No," I said. "I'll be at your office at five. Is that OK?" Dr. Hampton smiled to himself. He was wanting some excitement. I knew he could handle himself; he looked it.

At five I was parked in back of his office. Dr. Hampton came out and got beside me. "How can I help?" he asked. "And call me Heath."

"You're OK," I told him. "Tonight the blackmailer wants money from Larry. Last time Larry took the money to Wendy's in back. The man came up from behind, wearing big sunglasses and a cap. Larry saw his arm. It was white. He wore a ring, maybe a school ring. It happened fast, but Larry is setting up for a better look, but I am going to follow when he calls and park near if I can I have a camera and binoculars. If you want to ride with me, that would be good. Then next time we can work as a team."

"That sounds OK." Dr. Hampton smiled.

"Yes, that sounds good. I think it will be dark. It was last time. He wants less visibility," I said. "I'm hungry. Want something to eat?"

"Yes," he said.

"How about Wendy's?"

"Sounds good," and I drove there. We both ordered a salad and milk. I also ordered a fish sandwich and a frosty. He got some chicken nuggets and frosty for later. I had water. I kept a thermos and crackers in the car all the time. We ate and then drove around to the city pond and waited.

It was just getting dark when Larry called. "Chris?"

"Yes," I said.

"He wants me to be at Red Lobster in Conyers in back in one hour." It's seven now.

"Great," I said. "We are on it." I pulled out and headed to Red Lobster. I knew he was already there watching for a stakeout. It took twenty minutes to get there. I drove to the end. Lots of stores were open. Looking for anyone in their car, I passed one that locked perfect. I got behind a truck that helped hide my side. I could see all the back of Red Lobster, and we waited. I filmed all the cars there. With my zoom lens, I could get some good pictures. At eight nothing happened; then eight ten, a man got out of a blue Toyota and went to Larry's car. I was filming, and he stayed only a moment, then went back to his car behind Larry's and left. I was following. I wanted his tag number if I could get it. In town too many cars got between us, and I lost him. He was heading for Highway 136, so I hurried for it. I spotted him three cars in front. I just followed. When he got to Henderson Mill Road, he turned down. If I kept going straight, I figured he would know he was being followed. I parked at Henderson Restaurant and waited. Ten minutes later he came back and turned on the highway, and I let him have a good lead; then I followed another five miles, and he turned down a side street. I knew it wasn't long. I passed the street, then came back and went down it. His ear wasn't outside. It must be in a garage. At least we knew about where he lived. Now if my camera could see his tag number. I called Tom and let him know what was happening. He had a good fix on the cell phone and had intercepted a phone call from South Carolina. He played the tape to me.

"What's going on?" the voice said.

"I am to make a pickup at eight," the other voice said.

"They might try to follow you. Be very alert."

"I will," and that was all that was said.

"That's our boy," I told Tom.

"Yeah, I think so too." The street is Malcolm Way, 642. I had noticed a house for rent and decided to go check it out. Not now, I thought. If the man was watching, he might remember my green Honda. I took Dr. Hampton home. We talked a lot that evening. I was glad for his help.

I called Larry and told him we were on his trail. Now we would know whom to watch for good. He said, "Let's catch the bastard."

The next morning, I drove to 642 Malcolm Way. It had a closed garage door. Four more houses down on the other side of the street, a house was for rent, 671. See Bill Thompson, Covington Realty Co. I called Bill and asked, "How much is the rent?"

"Seven hundred twenty-five dollars with one month deposit."

I called Tom to handle it. "I got the Covington paper, Chris. It was written Harold Luke, a prominent banker, just came back from Japan. He was getting special treatment for his advanced herpes." Tom said he would not pay the blackmailer, and they let the information out. "That will put the scare in the people."

"Yeah, I'm afraid so," I said.

"I'll check on that house. Stay in touch," he told me.

"Will do," and hung up.

Later that day, Tom called. "Chris, here is a number to call if you need any help." I wrote the number down. "The name is Travis Breedlove. He can help with most things."

"Thanks, Tom," and I hung up.

Tom called again. "We have the house at 671. The key is at Covington Realty. They expect you."

"Good. I'll go there now." I picked up the key and went to the rental house. I had a good view of the house. I wanted to watch, but I didn't want to stay there all the time, and I thought about Travis and called him. "Can you come now?" I asked him.

"Yes," he said. I gave him the address. "I'll be there in an hour," he said.

"Thanks," and I hung up.

Dr. Hampton called. "Chris, can I help you with anything?"

"Not yet," I said, "but as soon as I know anything, I'll call you. Oh, Dr. Hampton, I have the house that was for rent. I'm there now watching."

"Good," he said.

Travis came, and we parked his car in the garage. "I'm Chris," and we shook hands.

"How can I help?" he asked.

"I'm watching that house for anyone. I would like to film anyone coming or going. They are blackmailing people and I want to catch them."

"No problem," he said. Then he went to his car and got a camera, binoculars, and a pistol. He put a chair near the window and sat. He got his camera ready. "Someone is coming out," he said. He got his camera ready, and the blue Toyota came out with one person in it. It was the same man that I saw at Red Lobster.

"I'm following him," I told Travis and went for my car. I got to Highway 136 and saw the blue Toyota down the road. I stayed behind a good distance. He pulled in to Kroger grocery store, and I got his tag number. While waiting, I called Tom and gave him the tag number. Thirty minutes later, the man returned with a buggy filled with groceries; then he went to a hardware store. I stayed way back and followed him to Highway 136 and let him get a long way in front of me. I called Travis. "Want a burger?" I asked.

"Sure, with some fries and large Coke," he said.

"I'll be back shortly," I said and hung up. I stopped at Burger King and got a fish sandwich, two salads, and a Whopper and fries, then went to the rental house. I decided to put a listening bug in the house. That night I would explore the place. I sat and talked with Travis until nine, then put my camouflage clothes on. I carried my stilts and a pistol. I went across the street, behind all the houses, and behind the house I wanted to check out. The ground sloped down, and there was a basement. Two windows were lit, and I put my stilts on and raised myself up to look inside. No one was in them. One was a bedroom; the other room was empty. I went to the side of the house and raised myself to look through the window. It had furniture, a bedroom suite. The door was open, and I could see a little inside the kitchen. I went around the house to the other side and looked in the den. I saw a man sitting, watching TV, eating pretzels. The phone rang, and I turned my hearing up.

"I'm calling people but only one other person will pay. You know I wouldn't hold out on you. Hell no, I wouldn't. When will he get here?" he asked. "Sure, if you think it will help." Then he hung up. No one was there except the one man. Now I needed to get inside that basement. There was a metal door on the back side of the house. I went to it and tried to get in. I used my burglar keys, and after a little while, I got in. The door was silent, and as I opened it, I felt good no one could hear me. There were several boxes there. I didn't open them but looked for a good place to put my bugs. At a vent, I put the first bug; then at the bedroom floor vent, I put another. I wanted to get inside to put my other two. I would have to wait for a better time. I went back to the window where the man was and watched a little longer.

When I got back, Travis had a sleeping bag on the floor and asked me if I learned anything. "I only saw one man there, but he talked on the phone, and someone else was coming. I'm going home," I told him. "You might as well get some rest. I don't think anything will happen tonight."

"OK," he said. "I'll be here." I left for the house.

I woke early and decided to have a good run. After six or seven miles, I decided that was enough and went back. Mom had eggs and pancakes ready. She went to work, and Brendon and Andrew went to school. Dad had left around five, and I didn't see him that morning. After eating, I showered and shaved, then went to see how Travis was doing. As I drove by the house we were watching, there was another car parked in front. It was a late-model Buick. The tag was South Carolina, number WEY 347. I pulled in our driveway and went in. Travis said they got in around four this morning. "They?" I asked.

"Yes, two people. They both had dreadlock ponytails. I think they are South Americans. They look shabby and wear baggy clothes." I wanted to retrieve my phone bug tapes and see what was going on but it would have to be dark. Dr. Hampton called. He had spoken to Dr. Amberham, and he and two patients had been called; and if they didn't come up with the money, they would have their names in the paper with Harold Luke.

"Dr. Hampton, if you want to help tonight, come over to 671 Malcolm Way."

"When?" he asked.

"When you get off work."

"That will be around five."

"That's fine," I told him, "or a little later."

Travis said, "Do you need me for a couple of hours?"

"No," I said.

"Then I'm going after some house food and a few things."

"Yes, go ahead. I'll just watch." Travis left, and I sat and watched; nothing happened.

Tom called around noon and said the house we were watching was rented to Benny Lane. He also owned a blue Toyota. That was our man, I told Tom. I was retrieving my bug tonight, and about the two men from South Carolina, tag WEY 347, "I'll check it out," he said. "Keep in touch."

I sat watching for hours, when Benny Lane came out and drove off. I decided to put a tracker on his car. Travis came back with a box of food. He had juice, cereal, snacks, and sandwich meat. "Hungry?" he asked.

"Yes," I said, and he fixed turkey sandwiches. We sat talking. Then Benny came back. It was seven, and Dr. Hampton came. "I'm going into the house tonight and retrieve my listening tapes. I want you, Travis, to watch my rear, and you, Dr. Hampton, to watch from here with binoculars. Anyone comes out, you can alert us."

"Sounds good," Dr. Hampton said. We talked about politics, weather, and lots of things.

When I figured it would be safe to go, "Ready?" I asked.

"Yes," they both said.

I got my stilts and put a black shirt on, and Travis and I went out the back door and came around the house and crossed the street. There were trees in back, and we went through them to Benny's house. We had our cell phones, and I was ready to go in. I first went to the side window where the den was and elevated myself up. I could see in, and there were two men that looked South Americans and Benny watching the TV. It looked clear, so I let myself down and went to the back door. I got the door opened and went in, shutting and locking the door behind me. I went to the vent where my tapes and machine were and got it and put a new one in. The phone rang, and I heard a voice speak like an islander, saying, "We are expecting a call anytime from three people. Benny has eighteen thousand, he says. That's all he has collected. He used two thousand. OK."

Benny then talked to someone. "No, I swear it. I only collected twenty thousand. I swear I wouldn't do that. I know you would," he said. "OK, good-bye then."

I heard a voice say, "Benny, Verez would skin you alive if you ever cheated him."

"I know," Benny said. "I wouldn't." I started back down, then went out the back door. It made a little noise, which worried me, but by the time I got the door locked and was back in the woods, nothing happened. I went into the house and listened to the tape. The first voice was Benny. He was calling Mr. Adair. "I am calling you about your daughter, Linda."

"What about her?" the voice said.

"Well, if you don't want the newspaper to know she has AIDS, you will pay me ten thousand dollars by Friday."

"Who is this?" he said.

"That doesn't matter. What does matter is if you don't want the paper to know, you will have the money by Friday."

Mr. Adair started cussing. "I won't pay you a cent."

"Then like Harold Luke, her name with yours will be in the paper." He hung up. The next voice was Benny calling a Mr. Vincent. "I am calling you about your wife, Donna."

"Who is this?" Mr. Vincent said.

"That doesn't matter. Your wife has AIDS, and if you don't want it in the paper, you will have ten thousand dollars by Friday."

Mr. Vincent said, "I don't have that kind of money."

Benny said, "Get it or her name will be in the paper with you and I know a big lawyer like you can get a little ten thousand dollars by Friday."

Then the voice said, "I'll call you tomorrow, good-bye," and hung up.

Another call came to Benny. "Hello. Hi, Verez, things are working. I have a pickup tonight and two more people working."

"Good," the voice said, and they hung up. That was all the calls, but there were lots of talking between Benny and Lewis and Val. Now we knew the names of the two men from the islands, Lewis and Val.

Dr. Hampton said, "I know all the people they are blackmailing. They are our most influential people in Covington. Do you need me any more tonight?"

"No, that's all for tonight. I'm going home too."

Travis said, "I've got it here. Go on home."

"Thanks," I told Dr. Hampton, "and I'll see you, Travis, in the morning."

"OK, see you," and we left. Everyone had gone to bed at home, but Dad came in the living room to say hello. It was about twelve. He went back to bed, and I watched TV for a while before going to bed.

The next morning, I had a good run. When I got home, I went to the basement for a good workout. I did lots of kicking, chins, and weight lifting. At eight I got ready to go relieve Travis.

When I drove by Benny's house, the car from South Carolina was gone. I parked inside the garage. "What happened to the Buick?"

Travis said, "One man left at seven forty-five. When he came outside, he looked around good, then he left."

I called Tom and asked if he had some tracking devices for the two cars. "I'll get them to you," he said. I told him what had been happening and that I was retrieving my tapes again tonight.

"When do you want me to pick up these three men?"

"Wait," he said. "I have someone on the people in South Carolina. A couple of days."

"OK." I played the tape I had collected the night before; then the Buick came back, and we watched as the man went in. That day went slow, and Dr. Hampton came back that afternoon. "I want to retrieve the tapes tonight," I told them.

After dark, Travis and I went exploring at the house. I put my stilts on and went to the side window. As I eased my way to look, I saw Val and Lewis. I turned my hearing up. Val said, "We better loosen the ropes up or it might kill him."

Lewis said, "Let the bastard die. Otto said to kill him." I could hear him moan all night. My mind started thinking. They must be talking about Benny Lane. I watched another ten minutes. Then Val went to a staircase door and went to the basement. I lowered myself down and went to a window and looked in. Benny was tied to a chair, gagged and passed out. His hands were wrapped and bloody. Val loosened the ropes around his hands and then went back upstairs. Blood was on the floor under Benny; then the lights went out.

I went over to Travis. "They have the American tied in the basement. His hands are bloody and bandaged. He is gagged and passed out now."

"Falling out amongst the thieves," he said.

"Yeah. I'm going after the tapes," I told Travis. "Rescue me if you have to," I said. "Call the doc and tell him what is going on."

"Will do," he said, and I took my stilts off and left them, then went to the back door. It only took a minute, and the door opened. I left it unlocked, and it made a sound when it opened. I waited for a light to come on, but it didn't. I went to the staircase and up a few steps to reach the vent where the tapes were, then put another one in and came back to the door. I passed Benny. He was not moving, but I could hear a loud breathing. I wanted to help him, but we had to catch all these creeps, especially the leaders. I locked the door and went back to Travis. We went through the trees, then between two houses, and crossed the street and went in the back door.

"What's happening?" Dr. Hampton asked.

I told him, "The American is tied in the basement. His hands are cut and bandaged. He passed out, and he is gagged, lots of blood under his chair."

I put the tape in, and we listened. The phone rang, and Val said, "Yes, you will pay or we will release this to the paper. No more excuses. Twenty thousand. What do you mean?" Val said, "I will call you back." Then Val said, "That was Linda Adair. She says you have been paid twenty thousand already."

Benny's voice said, "That's a lie. I only collected ten thousand."

Then there was noise, and the voice said, "Take him to the basement."

And for a few minutes there was noise, and then Val told Lewis, "Gag him."

"Please, Val, I have the money. I needed it bad. I'll get it," and then I heard him begging as they gagged him.

"You S.B.," Val said. "I told you what would happen if you got greedy. Get a knife," Val said. Lots of moaning. Then Val said, "Cut his hands. Start between the fingers and cut to his palm." Then lots of chair noise and moaning. "Wrap that hand," Val said, "before he bleeds to death." Then Val asked Benny, "Where is the money?" They must have taken the gag off Benny. When he screamed, "Gag him," Val said. Val told Benny, "If you scream again, I'll cut your noise off. Shake your head if you understand." A little later, Val said, "Take the gag off," and then a crying voice was begging.

"The money is in the freezer, wrapped. It's in the bottom, under some things."

Val told Larry, "Go see," and we heard someone going up the steps and opening a door.

A couple of minutes went by, while Benny begged, "Please, I'll work for nothing. You need me."

Then Larry's voice said, "Got it."

And Val said, "Gag him." Benny pleaded before he was gagged again. "Do the other hand," Val said. Lots of muffled sounds and chair noise. Val said, "Put a bandage on that hand. He is losing lots of blood."

Larry said, "I hate to kill him, Val."

"Shut up. You want Otto to get a hold of you?"

"Hell no," Larry said. "I still get sick thinking about him using that chain saw on that guy.

Val said, "And he would use it on you if you didn't do what he says."

"My Lord," Dr. Hampton said. "What kind of people are we dealing with?"

"Some mean ones," Travis said, "for sure." The tape was almost silent; then I could hear them going up the steps, and that was all. I called Tom and asked how things were going in South Carolina.

"It's working," he said, and I told him about Benny tied up. "Do you think he might die?" Tom asked.

"I don't know. He is passed out."

Dr. Hampton said, "I don't like knowing what is going on. I think we should close in on them." My phone was on loudspeaker.

Tom said, "You want backup?"

"I'll call you back," I told him.

While we talked, Travis said, "Someone is leaving." We went to the window. The garage lit up the driveway, and the Buick pulled out. Travis said, "We could take this one and it would be easy to get the other one when he returns." I thought about it; maybe we should. There was lots of blood on Benny.

"Let's do it," I said. "Travis, you go to the back, in case he runs. Dr. Hampton, you call us. Drive down to the highway so we can be ready for him. I'll go to the front door and get him to open. I'll tell him I broke down and need to use his phone."

"I'll go now," Dr. Hampton said.

Travis said, "I'll head for the back."

I pulled out of the drive and went to the front. Everyone should be in place. I parked above the house in case Val came back, and I went to the door. I knocked, but no one answered. I knocked and rang the doorbell.

After three times, the door opened. A man came to the door. "Yes, sir," I said. "My car has broke down. Can I use your phone?"

"I don't have one," he said. He started to close the door, and I pushed the door, and he went for a gun at his back. I grabbed the hand and kicked him in the balls. He let the gun go and bent over. I went in and shut the door. I threw him to the floor and put my knee in his back and called Travis.

"I'm in," I told him. "Come on in the front. It's unlocked. Shortly after, the door opened, and Travis came in.

"Did you call the doc?" he asked.

"I did." Travis had some ties, and we put one on Larry.

"Who are you?" he asked.

"The law. It doesn't matter," Travis said, "but you have trouble. If you will tell who the men are in South Carolina, you can be sure it will be better for you."

"Go to hell. When we get through with you, you will wish you never heard of us."

"Oh," Travis said. At that time he hit Larry in the liver with his knuckles, and the man doubled over like he was going to die. He tried to talk. Then Travis said, "I'll ask you again. Who is your people in South Carolina?"

Larry couldn't speak yet but barely got out, "Go to hell."

"That's a shame," he said and hit him again in the liver. Larry went to the floor moaning.

After a few minutes, Larry said, "You don't know these people and what they will do if I said anything."

I asked, "Like take a chain saw to you by Otto?"

He looked at me. "How do you know that?" he asked.

"We know," Travis said. "Let's take him downstairs and check on Benny." Larry looked surprised again. We helped Larry down the steps.

Benny was conscious now. We undid his ropes and gag. He begged, "Who are you? Look at my hands." I took the bandages off, and he was cut through his middle fingers to his palm on both hands. "He did this. Larry did that." I wanted to hit Larry. What a mess on his two lobster hands now. We helped Benny up and moved around. He couldn't stand by himself. After a couple of minutes, he could stand.

Then the phone rang; it was the doc. "Here he comes," he said.

"We're ready. Travis, stay down here. When he hollers, answer yeah. Before he opens the door, I'll get him."

I went upstairs and hid behind the sofa. The garage door opened, and I heard him close it and come in. "Larry, where are you?"

"Down here," the voice said. Val drew his pistol. He knew something was wrong. He went to the door and pointed down, then jerked the door open. I ran at him before he could turn. I hit him and knocked him down the steps. Travis grabbed him. I ran down. Val was putting up a good fight. It took both of us to subdue him, but by then we all had a few bruises. We tied him and called the doc.

"Come on in," I said. "We have a patient for you." Dr. Hampton pulled up and brought his bag in. We had helped Benny up the stairs. Dr. Hampton took the wrapped hands' bandage off.

"Oh, Lord," he said. "What a mess." He started with giving Benny a shot, put something on the hands, and bandaged them back up. Dr. Hampton said, "This man has to go to the hospital now. I'm calling an ambulance."

"Go ahead," I told him. He called 911. Travis and I went downstairs. "Let's separate them," I told Travis. "We better stay down here until the police leaves with Benny. Hey, Dr. Hampton, get them out of here and we will be quiet. Go with them to make a report. Maybe we can learn more about the South Carolina boys."

"OK, I'll call you later."

Travis said, "Chris, I can make them talk." We stepped outside, and he said, "I can make them talk and not hurt either of them."

"How?" I said.

"I'll be back in a couple of hours," and he went to the other house and left. I could hear the sirens coming. I had locked the basement and cut the lights off. I could hear the talking of Dr. Hampton and the men upstairs for thirty minutes; then the sirens started again, and it went quiet. I took Larry upstairs and left Val downstairs, tied and gagged. I cut the light off for him. I had Larry sitting, tied to a chair. I talked to him.

"You can help yourself if you talk. If not, you're in real trouble. You did the cutting to Benny and you can bet Val will tell it was you."

"I can't. Those men would torture and kill me someday and hurt my family."

Almost three hours later, Travis came back. I opened the door for him. He had a large cooler. I looked at him like what could he use to make them talk. "Come here," he said. We went out of hearing, and he said, "Look, Chris, don't worry. Let me handle this." What was he going to do? What did he have to torture them?

"Which one?" I asked first.

"Larry. He cut Benny's hands like that." He went to a door. It was a closet. "This will do," he said. "Let's put Larry in here." We took Larry to the closet. Travis undid his pants.

"And what are you doing?" I asked.

"Just watch," he said. He tied Larry down and said, "It's your last chance." After taking his gag off, Larry didn't say a thing. Travis reached into the cooler and took out a large rattlesnake and went to the closet. He held the snake at the head and middle.

Larry said, "What are you going to do?" Larry began to shake. Then Travis let the snake go, cut the light off, and shut the door. Larry started hollering. "I'll tell you, please let me out!" Larry said, "There is three people. Otto Dirking, Wheeler Sadler, and Loney Belcher. Let me out, hurry!"

"Where are they at?" Travis asked.

"Twenty three seventy four Allen Street, Aiken, South Carolina. Please let me out!"

Travis asked, "Want to know anything else?" He was recording what Larry had said.

"No," I said, and we opened the door. The rattlesnake was coiled in the corner. We got Larry out, and Travis reached in and got the snake and put him back on ice in the cooler. I smiled. That's how he did it. That was smart.

"Now let's put Val in there and make sure Larry is telling the truth." We put Larry in another room and shut the door; then we went to the basement and got Val. Then we took the gag off. Travis asked, "Who are you working for?" He spit at Travis. Travis slapped him hard. "OK, big man, let's see how tough you really are."

He went to the cooler and got the rattlesnake again, and when Val saw the snake, Val said, "I can't tell you. They will kill me."

Travis said, "OK, your little buddy here will keep you company." Travis was holding the snake at Val's face. Then he laid the snake down and cut the light off and shut the door. It was quiet for ten minutes. Then Val said, "Their name is Otto Dirking, Loney Belcher, and Wheeler. I don't know his last name."

"What is their address?"

"It's Aiken, South Carolina. I don't know the address number."

"That's it. Now we have both men on tape." Travis opened the door. The rattlesnake was on Val's foot. He got the snake and went and put him back in the cooler.

I called Tom, and he was waiting. I gave him the information. "That's where we are already," he told me. "Call the police. Speak to Sheriff Thomas. Tell him to come get those two and go get some rest. You earned it."

I called Dr. Hampton and told him what was going on. "Great," he said. "I sure thank you for all your help. I will call Travis. Thanks again and I'm going to bed. It's almost two."

"Good night," and I hung up. We called the sheriff and left. I shook Travis's hand and said, "Nice working with you."

"Me too," and we drove off.

The next morning, I woke early and went for a good run, then went back home. Mom was going to work. I kissed her and told her I loved her. Later that day, Tom called. "I have news. First, your friends in Baghdad, Rhonda and Lotus Halbin, got a reward and bought a house in Jabrin. Undrea is using your truck making a good living hauling and is giving us information about Al-Qaeda. Here at home, five men have been arrested for blackmailing and racketeering. Benny is in the hospital with his hands. He may not have full use of them and is cooperating with the authorities for a lesser sentence, and Dr. Hampton called me, and I thank you and Travis for your good work. Also, take a month or grow a beard and I'll talk to you."

"A beard?" I said. "A new assignment overseas?"

"Probably," he said, and we hung up.

The End

CPSIA information can be obtained at www.ICGtesting.com
Printed in the USA
LVOW050905081212

310385LV00002B/94/P